STRANGE TALES
FROM JAPAN

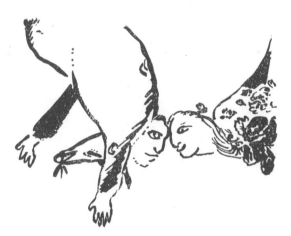

日本の伝説をめぐって

STRANGE TALES FROM JAPAN

99 Chilling Stories of Yokai, Ghosts, Demons and the Supernatural

Collected and retold by
KEISUKE NISHIMOTO

Translated by
WILLIAM SCOTT WILSON

TUTTLE Publishing

Tokyo | Rutland, Vermont | Singapore

Contents

Miraculous Strength

Pure Hearts

Strong Samurai

Unfortunate People

BOOK TWO: STRANGE TALES

Man-eating Demons and Yamanba

People Who Were Cursed

Living Heads and Skeletons

Ghosts' Requests

People Who Were Spared

Apparitions and Water

Shape-shifting Cats

Being Deceived by Foxes

Friendly Ghosts

Snakes, Wild Boars and Crabs

Preface

Some years ago, I found myself waiting on the train platform at Kiso Fukushima with a number of white-clad pilgrims. Kiso Fukushima is one of the main entry points to Mount Ontake, one of the holiest mountains in Japan, and these pilgrims apparently had finished their ascent of the mountain and were returning home. The worship of mountains is an ancient practice in Japan, influenced by the importation of Taoism in about the 5th century A.D., the native Shinto animist religion, and the esoteric Shingon sect of Buddhism. In the worship of Mount Ontake, the mountain is not so much considered the abode of a god, but a god itself; and thus, every tree, rock or pond on the mountain is holy and not to be treated lightly. In this way, the ascent and descent of the mountain is a form of worship. Groups of pilgrims are members of a *kou*, an organization of believers, and there are a number of these throughout Japan. It has been explained to me that the emphasis of the Mount Ontake religion is not dogma, but rather practice.

As I was sitting quite close to three or four of these pilgrims, I heard them discussing an incident that had taken place long ago; and before long they noticed my interest and were happy to include me in the conversation. It seemed that during the spring planting season, a young hardworking man had not returned to his house that night, and as there was no sign of him for two or three days, the villagers were alarmed and sent search parties out into the mountains and fields, but without result. Their judgment was that this was likely a case of *kamikakushi*, when an individual—often a child—is taken away by a god or a *tengu*, a long-nosed goblin that is often a mischief-maker. Oddly enough, a few days later, the younger sister of the man went out into the mulberry grove behind their house and found him there in a sort of stupor, emaciated and with hair that had turned completely white. He had no memory of where he had been or of what had happened to him. The astonished villagers were now absolutely sure that this had been a case of *kamikakushi*.

As the conversation went on, the man who was telling this story looked over at me from time to time, and must have noticed that my face betrayed some skepticism. He turned to me with a kind smile and said, "You know, you Westerners are much too rational. You must think that everything in this world can be scientifically proven. But there are worlds that we cannot see, and spirits and gods that live among us that only show themselves to us from time to time. You cannot imagine how foxes and badgers can have magical powers, but we Japanese have witnessed these things since ancient times. Perhaps you may experience some of this while you are out here in the Kiso area." With that, our train pulled into the station, we all made polite bows, and carried on with our individual journeys.

Introduction

I have sometimes been asked, "Where should I go to see the *real* Japan?" This is a reasonable question, especially considering the amount of travel time and the expenditure involved. And it is, perhaps, far more reasonable than asking where one might go to see the real America. New York? Boston? New Orleans? San Francisco? Dubuque? All of them are quite different, and all of them are quite American.

But the broad alternatives in Japan, I think, are more limited. On the one hand, there are the large urban centers of Tokyo, Osaka, and, to a lesser degree, Kyoto. In any of these places, you can check into a comfortable hotel, and once settled in, see the sights. Very likely, the concierge and others at the hotel will speak English and will arrange for a taxi or bus service, you will be dropped off at a famous temple or shrine or garden where you can see one of the city's main attractions, and take a lot of interesting photos to show your friends when you go home. No doubt, you will be well fed, get your quota of sushi, and maybe even some sake to boot. This is one way of experiencing Japan, and it is a fun and interesting one.

I would suggest, however, that the alternative—going rural—will give the visitor an experience far more in-depth of this unique country. In the countryside you will find no five-star hotels, but instead, traditional inns that may have been established centuries ago. You will not be sleeping in a bed as you would in an urban hotel, but rather on a Japanese futon on a tatami floor—just as comfortable, and the way Japanese have slept for over a thousand years. Instead of sushi or Kobe beef, you will dine on local traditional meals of in-season vegetables, herbs and river fish. And rather than the shower provided by most hotels, you will be treated to a typical Japanese bath, in which you can soak as long as you like. Rural villages in Japan also have their share of temples, shrines and gardens, and though perhaps not designed by famous architects (some are), they have a strong flavor of the area, and are not swarming with tourists. Finally, although you may have to struggle a little with your Japanese phrase book, and your host with his or her English one, you will find a true Japanese hospitality based on a unique experience for both host and guest. The same will be true in the tiny shops and noodle restaurants visited by the locals as well as by some Japanese visitors wanting to take a short vacation outside of the big cities. And while you can walk from village to village with just a light pack, trains in Japan will take you almost anywhere you would like to go. But you will not be hustled from tourist attraction to tourist attraction, and will have time to consider where you are.

🔺 🔺 🔺

Many of us like to read up on a foreign country before we visit it, and this, too, provides us with some interesting alternatives. In the case of Japan, English translations abound for almost all of the classics like the *Tale of Genji* or the *Pillow Book*, books on Zen Buddhism, or the best of modern literature. But in the case of the classics, many were written by aristocrats living in an ethereal and privileged world and vying for the coveted literary recognition; in the case of books on Zen or other kinds of Buddhism, the authors were often learned priests, often led by the desire to convince the reader of the legitimacy of their own sect; and with modern novels, you have pieces written from an author's own point of view. All of these are powerful pieces of literature and deserve to be read for that reason alone. But to what extent do they reveal the Japanese as a whole, the Japanese mind, so to speak?

Like the different venues for "seeing" Japan, there is a similar alternative for looking into the Japanese mind. This is *minzoku bungaku* or folk literature, also called *densetsu* or traditional tales. These consist for the most part of legends according to oral tales or literary documents, based on the belief of real happenings in the past in the surroundings of a particular locality. They are still passed on today, especially in the countryside, told by grandparents to their grandchildren on cold winter nights as the family sits around the brazier.

The word *densetsu* (伝説) literally means "traditional explanations," the word *setsu* originally meaning an explanation of the gods' answers to prayers. In the case of traditional tales, they are explanations of events that might otherwise be difficult to understand, often centered on a certain temple, shrine, rock or tree by the roadside. Unlike folk tales that begin with "long, long ago, in a certain place, an old man and an old woman…," *densetsu* name the place and sometimes the protagonists, so that no matter how exorbitant or fanciful the story, there is no need for a suspension of belief. What is important to our "seeing the real Japan" is that these stories were believed to be events experienced by local ancestors, perhaps not so distant, and this gives them an atmosphere of authority and continuity of place. And, although there may be no moral conclusions to *densetsu*, they do give insight into the lives of Japanese—both past and present—and to what kind of people they were and are—kind, warm, brave, and sometimes gullible or outright foolish.

Again, *densetsu* are not Hansel and Gretel folk or fairy tales, although there are plenty of these in Japanese folklore, called *mukashibanashi*, "stories of long ago." *Densetsu* instead may answer specific questions about why a rock at such and such a temple cried every night, or how a certain pond got its name, or why some people in Okinawa still shout "Eat shit!" (there is no polite way to translate this phrase) every time a baby sneezes. Or they may simply recount an amusing or scary event that took place in the local village at one time. But at the heart of every traditional tale is a remembrance.

Each story in this collection, with the exception of a few dating from far earlier collections, is identified by its place of origin, thus broadening the definition of the locale and its people. No doubt, some of them may have moved around with travelers from the various provinces during the 17th, 18th and 19th centuries when many people were on the road for pilgrimages or just out for a lark. Staying at the same inns far away from home, they might have entertained each other with strange stories from their hometowns, which would then be retold as the listener's own story at the next inn. But by and large, the place-names identified with each tale would prevent that sort of plagiarism.

Yanagita Kunio, the great folklorist of Japan, defined the difference between traditional tales and folk tales as follows:

> What is the difference between traditional tales and folk tales? I would answer that folk tales are like animals, and traditional tales are like plants. Folk tales go about here and there, but no matter where they go, they are perceived as having the same form or face. Traditional tales set their roots down to grow in one locality, and always grow up in that place. Sparrows or field buntings all have the same faces, but plum trees and camellias, tree by tree, are differing in shape, and thus are seen

and remembered individually. Many of the cute little birds of folk tales make their nests in the middle of the forests and thickets of traditional tales, but at the same time, the highly fragrant seeds and pollen of various traditional tales are carried off far away as well.... The strength of plants to flourish and grow strong is hidden in the land's earth and water, and in the brilliance of the sun. History puts these to use, just as in cultivating the soil in agriculture. If one regulates the tillage of history, it is natural that the traditional tales of mountains and fields are restricted in form.

Nihon no densetsu

Densetsu, then, provide an interesting complement to a hike or stay in the traditional Japanese countryside. Just as the Japanese will take trips to small local inns deep in the mountains to refresh their memories and feeling of who they really are, the foreign tourist can do the same from an outsider's view, and bolster his understanding by reading a number of traditional stories before covering up under his futon for the night, or while taking a break from the day's walk. Although they may not be the ones included in this book, every village or town will have its own collection of stories, if not printed, then imprinted deep within the local inhabitants' minds from the time they were children.

As Nishimoto Keisuke, the compiler and re-teller of this collection, wrote, "Behind every sad or scary or just interesting story, there are hidden principles that we cannot overlook, for the very essence of *densetsu* is a deep psychological truth that cannot be understood rationally. Evolved over a long period of time, they demonstrate the essence of what makes up the heart/mind of the Japanese."

🌲 🌲 🌲

It should be emphasized that the existence of the cast of characters appearing in these stories—ghosts, spirits, semi-supernatural animals, etc.—is not entirely denied by modern Japanese, even in large urban areas. The farmer who sees a fox on the edge of his rice field in the evening may be more inclined to think of it as a messenger of Inari, the god of fertility, rather than just a wild animal looking for a juicy mouse for dinner; and the lone shabby priest encountered in the mountains or even in a big city may be given wide berth, as he could be a *tengu* in disguise. Once in a park in Nagoya—the third largest city in Japan—my very modern Japanese companion identified two fluttering yellow butterflies as possibly spirits of the dead; and one spring, when I awoke to find a large black snake in my kitchen, my landlady informed me that it was likely the *nushi*, a sort of spirit master, of the area, and was to be considered good luck. (I admit to being happy enough as it slithered away.)

In this way, the stories collected here should not be thought of as simply interesting old tales, divorced from modern times. Their reality may be submerged, but perhaps not too far from the "real Japan." As my acquaintance at the railway platform said, "There are worlds that we cannot see, and spirits and gods that live among us that only show themselves to us from time to time. You cannot imagine how foxes and badgers can have magical powers, but we Japanese have witnessed these things since ancient times."

🔺 🔺 🔺

Go into any souvenir shop across the street from village train stations in Japan, and you will likely find a few copies (in Japanese) of local traditional tales for sale. These may be published by local societies for the preservation of local culture, or by town halls, or even by a local high school where students were given a project of collecting such tales from their parents or grandparents. In each case, the prevailing motive is preservation of the place, a physical and psychological definition of where a person is right now.

All of these stories, however, were collected into two volumes, *Nihon densetsu shu* and *Nihon kaidan shu*, by Nishimoto Keisuke, a scholar of Japanese folk and traditional tales. To him, I owe a profound debt of gratitude for his organization and presentation of the tales. I would also like to thank all the many others who have encouraged me in this work through the years. Their name is legion, and they know who they are.

William Scott Wilson

Book One:
TRADITIONAL TALES

Spirits and Ghosts

幽霊とお化けをめぐるお話

Flowers of the Sweet Olive Tree[1]

Long ago, in a certain village in the prefecture of Tottori there stood a single house owned by a samurai. One day, an old man went to the house for a visit as he and the samurai had been friends for some time. That night was the time for moon-viewing, and a large, round moon shone its bright light into the garden.

The two men extinguished all the lamps and sipped sake on the veranda as they gazed at the moon. From time to time, the fragrance of a sweet olive tree wafted by on a breeze. "Ah, what a pleasant scent," the old man said as he looked out over the garden. Just then, a young woman dressed in a white kimono appeared standing next to the sweet olive tree. Her long, disheveled hair fell over her pale white face, and she stared fixedly in the direction of the two men.

"That's strange," the old man said. "I must be getting a little drunk." He rubbed his eyes and started to stand up. Suddenly, the woman came up and abruptly thrust her face in between the two men.

The old man involuntarily let out a cry, but the samurai remained totally unafraid. "Go on, get out of here," he yelled, "or I'll cut you down!" The woman glided away and hid behind the sweet olive tree.

"Dear me!" the old man gasped as he breathed a sigh of relief.

"Oh, don't pay any attention to her," the samurai said to the old man as he filled a cup with fresh sake. "Here, drink your fill."

But after a while, the woman appeared again, and this time started to walk back and forth in front of the veranda. Now the old man could not even think about his sake. He looked at the woman and trembled all over. The woman suddenly stopped in front of the two men, leapt up onto the veranda, and glared and laughed at them.

A shiver went down the old man's spine, and he was speechless.

"You still don't understand what I mean?" the samurai yelled as he unsheathed his sword and slashed at the woman without warning. But the woman deftly dodged the blows and moved away just like the wind.

"Wait!" The samurai jumped down into the garden barefoot and chased after the woman. At last he came back, puffing and out of breath.

---

[1] *Osmanthus fragans var. Aurantiacus.* Jap., *Kinmokusei* (金木犀).

"What an annoying wretch!" he complained and spat disgustedly on the ground.

"She may be a crazy woman, but it wouldn't be right to kill her," the old man said.

"No, not at all. That woman's a ghost," the samurai replied. "When night falls, she appears like this all the time. If I leave the door open, she comes right into my room and gets up on the futon."

"What are you saying! Aren't you afraid?"

"Of course, I am," the younger man replied. "Even a samurai is afraid of something like that. But I've become used to her. And no matter how I slash away with my sword, it never has any effect. If I chase her, she just runs away like the wind."

"Well, so that's what they call a ghost! But why do you suppose a ghost comes here?"

"To tell the truth, I don't understand that myself."

Hearing that, the old man was afraid to stay a moment longer. Thanking his host for the sake, he quickly went outside. The moon was still shining brightly down. As he went around toward the front gate, his eyes fell on the large sweet olive tree that stood where the woman had been. A sweet and sour fragrance filled his nostrils.

Just then he heard the sharp sound of a branch being broken. Wondering what was happening, he peered over toward the tree and saw that the ghost was breaking off one of the many branches of the sweet olive tree.

The old man fled without another glance.

After that day, the ghost came every night and broke off another branch of the sweet olive tree. By the time she had broken all of them off, the tree started to wither. Strangely enough, when it had withered away completely, the ghost no longer appeared.

Soon after, the samurai passed away.

The Talking Futon

A long time ago in a town in Tottori prefecture, there was a small inn. One winter night, when one of the guests at the inn was sleeping, he suddenly woke up at midnight to the sound of human voices.

"Elder brother, you must be cold."

"Little brother, you must be cold."

The voices were those of whispering children.

"Well now, where would children be at this hour?" the guest wondered. "There's not supposed to be anyone else in this room."

Crawling out from under his futon, the guest peeped into the next-door room to see what was going on. But it was completely quiet, and not a sound could be heard.

"That's strange," he thought. "I'm sure I heard something."

The man got back under his futon once again and tried to go to sleep. But this time he heard the voices quite clearly right next to his ear.

"Elder brother, you must be cold."

"Younger brother, you must be cold."

The guest was shocked and leapt to his feet. He hurriedly lit a lamp, but there was no one else in the room. All he could hear was the sound of his own heart beating.

With the lamp still glowing, the guest lay down on his side. Then, once again, came the sad, whispering voices.

"Elder brother, you must be cold."

"Little brother, you must be cold."

Somehow, the voices seemed to be coming from right inside the futon.

The man shuddered in horror, brushed away the futon in panic, and nearly falling over himself leapt out of the room, running into the innkeeper.

"What foolishness is this? You were probably just having a dream!" the innkeeper exclaimed.

No matter how the guest explained the situation, the innkeeper refused to believe him. On the contrary, he got angry. "Let's not drag this out any longer. Do me the favor of getting out of here." And with that, he drove the guest from the inn.

The next night, however, a different guest staying in the same room also ran off at midnight, telling the same story.

"This is something strange," the innkeeper thought. "Could this be a ghost?"

The innkeeper went into the room himself and sat next to the futon for a while. Eventually, from the futon cover, sad voices began whispering.

"Elder brother, you must be cold."

"Little brother, you must be cold."

The innkeeper turned pale and ran from the room.

"What an eerie futon," he thought. "And what kind of terrible shop would sell a futon like this?" The next day, the innkeeper went to the used furniture store where he had bought the futon to make a complaint. There he heard a sad story.

On the outskirts of a town in the same prefecture of Tottori, there had lived a poor family of four. Some days before, after a long illness, the father had died in his sleep, and soon after, the mother had also passed away. This left only an elder brother six years old and a younger brother of four. Having no relatives to care for them, the brothers went day after day with nothing to eat, and shivered from the cold and empty stomachs under a single futon.

"Elder brother, you must be cold." The affectionate younger brother would try to pull the futon over his older brother.

"Little brother, you must be cold." And the elder brother would put the futon over his little brother.

But the cold-hearted landlord finally came, took the futon in place of the rent, and drove the children from the house.

The two boys, who had had nothing to eat for days, could not even walk. That night, as snow fell, they held each other in their arms under the eave of a nearby house and froze to death.

When the people of the town found out about this, they pitied the two boys and laid them to rest at a nearby temple dedicated to Kannon.[2]

"Is that what happened?" the innkeeper said. "What a miserable thing the landlord did."

He promptly set out to visit the temple dedicated to Kannon and formally read a sutra for the sake of the two little boys.[3]

It is said that after that, the futon never spoke again.

The Long-necks[4]

This happened about five hundred years ago, when a priest by the name of Kairyu was traveling through Japan, and arrived in the province of Kai.[5]

Kairyu was traveling along a road through the mountains when night closed in.

"There's nothing to be done about it," he thought. "I'll just rest here tonight."

The priest lay gently down on the grass by the side of the road and soon began to snore.

There was no way of telling how long he had been sleeping when he awoke to the voice of someone calling.

"Hello. Hello."

A woodcutter was standing over him looking down at his face.

"Venerable priest, you shouldn't be sleeping in a place like this," the man said. "There's a terrible ghost living around here who eats people. If you like, please spend the night in my small hut."

The priest accompanied the kind woodcutter to his small hut.

---

[2] Kannon (Sanskrit: Avalokitesvara). The Buddhist goddess of mercy.

[3] It is said that reading the Buddhist sutras for the dead helps them to find repose or salvation.

[4] Long-necks (Japanese, *rokuro-kubi*, 轆轤首). The *rokuro* is the Japanese potter's wheel, from which extends a long lathe connected to a kick-wheel. *Kubi* means "head."

[5] Kai: Yamanashi Prefecture.

In the woodcutter's hut there were three men and a woman. Though dressed in miserable attire, they were all perfectly courteous. The priest was impressed and questioned the eldest of the woodcutters.

"Are all of you from the capital?"[6]

"Yes," the elder man replied. "But we did something bad, and eventually killed some people. Reflecting on the crimes we had committed, we came here and are secretly living in the mountains like this."

This, the elder woodcutter stated in obvious embarrassment.

"You've spoken well," the priest said. "If your hearts are like this, even the dead will surely forgive you. In addition, I'll read a sutra and pray for the souls of the people who died."

So saying, the priest stayed up late that night, peacefully reciting a sutra. The night was at its blackest, and in the next room everyone was asleep.

"Well then," the priest thought. "Perhaps I should go to sleep, too." As he stood up, he accidentally glanced into the next room.

"Dear me! What is this?"

Instantaneously, the priest's eyes opened wide. Lined up under the futon were five headless bodies.

"Well now," he wondered. "Did the man-eater come in without my knowing it?"

The priest quickly entered the room, but strangely enough, there was no sign of blood.

---

[6] Kyoto.

"Then maybe these woodcutters are man-eating long-necks," he thought. "All right, then. I'll hide the bodies so their heads won't be able to come back."

The priest hid all of the bodies under the bedding and then went outside. Just then, he could hear the voices of people talking, coming from the nearby forest. When he approached the direction of the voices, something went whizzing by.

Five heads, wavering here, swaying there, flew all around, talking to each other.

The priest hid behind a tree.

"That good-for-nothing priest is nice and fat. He should taste really good," the long-neck that had guided the priest to the hut said.

"As long as he's endlessly reciting that sutra, we can't even get close," the eldest long-neck complained. "But the night is already quite late. He should be sound asleep by now. Somebody go and take a look."

The woman long-neck streaked away but returned almost as soon as she had flown off.

"This is terrible," she wailed. "There's no sign of the priest, and worse, our bodies are nowhere to be found."

"What!"

The eldest long-neck instantly took on a terrifying appearance. His hair stood up straight on his head, his eyes turned up back into their sockets, and he gnashed his teeth in a horrifying way. Even the priest felt a chill run down his spine.

"Without our bodies, we'll die for sure," the long-neck screamed. "But if this is the way it's going to be, we'll do that good-for-nothing priest the favor of tearing him limb from limb! Everyone go and look for the priest!"

With ghastly faces, the five long-necks flew off like will-o-the-wisps and started to search for the priest.

Soon, one of them found him hiding behind the tree.

"Hey, everyone! Have a bite of *this* body!"

The five long-necks flew in to attack, all aiming for the priest at once.

But the priest deftly pulled up a small nearby tree and knocked down the eldest long-neck.

"Aaagh!"

As the long-neck let out a yell, blood flowed from its head.

"Well, then," the priest called. "Come and get me!"

Brandishing the small tree, he struck at the long-necks one by one. Even though they were beaten again and again, the long-necks kept coming. The priest, however, had formerly been a samurai, and in the end the five long-necks were sorely beaten and fled in confusion.

Giving up on the priest, the five long-necks returned to the hut and collapsed, bloodied and battered.

"Well, what a waste of our time *that* was!"

The priest, who had defeated the long-necks and emerged unhurt, quickly walked down the mountain road in the early morning light.

The Ghost Cart

A long time ago, a strange incident occurred in the village of Koga, located in what is now Shiga Prefecture. When night fell in the village, a wooden cart would come out of nowhere, and with a weird creaking noise pass through the village to some unknown destination.

"This is a ghost cart, without a doubt," the townspeople agreed. "And they say that anyone who witnesses it passing by will incur some terrible retribution." Thus, when the day came to an end, the doors of everyone's homes were securely locked and people went straight to bed.

There was in this village, however, a rather bold housewife who thought to herself, "How can there be retribution for just seeing a ghost? I've a good mind to take a look and see just what kind of ghost rides in a cart."

That night, when everyone was sleeping peacefully, the housewife got up quietly, and opening the front door just a crack, waited for the ghost cart to come by. Outside, a bright moon shone a white light on the road.

Before long, the housewife could hear the grating sound of the ghost cart as it approached, and suddenly let out a faint gasp. A single woman with long straight hair and dressed in a white kimono sat in a cart which had only one wheel. Although no one was pulling the cart, it advanced steadily, creaking as it came.

While the housewife had thought that the ghost would have a frightening appearance, this woman was young and beautiful. As the housewife stared at the woman in a trance, the cart came to a standstill right in front of her house. In a panic, the housewife shut the door and crouched down behind it. But then, the woman whispered in a soft thin voice, "So you have dared to look at me, have you? Now go and take a look at the baby you hold so dear."

With a start, the housewife ran to the room where her baby had been sleeping, but there was no sign of the child. "Oh, no!" she cried. "Everyone, please wake up!"

The housewife turned pale, and shook her husband awake and everyone else in the house. In a panic, they all ran to the front of the house but the cart was nowhere to be seen. The husband was in tears. "Look what you've done," he yelled accusingly. But it was too late.

The housewife could not just simply give up on the child she loved so much. With tears running down her face, she wrote down her feelings on a piece of paper and posted it on the front door. "The person who did wrong by looking at the cart," it said, "was me. The child is guilty of no crime at all. If you will return my baby, I will accept any punishment, no matter how terrible."

The following night, the ghost cart creaked along and stopped in front of the housewife's door. Although she wanted to dash outside, the housewife held herself patiently in check. "If I look upon this woman again," she thought, "my child may be killed outright."

The woman in the ghost cart gazed fixedly at the paper posted on the door, and suddenly spoke with what seemed a very sad demeanor. "What a tender-hearted woman this mother must be. The defeat is mine. Although I had thought that I would never return this child, this time—just this once—I shall do so."

The housewife heard this from where she crouched inside the door, and hurried to the child's room, nearly falling over as she ran. And there was the child, sound asleep.

"Thank you, thank you." The housewife cried, quietly putting the palms of her hands together as the creaking of the ghost cart could be heard gradually going farther and farther away.

After this event, the ghost cart never returned.

Earless Hoichi

Long ago, there was a Buddhist priest named Hoichi who played the *biwa* and was living at the Amida Temple in Shimonoseki. The biwa is a musical instrument [much like a lute] in the shape of a loquat ["biwa" in Japanese] cut in half. Buddhist monks who sing sad stories while playing this instrument are called Biwa Buddhist Priests.

Hoichi was blind, but he was excellent at his vocation. When Hoichi played the biwa and sang, everyone would become spellbound and their tears would flow.

This happened one summer night.

The abbot had gone out to attend a funeral of someone in the town, and Hoichi was left alone, playing the biwa. It was completely quiet inside the temple, and only the sound of his biwa resounded through the halls. He was alone, and gradually became frightened. And for some reason, the abbot had not returned even though it was the middle of the night.

"The abbot hasn't returned…" Thinking this, he suddenly withdrew the hand that plucked the biwa. Now he could hear the footsteps of someone drawing near. "It must be the abbot," he thought, but as he listened carefully, the footsteps stopped short right in front of him.

"Hey! Hoichi!" someone said in a scary intimidating voice.

"Ye…Yes. Who might your honor be?" Shocked, Hoichi turned his face in the direction of the voice.

"I am a samurai who lives nearby. I have come to call on you at the order of my lord."

"As you can see, I am blind, so please forgive me," Hoichi said humbly. He was quite frightened, and his body shook with fear,

"You don't have to be afraid," the samurai said. "The fact is that my lord would very much like to hear you play your biwa. Well then, bring your biwa and come with me." The samurai's voice was not unpleasant, but was quite forceful.

Hoichi was led by the samurai's hand, and the two of them went outside. Hoichi had no idea of where or how they walked, but in a while the samurai let go of Hoichi's hand and said, "Alright, we've arrived."

There was the creaking sound of a gate being opened, and Hoichi was accompanied into what seemed to be a large sitting room. Around him there was, perhaps, a large number of samurai and women. Then an older woman said, "Hoichi, thank you for coming. Please let us hear your specialty, the story of Dannoura."

The story of Dannoura is one of events that happened more than 800 years ago. At that time, a sea battle took place in the nearby Dannoura Straits between the samurai of the Heike and Genji clans. In this battle, the Genji were victorious, and one by one the ships of the Heike were destroyed and sunk. The samurai, women, and even the children in those ships jumped into the sea and died. From that time on, it is said that a strange thing occurred in the sea around Dannoura. When night fell, pale white fires seemed to float up and ignite in the completely dark sea. When boats passed by, water-soaked samurai would appear from the bottom of the sea, throw the boats into confusion and sink them.

"Ah, how fearful! This must be the resentment of the dead Heike samurai." The people who lived nearby were frightened, and no one would go out in a boat alone.

After that, the Amida Temple was established, graves for the dead were erected, and prayers were said. And because of that, the sea ghosts seemed to no longer appear. Hoichi lived in that Amida Temple.

"Hoichi! Quickly play your biwa," the woman said again.

"Yes, well then…"

Hoichi cradled the biwa, and began to sing calmly. The plucking sound of the biwa and his beautiful voice echoed around the room. It must have been a remarkably sad song, for each time he raised his voice and shook his head, one could hear sobbing here and there. Especially in those places that told of the Heike being driven back and the little children jumping into the sea, all around raised their voices and cried.

Up to now, Hoichi had plucked his biwa many times, but until tonight no had heard him play so passionately. And even after he had finished the song, the weeping and sobbing could be heard for some time.

"Hoichi, we enjoyed hearing your song very much, and our lord was extremely pleased. Please come again every night and play again."

"Yes, well thank you very much."

But when Hoichi stood up, the woman quickly raised her voice, "But by no means tell anyone that our lord is here."

"Ye, yes. I will tell no one."

That night, the samurai once again took his hand and secretly returned him to the temple.

Thus, Hoichi set out for the lord's mansion the next night, and the night after that. About then, the abbot noticed that Hoichi was always slipping out of the temple about midnight. But even though the abbot questioned him, "Say, Hoichi, where are you going at night?" Hoichi only remained silent.

Finally, one night, the abbot decided to try to follow Hoichi. It was about midnight when a single samurai arrived at the temple. He was wearing fine armor, and was clearly high-ranked. Not noticing that the abbot was following them, he left the temple with Hoichi. However, as bad luck would have it, it was raining and outside of the temple the night was totally dark. After he could walk no longer, the abbot lost track of the two men.

"Where could they have gone," he wondered. But as he looked around restlessly, he heard the sound of the biwa being plucked in the direction of some graves. Surprised, the abbot ventured near the graves. There, pale white fires flitted around the gravestones; and seated in front of those gravestones, Hoichi was singing and plucking his biwa. The abbot was so frightened that his body shook and his voice caught in his throat.

"Ho...Ho...Hoichi!" At last, he could say only that, and putting his arms around Hoichi, hurried him back to the temple. There, he quickly changed Hoichi's drenched clothes and had him drink some hot water.

"Hoichi, listen carefully," the abbot said sternly. "The place you have been going to every night is the graveyard of the Amida Temple. You have been playing the biwa in front of the graves of the Heike samurai. You poor thing! You have been manipulated by the spirits of the Heike. If things remain in this way, they will surely kill you."

When Hoichi heard this, he turned completely pale, and told the abbot everything that had happened up until then in detail.

"Alright, alright. I'm going to help you." So saying, the abbot had Hoichi take off all of his clothes, and wrote verses from a sutra in India ink over his entire body, including his face and his hands. "With this," he said, "due to the sutra's power, the dead will not be able to see your body. But if they hear one word from your mouth, the Heike spirits will tear you limb from limb."

Thus, the abbot strictly warned Hoichi.

Well, the next night, the abbot had some errand, left for the town, and Hoichi was sitting intently inside the temple when the samurai arrived.

"Hoichi, Hoichi! I've come for you!"

But there was no response. The samurai abruptly entered the room and began to search for Hoichi. Nevertheless, his body could not be seen because it had been covered with the writing from the sutra.

"Hoichi's biwa has been left here and, huh, I can see his two ears. Well, there's nothing to be done. Tonight I'll just go back with these ears." With this, the samurai grasped Hoichi's ears and forcefully ripped them off of his head. Hoichi instinctively was about to cry out, but knew that if he did, he would be killed. Enduring the pain, he bit his teeth for all he was worth.

At last, the abbot returned. He had been worried about Hoichi, and had hurried back to the temple. But what was this? Hoichi had collapsed in the middle of the temple, and the place was covered in blood.

"Hoichi! Be strong!" The abbot put his arms around Hoichi and sat him up. When he looked, he could see that Hoichi's ears had been ripped off, and that blood was profusely flowing from the wounds. "Hoichi, please forgive me! I forgot to write the sutras on your ears. But you forbore, and after this the dead will not return again."

"Abbot, I was scared!" And with this, he fell into the abbot's arms.

"Now, now. This must have been truly frightening, and you must be in pain. *Namu Amida Butsu. Namu Amida Butsu.*" While the abbot chanted the sutra, he dressed Hoichi's ears, and thanks to that, the wounds gradually got better.

Eventually, this story spread around Japan, and many people came from all over to hear Hoichi play the biwa. Afterwards, Hoichi became the most famous biwa playing priest in all of Japan.

As Smooth as an Egg

In the Akasaka section of Tokyo, there is a steep road called the Kii Province Slope. Many years ago, there was a deep canal on one side of this road, while on the other side a line of mansions continued all the way to the top. It was a lonely place even during daytime, and after the sun set almost no one traveled along the road. There were rumors that badgers lived in the area that deceived and played tricks on people in any way they could.

One night, however, an old man was making his way up this road on some urgent business. It was a moonless night and the area was completely dark. Nevertheless, the old man moved along, holding a lamp to guide his footsteps.

Halfway up the hill, he could barely make out someone standing by the side of the moat.

"Could this actually be a ghost?" he wondered.

Nervously, the old man moved the lamp toward the person. Even in the darkness, he could see that it was a woman who was facing the moat and crying.

"Excuse me, but what's the matter?" the old man asked gently. But the woman, who was crying pitifully, did not answer. When he looked carefully, the old man could see that the woman seemed to be quite young, and that she was perhaps the daughter of some upper-class family. Her kimono, he noted, was of the highest quality.

"No doubt she's here for some very serious reason," the old man concluded, and forgetting all about his urgent business he walked up to the woman's side.

"Listen," he said softly. "You shouldn't just stand there and cry. Try to tell me what the matter is. I'll do whatever I can to help you."

Hearing these words, the woman raised her voice and cried even more violently. It seemed as though she would jump into the moat at any time.

"Wai ... wait! You mustn't think about dying," the old man stammered. Shaken to his core, he put his hand on the woman's shoulder to stop her from jumping. With that, the woman suddenly stopped crying, and with her hands still covering her face, she turned around. Then, in an instant, she let her hands fall to her waist.

"Ahhh!" The old man stumbled backwards, his breath caught tight in his chest. The woman's face was as smooth as an egg, with no eyes, nose or mouth.

"Some ... somebody help!" the old man cried and ran tottering up the slope, oblivious to where he was going.

The old man had no idea how long he had been running. Then, suddenly, he saw a small flickering light up ahead. "I'm saved!" he mumbled. "Thank the gods!"

The old man finally managed to stagger up to the light, and saw that it came from a small soba shop at the edge of the road. Wasting no time, he entered the shop, breathing hard and in a state of shock.

"What's the matter?" said the shop owner, who was standing over his stove.

"Ah, ah, ah...." The old man was out of breath and hardly able to say anything.

"Have you been robbed?"

"I ... I ... I saw her." The old man was finally able to get something out of his mouth. "A wo ... wo ... woman!"

"Really?" the shopkeeper replied. "What did she look like?"

The old man nearly went crazy just thinking about her face.

"Did she look anything like this?" the shopkeeper asked, and he turned towards the old man and stroked his face. In an instant, the man's face had become as smooth as an egg. Then the lamp went out.

The old man screamed something in a high-pitched voice, and fainted dead away.

Demons and Wolves

鬼とオオカミをめぐるお話

The Demon of Rashomon

Many, many years ago in the ancient capital of Kyoto, there stood a large roofed gate called the Rashomon. At some point, a terrifying demon began to live inside the structure of this gate, and the rumor was that it ate passers-by. Even in the daytime, no one walked by or through this gate, and when the sun set no one even came close to it.

There was at this time, however, a very powerful samurai, already famous for having subdued the demon of Mount Ooe, by the name of Watanabe no Tsuna.

"All right," he thought when he got wind of this rumor, "I'll go and see this for myself."

So saying, one night he mounted his horse and rode off. At his waist he had his famous sword, "The Demon-cutter."

Very soon the Rashomon came into view. The great roof of the gate towered above him in the dark night sky, and the entire area was as silent as a grave. Tsuna momentarily looked up at the gate, but did not find it particularly frightening.

"It is a little uncanny," he murmured to himself, "but I don't see anything that looks like a demon around here." Then, just as he was about to return home, "Excuse me," a woman's voice came from behind him.

Turning around from where he sat in his saddle, he found that the voice belonged to a pretty young woman.

"Please could you accompany me to my house in the Gojo area? I was on my way back from an errand and the sun suddenly went down. Now I seem to have lost my way."

Tsuna thought that it was rather strange for a young woman to be walking by herself in such a lonely place, but he dismounted and said, "How unfortunate. Yes, I know the Gojo area quite well. Let me help you onto my horse."

Just as the woman seemed to be stepping into the stirrup, she suddenly transformed into a terrifying demon, took Tsuna by the neck, and began to fly into the sky.

"Now I've done it!" Tsuna choked. He quickly tried to wrestle himself free from the demon's grip, but to no avail.

Laughing fiendishly, the demon rapidly flew higher and higher.

Tsuna was desperate. He unsheathed his sword, and with a great shout struck out at his captor.

"Yaah!" the demon shrieked, and instantly Tsuna fell with a thud on the roof of the Rashomon. A second later, a severed hairy arm landed next to him.

In the black night, he could hear the demon screaming, "You may have cut off my arm, but beware, I'll be back for it in seven days!" The screams seemed to be coming from farther and farther away, but at last everything was silent.

"Well now," Tsuna thought to himself. "So this is the arm of a demon." Picking up the arm, he found that it was as hard as steel and covered uncannily with hair. The fingernails were like the sharp points of lancets.

"Well, I've gotten something interesting here," he said to himself. "I think I'll bring it home."

Tsuna returned home, put the demon's arm in a strongbox and locked the box securely with a key. Then he commanded his retainers to be on the lookout for anything strange around his mansion.

The sixth day passed. Then, in the evening of the seventh day, a little old lady arrived at Tsuna's gate.

"Hello! Hello!" the old lady shouted as loudly as she could. "I'm Watanabe no Tsuna's aunt! I haven't seen him for a long time and have come for a visit. My home is way out in the countryside and I'm quite tired. Would you please let me in?"

"The lord has given strict orders that no one – no matter who – is to be allowed in," the gatekeeper on duty yelled back. "So I'm afraid that even his relatives are not welcome." And with this, he was about to go out and drive the old lady away.

But she suddenly burst into tears and sobbed, "How cold-hearted he is to say such a thing. I've cared for him and spoiled him since he was little, and now he's going to drive me away. That's too much. That's just too much!"

The watchman was confused and went to his lord Tsuna to report what had occurred.

"What? My aunt, you say?" Tsuna interjected. "Bring her here right away!"

The old lady entered the room and grasped Tsuna by the hand.

"Ahh, Tsuna. I've wanted to see you for so long."

"I'm so glad to see you, Auntie," Tsuna replied, and happily took her by the hand as well.

"By the way," the old lady said with a worried look. "Why aren't you letting anyone into your mansion? Has there been some sort of trouble?"

"Yes, the fact is, that a demon may be on its way here."

"What? A demon, you say?"

The old lady seemed quite shocked as she looked intently into Tsuna's face. For his part, Tsuna then told her the entire story, detail by detail.

"Is that so?" she finally exclaimed. "You really cut off a demon's arm? That's just like a nephew of mine! I'd like to see just what a demon's arm looks like!"

"Oh no," Tsuna returned. "That's the one thing I can't do. The demon's coming back for it, you know."

"Ahh, don't be so unfeeling," the old lady cried. "Looking at it for just a second won't hurt. I'm an old lady and don't know when I'm going to die. I would just like to see something like that once in my life!"

Hearing his aunt talk in this way, Tsuna felt that he couldn't refuse. "All right," he said hesitantly, "but just for a second."

Taking out the box, he released the lock and showed the old lady what was inside.

"Oh, my! This is a demon's arm? How frightening!"

As she looked intently inside the box, however, the old lady suddenly grabbed the arm and flew up towards the ceiling. "Tsuna! You see?" she screamed. "I've come back for my arm!"

The old lady's face instantly turned into that of a horrifying demon. Breaking through the window in the ceiling, the demon danced up into the sky.

"Wait! Wait!" Tsuna unsheathed his sword and raced after the demon, but the figure became smaller and smaller. Soon, the sky was completely black.

Then came the fiendish high-pitched laughter, which also slowly faded away.

Tsuna stamped his feet and cursed, but it was all over. Nevertheless, possibly from its fear of this dauntless samurai, the demon never appeared again at the Rashomon.

The Old Lady Who Turned into a Demon

Long ago, in the village of Nonoguchi, which was in the old province of Tamba, there lived a man by the name of Yoji. He lived with his grandmother, a woman who had reached the incredible age of a hundred and sixty. Despite her age, this woman's eyes were clear and her hearing quite sharp. Her teeth were as strong as rocks, and she could crunch away at anything from hard beans to brittle rice cakes.

"What a healthy old lady!" the elderly of the village said. "I'd like to be as strong as she is!" How jealous they felt.

After some time, however, the old lady stopped eating rice. Up until this point, she had been able to eat as much as the young people in the village, so this was somewhat strange.

Yoji was worried and said, "Grandma, if you stop eating rice, I'm afraid you'll die."

"What are you talking about?" she said. "Not eating rice is all the same to me," and it seemed as though she had stopped eating rice for good.

By abstaining from eating rice as she did, the old lady rapidly lost weight. Her eyes sank into her head, her teeth stuck out like sticks, and she began to look like an old ogress. Somehow, she was turning a blue-green color right to her eyes. The strange thing, however, was that her bones—and only her bones—were getting thicker and thicker.

About this time, the old lady's behavior was also becoming rather strange. At midnight she would suddenly get up, look like she was peering around, then look at Yoji's face and start chuckling.

This naturally worried Yoji, and he was unable to sleep well at night.

One night, Yoji suddenly woke up and saw that his grandmother was about to go outside. "Where would she be going at midnight?" he wondered.

Yoji quietly got up himself and secretly followed the old woman. His grandmother was unaware of what he was doing and walked quickly on alone without looking behind. The speed of her steps was almost inhuman.

The old lady finally stopped when she got to the graveyard just outside the village. To lose sight of her now would be a disaster, so Yoji moved along quickly, then hid behind a large cedar tree. "Uh oh, where did she go?" he wondered. He had looked away for a moment and the old lady had disappeared. "I'm sure she was right over there."

Yoji looked around restlessly, then he heard the sound of something being crunched or chewed from the direction of the graves. Fearfully, he looked carefully among the grave markers.

Then … what was that?

There was the old lady—his grandmother—her hair disheveled, chewing on human bones! Human bones, dug up from the graves—bones of hands and feet and full skeletons—were strewn all over the ground.

"Aah!" When Yoji unthinkingly let out a groan, his grandmother suddenly whirled around and glared at him with a horrible expression.

"What have you seen, my boy?" In the very instant she said this, the old lady ran through the gravestones with the bones still in her mouth, and headed toward the mountains in full flight.

That was the last time anyone ever saw the old lady, and nobody knew where she went. It was rumored among the people of the village, however, that she had turned into the demon of Mount Oe.

Adachi Plain

A long time ago, there was a monk who was traveling alone. Just as he reached a broad, wild area by the name of the Adachi Plain, the sun went down and night fell suddenly upon him.

"This is not good," he thought. "I'd better find some lodging for tonight in a hurry."

The monk walked along quickly, but the grasses and reeds reaching his shoulders were thick and dense, and there was nothing that even resembled a road. He pushed on, however, parting the grasses and stumbling over roots as he went.

"I wonder if I could at least see lights from a house," he thought to himself. Stopping for a moment, he looked for any horizon he could make out, but the night was completely dark and he could see nothing at all. Just then, the wind picked up and a warm breeze lightly shook the grasses and the branches of the trees.

"There's nothing to be done," he mused. "I'll just have to sleep here tonight." Looking around, he found a large cedar tree and propped himself up against one of its roots. Then, suddenly, he spied a faint light between the swaying grasses.

"What a blessing! I'm saved," he said, relieved.

The monk walked hurriedly in the direction of the light, and found, in an opening in the grasses, a cave where an old lady was spinning cotton into thread. "Good evening," he said politely. "I'm on a journey and have lost my way. Would you let me stay here just one night?"

"Well, well. If a place like this will do, you're welcome to spend the night." The old lady let the monk come into the cave, which chilled him to the bone, and was without even the hint of a fire. "I've just run out of firewood," she explained to her visitor. "I'll go out and collect some. Just wait here a little while, please."

So saying, the old lady was about to leave the cave when she turned around with a terrible look on her face and exclaimed, "Do not on any account look into the next room until I return!"

After the old lady went out, the monk sat quietly in front of the fireless hearth. But there was no way he could not feel uneasy about what might be in the next room. When you're told not to look at something, you want to look at it all the more.

Through a crack in the door, the monk stole a look into the next room. And inside—inside was a mountain of human bones piled high, and the room itself was splattered with dark red blood.

"Ah!" he gasped. "This old lady must be a man-eating demon!" Leaping out of the cave, the monk ran as fast as he could go without looking back once.

"I told him not to look," the old lady screamed when she returned, "but he seems to have peeped inside anyway! Now I'll kill him for sure!" In the twinkling of an eye, her face turned into that of a demoness and she ran off in pursuit of the monk.

The monk did not know where or how he was fleeing. Looking back for a second, he saw the terrifying ogress, her fangs jutting out and her white hair completely disheveled, gaining on him with every leaping step she took.

Suddenly, he tripped over a tree root and fell to the ground. "Ahh, this is the end," he murmured. But taking out the statue of Kannon[1] he carried in his backpack, he prayed with all his might. Suddenly, a ray of light fell from the sky, hitting the ogress with a jolt.

With an earth-shattering scream, the ogress, who was on the verge of grasping the monk's throat, died on the spot.

When day broke, the monk awoke from his dream, and looking around found himself still in the pathless Adachi Plain. Getting up from the root of the cedar tree where he had lain the night before, he felt a slight shiver go down his spine. Shouldering his pack, he hurried on in the early morning sun.

---

[1] Kannon: The Buddhist goddess of mercy, who, according to the 25th chapter of the *Lotus Sutra*, will come to the aid of those who call out her name.

Messengers from Enma, the King of Hell

A long time ago, in the ancient province of Yamato, there was a merchant by the name of Iwajima. One day, on his return from some business, Iwajima was walking along the bank of Lake Biwa when he suddenly felt ill, and was unable to take a single step farther. He threw up everything he had eaten that day, and his head hurt so that he thought it might split in two.

"Am I going to die right here?" he wondered. Leaning against a nearby tree, he sank to the ground.

Just then, he saw three demons coming toward him from the other direction. Each had a mouth that split its face from ear to ear, and large protruding fangs.

"If I stay here, I'll be eaten alive," Iwajima thought, and he ran off, tottering on unsteady legs. Feeling as bad as he did, he could not run as fast as he needed to, and the demons quickly caught up with him.

"Wait! Wait!" one of the demons cried. "You don't have to run away. We're not going to hurt you."

Hearing this, Iwajima was more than a little relieved, and said, "Well then, where are the three of you going?"

"Well, we are messengers from Enma, the king of Hell," the red demon said. "We're looking for a man around here who's about to die."

"Goodness! Then who is this man and where is he from?" asked Iwajima.

"He's a man by the name of Iwajima from Yamato," came the reply.

"What! Iwajima?" Iwajima turned pale and squatted down in shock.

"Hey!" The blue demon looked questioningly at Iwajima's reaction. "What's the matter?"

The situation was desperate but Iwajima said quite frankly, "I'm your man."

"What?" one of the demons blurted out. "You're Iwajima?" The demons looked at each other and smiled.

"Yes! But why do I have to die?" Iwajima asked in a loud voice, forgetting that he was ill. "I've done nothing wrong."

The demons were surprised at his vehemence, and looked up and down, avoiding his face.

"Don't be angry," the red demon said. "It was Enma who sent us to bring you back to Hell, and because of you we've had a hard time of it. We went to your house to take charge of you, but they told us you were gone on business. We were afraid we were going to be beaten by Enma, so we've spent the entire day running around after you, but couldn't turn up a clue. Thanks to you, we've spent the whole day in a fruitless search and now we're famished. Say, you haven't got anything to eat, have you?"

"Unfortunately, I'm on my way back from a business trip," Iwajima replied, "and have nothing with me here. But why don't you come to my house? If you will, I can serve you anything you like."

The demons were overjoyed at hearing this and returned with Iwajima to his home.

"Well then, tell me. What can I get you? Sake? Rice? I can provide whatever you like, and lots of it, too." Iwajima smiled. His spirits had completely recovered, and he now felt perfectly fine.

"I don't like to trouble you," the blue demon said, "but can you bring us some beef?"

"What? Beef!" Iwajima exclaimed. "That's no problem at all. I'll buy you some right away." With that, he instructed his household to go out and buy a cow. Now, at that time a cow was a very expensive animal and you could not buy one without a great deal of cash. Nevertheless, such an outlay was far better than being carted off to Hell.

"Oh, my! Excuse our manners, but…." The demons gulped down

this gorgeous meal in the twinkling of an eye.

With that, the blue demon began to look rather troubled. "Having received a feast like this from you," he began, "it would be a poor thing now to take you off to Hell. But if we don't, we're going to be in for some rough treatment from Enma. Hmm. This is a real problem."

The other demons agreed, and the three of them fell into deep thought.

Suddenly, the red demon clapped his hands and said, "I've got it! Instead of this man, we'll just carry back another one."

"Yes, yes!" the other two quickly agreed. "An excellent idea."

Iwajima felt bad for the man who would become his substitute, but on the other hand he would not have to take part in dying himself. So he remained silent.

"All right, then, it's settled!" the blue demon exclaimed. "Let's go out and find a stand-in. Listen, Iwajima, that was a real feast!"

The three demons then returned in good spirits. And thanks to his substitute, Iwajima lived to be over ninety years old—a long and happy life.

The Old Wolf Lady at Saki no Ura

A long time ago, there was a small fishing village called Saki no ura in the ancient province of Tosa. Near this village there was a steep mountain by the name of Mount None. Hundreds of ferocious wolves lived on this mountain, and they killed and ate travelers who passed over the road at night. The villagers were understandably terrified, and when night fell no one would even walk from one house to another.

Once, however, there was a courier who happened to be on this road just as night fell. Shouldering a wooden pack containing the letters in his charge, he jogged over the steep mountain passes, repeating a sort of rhythmic chant as he went along.

"Ei-ho! Ei-ho!"

Inside his pack this particular night was an important letter from the local lord.

Just as the courier was passing a large cryptomeria, he heard what sounded like the painful groan of a woman.

"That's a strange thing to hear at a time like this," he thought.

The courier stopped and then walked slowly in the direction of the moaning voice. He could now hear that it was coming from inside a small but dense thicket in front of his eyes.

Hesitantly, he held up his lamp to see. And there was a young woman collapsed on the grass. Holding her distended belly, she was panting and gasping for breath.

"Excuse me," he said softly, "what is the matter?"

"I was on an errand to the next mountain," she said, "and my belly began to hurt. I think I'm about to have my baby…." And with that, she held her belly again and seemed to be in terrible distress.

"This is terrible," the courier thought, cradling the poor woman's head. He had to quickly deliver the important letter he was carrying, but on the other hand he could not simply abandon a woman in pain. At the same time, he had no idea how to deliver a baby. And if he hesitated too long, the baby was going to be born anyway.

As a stopgap, the courier gathered some grass for a bed beneath the cryptomeria, and got the woman to lie down and rest there. Her condition became worse and worse, however, and she cried out as though she was being murdered.

Suddenly, the howls of approaching wolves could be heard coming from here and there, as though they were joining her groans in chorus.

"We're in for it now," the courier shuddered. "We've been discovered by the wolves!"

The courier unsheathed his sword and took a stance so that he might protect the young woman. Low growls came from nearby and numerous fiery eyes began to gleam in the dark.

Suddenly, one of the wolves let out a sharp howl and instantaneously leapt toward the courier. The courier quickly jumped to the side, away from the animal's path, but now there were wolves coming at him from the front and behind. Brandishing his sword, he flailed away at them in any way he could. The wolves he was able to strike yelped in pain and ran away, but immediately other wolves would appear and join the attack. It seemed clear that a single courier was not going to be able to hold them off for long.

Just when the courier was thinking he could not stay on his feet much longer, one of the wolves suddenly barked in a near human voice, "This fellow's pretty tough. We'd better call the old lady at the blacksmith's shop in Saki no ura."

No sooner was this pronounced than he ran off like the wind, the other wolves following him in one great pack.

"We're saved!" the courier panted and sat heavily on the ground.

Perhaps because she had been frightened by the wolves, the young lady lay absolutely still, her eyes shut tight.

It occurred to the courier that if they didn't escape now, the situation might turn for the worse, but just as he began to take the woman up in his arms to carry her away, the wolf pack closed in again. At the head of the pack was an old wolf that seemed to be its leader, and its expression was truly frightening.

"All right," the courier thought. "If this is the way it's going to be, I'll take out the leader first." Once again, he brandished his sword, and in a flash struck at the head wolf. The wolf, who was caught unawares, let out an ear-splitting howl of pain and fled.

Their leader had run away, so there was nothing to be done. The other wolves leapt away in full panic.

The courier was certain that the wolves would not be coming back, and relieved, went back to where he had left the young woman. At the first hint of dawn, she finally gave birth to a baby boy.

The courier then accompanied mother and son to the village without incident.

The next day, the courier went through Saki no ura again on his return from delivering the letter, and suddenly remembered the events of the night before. "I'm sure the wolves mentioned an old lady at the blacksmith's shop," he recalled. When he asked a villager who was passing by if there was a blacksmith's shop in the vicinity, the man replied, "The blacksmith shop? It's right over there."

Walking over to the front of the shop, he found that there was some sort of commotion going on inside. "What's the matter?" he asked one of the members of the household.

"The fact is," the man answered, "that the old lady of the house was injured by the tusk of a wild boar last night." When the courier inquired about the nature of the injury, the man replied with a grimace, "It was an injury to her head; a terrible wound."

"Just what I thought," the courier mused, and deep inside clapped his hands in satisfaction. Then, with an innocent expression on his face, said, "Well, that's a terrible disaster. But I happen to be a doctor, and if you like I'll take a look at her."

"That would be a blessing," the man said. "Please come in."

The man happily led the courier to the room where the old lady was lying down and groaning, her hands tightly grasping the edge of the futon.

The courier sat at her pillow and looked at the old lady's face. "This is a sword wound for sure," he thought. Swiftly taking the short sword he had hidden in his robe from its sheath, he stabbed the old lady right through the heart.

"Take that, you old wolf!"

He did this with such speed that the people of the household had no time to intervene. The old lady gave a shriek and died on the spot.

And then it happened: hair suddenly began to grow from the old lady's body and her face turned into that of a wolf right before the onlookers' eyes.

The courier explained the events of the night before to the shocked members of the household. "Well, this thing must have eaten our old granny as well," one of them said, and looking under the bed they found a pile of human bones mixed with an old lady's gray hair.

The cryptomeria where the young lady gave birth is still standing, and its leaves have become talismans for local women who are about to have children themselves.

Kappas

河童をめぐるお話

The Kappa's Promissory Note

A long time ago, there was a *kappa*[1] that lived near the village of Nishikawatsu in the ancient province of Izumo.

One day, a horse was at the riverbank nibbling grass when the *kappa* appeared, grabbed the horse's reins and tried to pull it into the river. The horse was startled and abruptly ran off, pulling the *kappa*, which was still grasping the horse's reins, along with it. Slipping and sliding, the *kappa* was dragged right into the middle of a vegetable field.

"Hey! A *kappa*!" yelled the farmers who were working in the field. "Let's get it!" And throwing down their spades, they chased after it.

Regardless of how nimble *kappa* usually are, they are quite helpless once on land, so the farmers quickly captured it and tied it up with a coarse straw rope.

"What shall we do with it?" one of the farmers asked.

"It's nothing to us," another replied. "Let's kill it!"

"Yeah," another farmer added. "These things will pull the living liver right out of a human being." Accordingly, all of them started beating the *kappa* and were ready to put it to death.

"Wait, please!" the *kappa* cried. "If you'll spare my life, I'll do anything you say."

The *kappa* begged so earnestly that the farmers decided not to kill it, but to make it work at the village headman's house; and for a short time, the *kappa* worked hard, sweeping around the house and weeding the fields.

Nevertheless, it's a *kappa*'s stock in trade to pull a human's liver right out of his anus, and in spite of himself the *kappa* absentmindedly started thinking about getting his fingers on the anus of one of the farmers.

"No, no!" it admonished itself. "That sort of thing is going to get you killed!" and he rapped one of his hands hard with the other.

---

[1] A *kappa* is a green imp-like creature, usually described as about the size of a 5-year-old child, living in ponds and streams. It has a sort of saucer on the top of its head which must be filled with water or it becomes helpless. It is said to sometimes pull children or other animals into deep water where they might drown. Its favorite food is cucumbers.

As for the farmers, those who worked in the field with the *kappa* could not help feeling uneasy. They never knew when, in a careless moment, the *kappa* might pull their livers right out of their anuses.

In talking this situation over with the village headman, they decided to make the *kappa* write a promissory note, and then return the *kappa* to the river. A promissory note, in this case, was a promise not to misbehave written on paper.

"Listen, *kappa*," the village headman said. "As long as you're around, the farmers won't be able to settle down to work. So we've decided that if you'll write a promissory note declaring that you won't pull out people's livers any more, we'll let you go back to your river."

Hearing this, the *kappa* was overjoyed. "Good enough!" it exclaimed. "What's more, if anyone falls into the river and is about to go under, if that person will yell 'Izumo Nishikawatsu Village' three times, I'll come to his aid right away."

Thus, the *kappa* was able to return to its river, and the villagers had a way to keep from drowning if they fell into it.

The promissory note is said to remain in Nishikawatsu to this day.

The Kappa's Ointment

A long time ago, there was a doctor by the name of Mondo no kami Morikiyo, who was a retainer of the great warlord Takeda Shingen. One day, he was riding his horse across a river when, halfway across, the horse came to a halt and could not move.

"What's this?" the doctor exclaimed. Looking down into the water, he saw a long yellow arm looming out of the depths, its hand firmly grasping the horse's leg.

"Hey! Let go!" the doctor yelled, but the hand only grasped the horse's leg more firmly. The doctor unsheathed his sword and, in a flash, cut off the arm. The horse, now freed, easily crossed over to the opposite bank of the river. The arm, however, was still firmly attached to the horse's leg.

"A ha!" the doctor thought. "This is the arm of a *kappa*. I've come into possession of something quite interesting." And detaching the *kappa*'s arm from his horse's leg, he returned home.

That evening, just as the doctor was getting ready to go to bed, something slipped quietly into his room.

"Who are you?" the doctor demanded as he quickly grasped the sword beneath his pillow. "Identify yourself!"

"It's the *kappa*," came a feeble voice.

"What! The *kappa*?" The doctor lit the small lamp at his bedside and a found a one-armed *kappa* with a pale face seated on the floor.

"I beg you to forgive me," the *kappa* began. "I promise I'll never play tricks like that again. Please just give me back my arm."

"I'm hardly going to give you back your arm," the doctor scowled. "Perhaps I should take your other one now."

"No. No, please don't do that," the *kappa* pleaded. "If you will just give me back my arm, I will teach you how to prepare the most effective ointment in the whole of Japan. Here is a sample."

"All right, I'll give you back your arm," the doctor said. "Let's use it as a trial to see if this ointment really works or not."

The *kappa* took the arm, attached it to its former place on his body, and then applied the medicine where the cut had been made. Miraculously, the arm was restored to its former condition and the wound disappeared altogether.

The doctor was duly impressed. "I see," he exclaimed. "This ointment really does work. Will you teach me how to make it?"

With this, the *kappa* taught the doctor exactly how the medicine was made.

In gratitude, the doctor smilingly offered the *kappa* some sake as a show of goodwill. But just as he went to get the heated bottle and cups, he suddenly woke up.

"What? Was this just a dream?" In confusion, he looked next to his pillow where he had placed the *kappa*'s arm, but it was not there. "This is awfully strange," he thought.

The doctor jumped up and hurriedly ran out to the veranda. And there, dripping with water, were the maple leaf shaped footprints of a *kappa*.

The next morning, the doctor promptly prepared some of the medicine just as the *kappa* had taught him and went to the castle where the lord was residing. There, he applied it to the wounds that some of the samurai had received in battle, and then stepped back. To his amazement, the pain the men had felt for days was completely gone, and the wounds had disappeared as though they had never been there.

The doctor nodded to himself in quiet understanding.

At this point, the doctor left the service of the lord, and setting up shop started selling his medicine, which he called "the *kappa*'s ointment." Soon, the reputation of this medicine spread and people with one kind of wound or another came from all over the country to purchase it.

The doctor then became a pharmacist, taught the secret preparation of the *kappa*'s ointment to his children and grandchildren and his little shop prospered for years to come.

The Kappa's Return of a Favor

A long time ago in the ancient province of Hida, there lived a farmer in the village of Kawai by the name of Chohei.

Early one summer morning, Chohei went to check on his cucumber patch. Although it had been full of cucumbers up until the day before, he now found that a full half of them were gone.

"What's this?" he stammered. "Who could have done such a thing?" Chohei was outraged and decided that from that evening on he would begin staying overnight and standing watch at the small field. To this end, he built a small camouflaged hut in the corner of the patch and stood guard throughout the entire night, his eyes as big as saucers.

By dawn the next morning, no one had come.

"Well, maybe my being here tipped off the thief," he thought. Then, just as he was rubbing his sleepy eyes and looking blankly around, he saw a small animal, about the size of a two-year-old child, squatting in the middle of the field, its hands moving energetically back and forth.

"A hah! That must be the culprit!"

Chohei stealthily approached the scene and saw that it was a dark reddish *kappa* eating cucumbers as though in a trance. Right before the farmer's eyes, a pile of cucumbers was rapidly disappearing as quickly as the *kappa* could consume them.

Chohei grabbed his staff, and circling around to the *kappa*'s rear, took careful aim at the dish on its head.

"Hyaa!" Chohei made perfect contact with the dish, and there was nothing more the *kappa* could do. Its eyes rolled around in their sockets, and it collapsed on the ground.

Chohei bound it up with a straw rope, threw it over his shoulder and returned home.

To make sure that it did not escape, Chohei tied up the *kappa* again, this time around its arms, and fastened it to the front of the house.

For the *kappa*, this was a terrible turn of events, and all the people of the village came quickly to take a look for themselves.

"Just as you might imagine, *kappa* have really strange heads," one villager remarked. "They look just like *karasu tengu*."[2]

"So that's the hand that takes off with the anuses of human beings," said another.

As the villagers bantered back and forth about the *kappa*, they poked it with the ends of their staffs and started to give it a beating. With each blow, the *kappa* emitted pitiful little cries and apologized for its actions as well as it could. But the villagers were amused by this sport and tormented the creature all the more.

When evening fell, Chohei's wife came out to the front of the house to scatter some water.

"Please, ma'am," the *kappa* pleaded. "Won't you unfasten these ropes for me?"

"There's no chance of that," the lady replied. "You've eaten the cucumbers that are so hard for us to grow. Do you think we can forgive you for that?"

Chohei's wife took the water-filled ladle and rapped the *kappa* on the head. But what then? Some water spilled into the *kappa*'s dish and the situation took a different turn. The *kappa* instantly regained its strength and tore off the ropes. Leaving its left arm that it could not disengage, it ran off to the river without looking back.

The next morning, when Chohei went out to his cucumber patch, there was the one-armed *kappa*, looking small and quiet, seated on the ground.

---

[2] *Karasu tengu*, the more primitive and dangerous *tengu* whose head resembled those of crows.

"Haven't you learned anything?" Chohei yelled. Taking up his staff, he got ready to give the *kappa* a sound beating, but the little animal quickly put out his one hand in supplication.

"Wait!" it cried. "I'm a *kappa* that lives in the river over there and I promise I'll never steal your cucumbers again. In return, please give me back the arm I left at your house yesterday."

The *kappa* seemed so utterly downcast, that even Chohei felt sorry for it. "All right," he declared. "If you promise never to do such bad deeds again, I'll give you back your arm." Taking the *kappa* back to the house, he returned the arm to the little creature. For its part, the *kappa* was so happy that it shed tears and quietly returned to the river.

The next morning when Chohei got out of bed, he discovered that there were five or six river fish strung to the drying pole that hung under the eaves.

"That is strange," he thought. "Who would have done this?" But the next morning, and the one following, again the fish were hanging there. "Ahh, this must be the *kappa*'s way of thanking me for his arm."

Chohei realized that this was the *kappa*'s doing, and thanks to the *kappa*, he now had fresh fish to eat every day.

After a while, however, the wooden drying pole began to bend with the weight of the fish, so Chohei replaced it with an iron one. But the following morning the fish were not there.

Kappa hate iron more than anything else in the world, and out of fear will never get close to it.

"Ahh, that's right," Chohei remembered, and quickly replaced the iron pole with a wooden one.

But the *kappa* never returned, and from that time on, if Chohei wanted fish to eat, he had to go and catch them himself.

The Ninety-ninth Pass

In Oita Prefecture on the island of Kyushu, there is a mountain road that winds over a place called the Ninety-ninth Pass. Directly below the pass is a deep pond inhabited by *kappa*. The pond is always filled with perfectly blue-green water, and just a glance at it will make you feel uneasy.

Since times past, however, when people went to swim or fish in this pond, the *kappa* would rarely appear, but would rather sink down to the bottom of the pond and stay there until the humans left.

But one evening, a farmer came to the pond to wash his horse. As he was scrubbing the animal, something suddenly began to jerk on its reins, which were hanging down in the water. Taken aback, the farmer could only pull on the horse's tail.

The horse, too, was surprised, and leapt quickly up onto the bank of the pond. In that instant, there was a loud splash and something was thrown up beyond the water's edge.

It was a *kappa*, with the telltale dish right on the top of its head.

"You scoundrel!" the farmer yelled, and quickly started to grapple with the animal. There was no time for the *kappa* to dodge, and in no time at all it was turned upside down and all the water in its dish spilled to the ground. Without that water, of course, the *kappa* was helpless.

The *kappa* was soon pinned to the ground, and the farmer had it by its throat.

"That … that hurts!" The *kappa*'s eyes rolled up to the back of its head, and it put the palms of its hands together as if in supplication.

Even this farmer, who was rough by nature, felt pity for the creature and relaxed his hold.

The *kappa* got up, but then got down on its knees before the farmer and placed its hands on the ground. "I promise I won't get into any more mischief again," it said in a low voice. "Just please let me go. In return, I'll give you my most valuable possession."

When the farmer heard this, he couldn't help but feeling pleased. "What in the world could be valuable to a *kappa*," he wondered.

At this point, the *kappa* said, "I don't have this treasure right here. It's put away in my house, so perhaps you wouldn't mind going there to get it. "If you go on up this mountain path," it continued, "you'll find my place just to the right of the pass. Take this letter and jar, and just give them to the *kappa* who will be there."

So saying, he handed a letter and a jar to the farmer and disappeared.

The farmer considered this to be a little suspicious, but thought that he might as well go along with it, and so started up the mountain path.

His misgivings, however, soon got the better of him, and besides, there was something horribly smelly coming from the jar.

"This is just a bit strange," he said to himself, and so opened the envelope to read the letter on which was written:

As you, my honored boss, have ordered, I have gone out
to collect one hundred human anuses. In this jar you will find
ninety-nine, and you can take the one hundredth from the man
who is delivering this to you.

"What the …?" Barely able to control himself, the farmer threw the jar away and ran back down the mountain at full speed. Arriving home, he broke out in a fever and had to stay in bed for a week.

After this event, this place was called the Ninety-ninth Pass, and thereafter people avoided both it and the pond below.

The Kappa and the Gourd

A long time ago, there was a village headman who lived in a place called Kita Arima. Now, this headman had only one child, a daughter so beautiful that all the young men of the village fervently hoped to become her husband.

One summer, the water in his rice fields had dried up for some reason.

"The river is full of water," the headman thought, "so this is very strange."

On going to investigate the matter, the headman found that it was only the water in his own rice fields that was lacking. All the other rice fields were brimming with water, right to the edges.

"Perhaps the ditches to my fields are stopped up," he said to himself, and he had the ditches to his fields repaired so that the water would flow into them freely.

However, the water still did not enter his rice fields, and without it the rice plants were going to wither and die.

The headman put his head between his hands and thought the matter over with some dismay. "There's really nothing I can do about this except consult the village gods."

So every morning, the village headman, accompanied by his daughter, went to the local shrine and prayed, "Please, won't you let the water into my fields?"

Then, one night the village gods appeared to him in a dream. "There is a *kappa* living in the Arima River," they informed him, "who desires your daughter. If you give your daughter to the *kappa* as a bride, the water will quickly flow again."

The village headman woke up from his dream with a start, his entire body wet with sweat. "This is ridiculous," he thought. "does anyone really believe that I would marry my very own daughter to something like a *kappa*?"

The next morning, the headman got up early and went to inspect his rice fields. Water was flowing freely through all the fields, and the rice plants were green and luxuriant. Except for his. Looking sadly at his own rice fields, the earth was dry and cracked and the rice was badly withered.

Completely dejected, he walked along looking at the ditches when, uh oh, there was the *kappa*, sitting at the outlet of the main ditch. With both hands, it firmly stopped up the entrance so that no water could come through.

"Of course," the headman whispered under his breath. "It's just as the village gods said."

"Master Kappa," he said politely, bowing his head. "I humbly implore that you let the water into my fields."

"Absolutely not," the *kappa* replied with a stern expression. "The water will flow again when you give me your daughter as a bride."

"Ahh, this is horrible," the headman sighed, and dragged his feet homeward.

Utterly depressed, the headman sat looking at his daughter. "The

truth is," he mumbled, "that the *kappa* wants you for his wife." Thinking that he would not inform anyone of this matter, he finally confessed the uncomfortable situation in full.

His daughter, however, just looked at him and said, "If that's the problem, don't worry about it. Just leave it to me." That said, she grabbed a gourd and ran out of the house.

Soon after, the headman's daughter stood on the bank of the Arima River and called out to the *kappa*, "Hey, Master Kappa! Is it true that you want me for a bride?"

Suddenly, the *kappa* stuck his head out of the water. "I love you so much I can hardly bear it," it said, and its blue-green head turned even more so.

"All right," agreed the headman's daughter. "I'll marry you, but in return you must fill my family's rice fields with water."

"Wonderful," the *kappa* exclaimed. "Now there's no reason to hold the water back."

"There's one other thing," the headman's daughter added. "This gourd that I've brought along contains my fate. Only when this gourd sinks beneath the water will I be able to become your wife." With that, she threw the gourd into the river.

A little while later, water filled the headman's fields and his rice plants began to revive and grow luxuriantly green.

The *kappa* had thought that the gourd would sink quickly, and allowed the water to rise and increase, but the gourd showed no signs of sinking. This stands to reason as such a light thing as a gourd is not likely to sink at all.

So thanks to the headman's daughter, the Arima River is always full of water, even when it does not rain. And in the fall, just when the rice is ripening, you can see a single gourd rising and falling, falling and rising, as it floats lightly downstream.

Tanuki and Foxes

タヌキとキツネをめぐるお話

The Priest That Was Eaten by a Dog

A long time ago, in the ancient prefecture of Tosa, there was an old temple located in the countryside called the Saifukuji. There were almost no houses close by the temple, and the surrounding scenery was limited to rice fields and forests. It was said that at night, *tanuki*[1] that transformed into human form often appeared, and as a result no one ever approached this place after sundown.

But one evening, a farmer who was about to return home from watering his fields, caught a glimpse of the priest of the Saifukuji standing on one of the footpaths a short distance away. The priest was squatting down and appeared to be in some pain.

"Honored Priest," the farmer called, hurrying to the priest's side. "What's the matter?"

"Well, you know," the priest replied, "some of the villagers invited me to some celebration but I've twisted my ankle and can't walk properly. I feel terrible asking you this, but could you carry me to the village?"

"What a shame," the farmer said. "Just hop on and hold on tight."

The farmer hoisted the priest up on his back with a grunt, but was surprised at how light the man felt.

"Honored Priest," he said with concern. "You've become quite thin, haven't you?"

"I've got old," the priest remarked pitifully. "I just can't eat as much rice as I used to. Yes, I've become awfully thin."

Nevertheless, the farmer thought it suspicious that this formerly plump priest now seemed to weigh so little, and wondered if a *tanuki* had not transformed itself into the priest. With these doubts, he lightly touched the holy man's foot with the tip of his finger.

And just as he thought, the man's foot was covered with hair.

"A ha!" he said to himself. "A *tanuki*!"

"Honored Priest," the farmer then said nonchalantly. "Your foot seems awfully swollen. If you don't apply something cold to it soon, you're not going to be able to walk again for some time. I'm going to hasten my pace, so let me tie you tightly to my back with my sash."

---

[1] Known as a raccoon dog, a *tanuki* inhabits the mountains and fields of Japan.

So saying, the farmer loosened the sash of his kimono and tied it securely around the priest's back. Then he held on to the priest's feet tightly enough to make them uncomfortable. Returning to his house, the farmer put the priest in his own room, but then locked the door with a key.

Now, if this was really the priest of the Saifukuji, things were going to be a bit uncomfortable, so the farmer sent someone off to the temple to see if the real priest was there. And the priest was indeed at his temple.

"This is the last time you'll fool me," the farmer muttered. He then brought in his best hunting dog and let it into the room where the "priest" was sitting. The dog, whose specialty was *tanuki*, took one look and emitted a low growl. The priest, now recognized as a transformed *tanuki*, began running around the room, trying to escape, but the door was locked and there was no way out.

In the melee that followed, the dog killed his opponent, and when the farmer at last entered the room, there lay the corpse of a large and very old *tanuki*.

The God Inari and Yasubei

Long ago, in the mountainous area of Joshu, there was a farmer by the name of Yasubei who lived in the small village of Odo. He was an honest man and a hard worker, but work as he might, his life never became what you might call comfortable. So one day, he went off to pray at the shrine dedicated to the god Inari,[2] which was located at a mountain behind the village.

"Holy Inari," he begged, "could you not turn me into a wealthy man? If you would do such a thing, I will build the best shrine in Japan for you and worship you always."

After this, Yasubei continued to come to the shrine every day for twenty-one days, and prayed to the god Inari for all he was worth. But by the twenty-first day, nothing had changed.

"What is this?" Yasubei muttered. "Is the god Inari so unreliable?" Disappointed, he went back to work in the fields as usual.

On his first day back in the fields, however, he looked up to see a man riding along on a horse in a carefree manner, singing as he passed by.

A lot of people came by on their way to relax at the Kusatsu hot spring, and as Yasubei watched the man pass by, he thought to himself, "How nice! I wish I could go to that hot spring just once in my life."

Even as he thought this, he continued working hard in his field. Then, taking out a cold, miserable box lunch, Yasubei sat down on the footpath between the fields and absentmindedly watched the clouds as they drifted past. Suddenly, he felt quite exhausted and dozed off. In his dream, a man with pure white hair appeared before him.

"Yasubei!" the man said abruptly. "You are indeed an honest and hardworking man. Tonight I'm sending the god Inari to your house, and you may ask for whatever you like. But be sure not to take the god lightly, no matter what happens after this."

Yasubei woke up with a start, but the old man was nowhere to be seen.

"Huh!" he murmured. "A dream, I guess." And with that, he picked

---

[2] The Shinto god of grains and fertility.

up his hoe and went back to work.

That night, Yasubei sat before his poor meal, when he suddenly noticed that a fox, the messenger of Inari, was sitting squarely before him. "Well now!" he thought. "This is just as the old man said!"

"How about some white rice and a little raw sea bream?" Yasubei happily asked. In an instant, the fox disappeared, but just as quickly brought in white rice and raw sea bream.

This was the first time Yasubei had ever eaten such a delicious meal. Chewing his food carefully and slowly, he savored every bite.

From that time on, thanks to the visit of Inari's messenger, Yasubei's life quickly improved. But the hard worker that he was, Yasubei continued to work diligently in his fields, just as before.

One day, Yasubei thought that he might give up his life as a farmer and go into business. That very evening, on his return from his fields, he immediately asked Inari to bring him the materials for making sake. Instantaneously, the materials arrived. Yasubei brewed some sake and found that it was delicious. He thereupon put a signboard reading "Sake Shop" in front of his house, and began to sell his brew. The taste of his sake immediately became famous, and guests crowded into his shop from morning till night.

Eventually, Yasubei got married, built an even larger shop and welcomed crowds of visitors who came from far and wide. In this way, before many years had passed, he became the wealthiest man in Joshu.

Later, Yasubei changed his name to Kabe[3] Yasuzaemon and lived a life as luxurious as that of any lord. But he kept his promise to Inari, built a beautiful shrine for the god, and filled the shrine with offerings for as long as he lived.

After Yasubei passed away, however, his descendants treated the god lightly, and only occasionally brought offerings to the shrine. Because of that, the sake shop that had prospered so exceptionally finally went to ruin, and now, they say, only the remains of Yasubei's mansion remain.

---

[3] Kabe (加部) is a name indicating increase.

The Honored Fox God

A long time ago, in the ancient province of Iyo, there lived a lord by the name of Kono Michiyoshi. One day, Michiyoshi went to his wife's room, only to be dismayed at finding there were two women in the room, both claiming to be his wife. From their faces to their gestures to their voices, they were identical. The lord, as might be imagined, was quite shocked.

"What?" he asked neither one in particular. "Did you have a twin?"

"Not at all," one of the women responded. "And I don't have older or younger sisters either."

"Well then, who is this other woman?" Michiyoshi inquired.

"My lord, what are you saying?" the other women interjected. "It is I who am your real wife!"

"No, I'm your wife," the first woman broke in. "That woman is an imposter!"

Michiyoshi became more and more confused. The more he looked at the two women, the more they seemed completely identical, and there was absolutely no way he could distinguish one from the other.

"This is terrible," he thought. "What if this is what they used to call the split soul disease?"[4]

Michiyoshi quickly sent for a famous doctor to have the women examined, but that learned man could find no cause for this predicament either.

Finally, Michiyoshi decided to shut each woman in a separate room and to see what he could find out from there.

"Even if they look exactly alike," he reasoned, "if I separate them, I should be able to find some discrepancy one way or the other." For some time he carefully watched exactly how each one ate her meals, and even how each one slept. After a while, one of them did indeed seem to look a little suspicious.

---

[4] The split soul disease, *rikonbyo* (離魂病), occurs when the soul divides into two, and one half takes on another body; or when the yang soul separates from the body, leaving only the yin soul, and takes on another body. *Ri* means to be divided from, while *kon* means the yang soul, as distinguished from the yin soul.

One day, the wife in question began to roll the sweet potato on her plate over and over again. Then, in what seemed to be a bit of confusion, she picked it up with her fingers and popped it into her mouth.

"Hmm," Michiyoshi thought. "This, without a doubt, is the imposter. My wife would never eat anything with her fingers."

He then ordered one of his retainers to tie up the woman.

"A hah!" Michiyoshi declared. "You are indeed the imposter. Confess, or I'll cut off your head!" With this, he unsheathed his sword and brandished it in the woman's face.

Having her head cut off was not a pleasant prospect, so the woman who had insisted that she was the lord's true wife finally transformed herself back into the form of a white fox, tail and all.

"Just what I thought! You're a fox!" Michiyoshi shouted. "How could you have dared to trick me?" Completely outraged, he lifted up his sword and was ready to cut off the fox's head.

Just at that moment, however, there was a great commotion at the front of the castle. A large crowd of foxes who had transformed themselves into human shapes had approached the castle gate and were very upset.

"Please, Lord Michiyoshi," they implored. "Please don't kill the fox before you. He is actually Kiko Myojin, the Honored Fox God, and the leader of all the foxes on the island of Shikoku. If you kill this fox, all manner of disaster may befall you. Think for a moment," one of their representatives continued, "how miraculous his power of transformation is. Why, he even fooled a great lord like yourself. We beg you not to kill him!"

The foxes made such a plea that Michiyoshi was quite moved.

"All right," he said. "If he is such a great leader, I will forgive him just this once. But all of you are banished from the island of Shikoku. I cannot permit you to live here any longer."

So saying, Michiyoshi released the fox. And this is why there are no foxes on Shikoku even to this day.

The Great God Shinpachi

Long, long ago, in the ancient province of Awa, the chief of all the *tanuki* lived in a place called Sako. This *tanuki*, whose name was Shinpachi, was never beaten in any of the *tanuki* wars or competitions in physical transformations, and its name was known all over the island of Shikoku.

At this time, there was a samurai employed as a gunner whose house was near the cave where Shinpachi lived. Shinpachi found it extraordinarily amusing to play pranks on this samurai, and did his best to surprise the man at night by appearing as flying balls of fire or one-eyed Buddhist acolytes.

But the samurai knew that these things were nothing but the *tanuki's* mischief, and paid them little attention.

As time when on, however, Shinpachi would appear at the samurai's house transformed into a large serpent or some sort of monster and cause an uproar among the servants.

This finally made the samurai angry.

"All right, that's enough," he thought. "It's time to do something about this."

Soon after, the samurai got up late one night to go to the bathroom. As he was washing his hands, he noticed a light coming from beyond his garden.

"Well," he muttered to himself, "this is one of Shinpachi's tricks." Returning to his room, he took out his musket and quietly approached the place from where the light had come. As he quickly went to the spot, and hid in the shadows of some trees, he suddenly saw a beautiful young woman applying make-up to her face in front of a mirror stand.

"Huh!" he grunted. "Does that *tanuki* think I'm going to be taken in by that?"

The samurai loaded a ball into his musket, took careful aim at the woman's chest and pulled the trigger. In that instant, both the woman and the light disappeared.

"Damn!" he burst out. And shouldering his rifle, he returned home.

The samurai waited until dawn and then went down to the shallow ravine where the events of the night before had taken place. There he

found a large woman-sized stone with a bullet hole right in its center.

"What!" he muttered. "Made a fool of by Shinpachi again?"

Outraged by the whole affair, the samurai started to return home when he heard the voice of a young woman singing coming from a nearby bamboo thicket.

"Well then," he thought, "can there be someone's house in a place like this?"

The samurai thought this was a bit strange, but pushing through the bamboo thicket he spied a solitary hut in a narrow clearing. Inside, there was an old lady singing and spinning thread on a spinning wheel.

Thinking this was more than suspicious, the samurai made as if to aim his gun, when both the hut and the old lady disappeared like smoke.

"You know, this Shinpachi's art is truly impressive," he thought to himself. "But the next time I see him, I'll send him straight to hell." The samurai was as impressed as he was angry, and in this mood returned home.

On the way, however, a rainstorm suddenly came up, dampening his musket and rendering it inoperable. Holding the useless weapon in disgust, he looked up to see a lovely young woman holding out an umbrella.

"If you like, sir," she said with a polite smile. "Please get under this and stay dry."

The samurai peered at the young lady, and found her to be

exceedingly attractive. Forgetting all about Shinpachi, he happily walked along with her under the umbrella.

In the next moment, however, he became suddenly aware that the young woman had gone, and what he had thought to be an umbrella was in fact an old long and narrow wooden grave marker.

This was more than the samurai could bear. From that day on, instead of reporting to the lord's castle, he went out hunting for Shinpachi. But undaunted, the *tanuki* would do things like eat the balls shot from the musket right before the samurai's eyes, or suddenly pull his hair from behind.

But perhaps Shinpachi's luck ran out, too, because one day, while transformed into human shape, the *tanuki* was finally shot by the samurai, and fell down dead.

It was, however, the chief of all the *tanuki*, and he lay dead in a human form for three whole days. The samurai, of course, was sick with worry those three days, thinking that he had truly shot someone, and was unable to eat even a bite of rice.

After that, Shinpachi was celebrated as the Great God Shinpachi, and his shrine is full of visitors to this day.

The Fox and the Horse Driver

A long time ago, in a place called Oki no Su in the ancient province of Enshu, there lived a horse driver by the name of Toju. He worked every day by mounting his customers on horses and accompanying them to their evening's lodging.

One day, Toju had finished his day's work and was leading his rider-less horse back home. He had a rather beautiful voice, and as he traveled along the mountain road, he was singing his heart out.

"Excuse me," a voice suddenly came from behind. "Mr. horse driver...."

Toju turned quickly around, and beheld a beautiful young woman standing in the middle of the road.

"I'm sorry to bother you," the young woman said in a slightly coquettish way, "but would you let me ride on your horse? In return, I'll treat you to a really nice meal when we arrive at my house."

"Well, it's my job to have people ride my horse," Toju replied. "Please, go right ahead." And he lifted the woman up into the saddle.

The young woman's complexion was white and very clear. The horse rider gazed at her in spite of himself and was deeply impressed by her beauty. A lovely fragrance wafted from her delicately powdered face and Toju unconsciously narrowed his eyes.

"One rarely encounters a young woman like this," he mused. "I wonder what kind of house she lives in."

Lost in thought, Toju led the horse and his guest down the mountain and came to a corner in the road.

"That's my house over there," she said, pointing her finger in the direction of a faint light.

"Huh," Toju thought. "Can there really be a house in a place like this?" He considered this a little strange, but when he led the horse in the direction of the light, there was, indeed, a large mansion at the end of the path.

As soon as Toju had taken the young lady off the horse, some maidservants appeared and washed his feet. He was then accompanied into the drawing room, where a gold flower vase filled with plum flowers had been placed in an exquisite alcove.

A fragrance impossible to define filled the rooms.

"Please, don't stand on ceremony," the young woman encouraged him. "Please eat as much as you like."

The maids brought in sake and a regular feast, the likes of which Toju had never eaten in his entire life.

As Toju drank and ate as though in a trance, the young lady once again entered the room. "You truly helped me a great deal," she said quietly. "When you have finished your meal, please come and take a bath."

"No, no!" Toju interjected. "This meal has been perfect! I don't need anything more."

Toju stood up nervously, and started to make his way to the door.

"Don't be so polite," the young lady giggled. "Please, this way."

"Goodness, she's beautiful," Toju thought, and once again as if in a trance followed the woman to the bath.

The bath was huge, and the fragrance of wood filled the room.

Toju at last felt completely at ease, and with his eyes closed sang away at the top of his voice.

Toju had relaxed in this happy way for some time when he suddenly felt a chill and opened his eyes.

"What!" he yelled, and stood up immediately.

What he had thought was a bath was, in fact, the middle of a pond. Around him, where the mansion should have been, was not even the hint of a house.

Shaking in disbelief, Toju crept out of the pond. By the side of the road were scattered a number of large leaves, each holding a neatly placed piece of horse dropping.

"Ahh," he cried. "What I thought was a delicious meal was nothing but horse dung!" A shudder lurched through his entire body, and he began to throw up violently. But there was nothing really to be done.

Suddenly, Toju was aware of a small statue of the fox god[5] standing in a grassy thicket nearby.

"Yaah!" he yelled. "This was the trick of some fox living around here!" Toju kicked the statue with everything he had, which unfortunately did not settle his stomach. "We'll see about this," he thought. "I'm going to take my revenge." And taking the reins in his hands, he angrily returned home.

Toju felt sick for some time after that, and was unable to eat anything properly for a number of days.

About a week went by.

Then one day, on his way back from accompanying a customer, he was passing by the place where the statue of the fox god had been, when, "Excuse me," said a woman's voice from behind.

"A ha!" Toju thought to himself. "It's the fox!" Turning around, he saw that it was a beautiful young woman.

"May I be of some service to you?" he said with a deliberately innocent face.

"I'm sorry," she said. "But could you accompany me to my home?"

"Of course! Of course!" Toju replied, and lifted the young lady up on the horse. He was absolutely certain this was the same woman. Walking along beside the horse and its rider, he considered what he

---

[5] The fox god, *inari sama*. Technically speaking, the fox is the messenger of the god Inari, not the god itself, but this is often a point of confusion among the Japanese people themselves.

might do to take his revenge.

After a while, the large mansion came into view.

"This is my home," the young lady said kindly. "Please come in and rest awhile."

"Huh! Does she think I'm going to be fooled again?" Toju grumbled to himself.

He then turned to the young woman. "The fact of the matter is," he said in a humble manner, "I'm the horse driver you employed not long ago. At that time, you treated me to a fine meal. In return, I'd like to do the same for you today."

The fox, still in the form of a young lady, was taken aback, but quickly rethought the situation.

"Well, there's no reason to believe that human beings consider horse dung to be delicious," it mused. "So maybe I can really eat something good here."

And so the two went on to the horse driver's home.

"Hey!" Toju yelled to the people at his house. "We have a guest, so hurry up and prepare a good meal for her." Winking to his servants, he accompanied the young woman to a room.

"I'm going to have it brought to you right here," he said graciously, "so wait for a while, please."

So saying, he closed the door to the room, and threw some hot pepper and pine needles onto the fire in the brazier. In no time at all, yellow smoke enveloped the room.

"I'm awfully sorry," he apologized. "I'm having a hard time lighting this fire."

"Don't think anything of it," replied the young lady, who was sitting with a demure expression.

"This is one audacious fox," Toju said to himself, thinking back to how horribly he was humiliated before. Now, all he wanted to do was to give it a sound beating, but with great restraint told himself to wait patiently.

"No, this isn't working," he announced. "I'm going to go and get a fan."

With this, Toju left the room but locked the door from the outside. Chuckling to himself about how successfully his plan was proceeding, he peeked into the room through a crack in the door. Smoke was now pouring out of the brazier and completely filling the room where the young lady was still sitting.

"Yes, this is going quite satisfactorily," he laughed quietly.

Just then, the young lady stood up and tried to open the door. But it wouldn't budge. With a curse, the fox instantly returned to its original shape. Choked terribly by the smoke, it ran around the room, desperately trying to get out. In its confusion, its tail brushed against the brazier and caught fire, causing it to yelp piteously.

The fox was now running wild in panic. Seeing this, Toju let out a deep sigh of satisfaction.

"How about it?" he yelled from outside the room. "Have you learned your lesson?"

The fox could only bark sadly, but nodded its head up and down and put its front paws together as in supplication.

Somehow, Toju began to feel sorry for it now. "All right, I'll let you go," he yelled. "But you must promise never to play tricks on people again," and he opened the door.

The fox nearly fell over as it leapt outside, and, with its tail still on fire, ran out of sight in the twinkling of an eye. And, it is said, that it never bothered a human being ever again.

Rivers and Lakes

池と川をめぐるお話

Otowa Pond

At the foot of Mount Myoken in Niigata Prefecture, there is an old temple called the Chofukuji. A long time ago, a young woman came from an unknown village to visit this lonely place. Though her straw sandals were quite ragged and her kimono torn here and there, she was a beautiful woman with a pale complexion.

Kneeling down in the garden before the main hall, she began to pray with great intensity. All around her was completely quiet, and nothing else could be heard but the soft yet compelling voice of her prayer. After a while, the sun set and the temple grounds were enveloped in darkness.

When she had finished her long supplication to the Buddhas, the young woman stood up and started to leave. But at that moment, the priest came out from the main hall and advised her against such an idea.

"Listen," he said "It's dangerous for someone to travel on these mountain roads alone at night. If you like, why don't you stay here for the evening?"

"Thank you so much," the young lady replied, bowing politely to the priest. Accepting his kind invitation, she remained at the temple for the night.

The following morning, when the priest awoke, he found that his guest had already got up and that a fire was burning brightly in the hearth.

"What a forthright young woman," the priest mused.

The priest was quite pleased with the young lady, but was surprised when she suddenly put her palms together in front of him, and begged to be heard.

"My name is Otowa," she began. "For reasons I would rather not explain, I cannot return from where I came. If you'll let me stay here, I'll do anything you ask."

Though there seemed to be some major problem here, the priest asked nothing about it.

"Yes, of course," he replied. "You can stay here as long as you like." He gave her permission to remain at the temple and made no further inquiries.

Otowa turned out to be a very hard worker. She swept the temple and its garden every day and prepared the meals, all of this by herself and with great vigor.

But one spring day, Otowa went off to Mount Myoken with some of the young women from the nearby village to pick bracken.[1] Totally absorbed in her work, at some point she became separated from her friends and eventually found herself lost deep in the mountain. She called her friends' names as loudly as she could, but there was no answer.

After a while, it got dark.

"I've got to get home soon," she worried.

Pushing her way through the tall grass, Otowa walked on almost blindly, all the while being cut by the thick thorns and brambles. Losing track of time, she finally spied something shining in the midst of a thicket. Shouldering her way through the thick vegetation as fast as she could, she suddenly came upon a large pond. Stepping down to the edge of the pond, she cleaned her feet in its cold clear water.

At that moment, the surface of the pond became dark, the water began to move back and forth, and all at once a large dragon danced up before her. Its eyes shone in flaming disks and blue flames belched from its mouth

"Otowa!" the dragon boomed. "I am the *nushi*[2] of this pond and I have been waiting for you. I have now very old and must soon rise up to Heaven. You are to be my heir and to become the *nushi* in my place."

Otowa was so frightened that she could say nothing. When she was finally able to find her way back to the temple, she fell down on her bedding and went straight to sleep.

Six days went by, but on the morning of the seventh, the temple was visited by a violent storm. Otowa got dressed and then went to kneel before the Buddha.

"Otowa," the priest said, kneeling down next to her, "you should recite a sutra along with me." Together they chanted with all the concentration they could muster.

---

[1] *Warabi*, a kind of fern sprout that is often soaked and then lightly boiled in thin soy sauce.

[2] Owner, proprietor or master. According to Japanese folklore, lakes, ponds and other water bodies will have such *nushi*.

Outside, the storm gathered even more violently, and the dark sky crackled with lightning. All of a sudden, a monstrous peal of thunder seemed to shake the entire mountain. The roof of the temple was encircled by an erratically blowing wind and instantaneously the dragon appeared.

"I've come for you, Otowa!" it bellowed.

At this fearful sight, even the priest – who was after all a Buddhist – lost his breath for a moment. But quickly recovering, he looked sharply at the dragon, eye to eye.

"Lord Dragon," he called. "Why don't you calm down a little. If you take this form, everyone is going to be frightened of you. When you come to greet someone, you must take the form of a human being." This said, he went back to intoning the sutra at the top of his voice.

"All right, I understand," the dragon said, becoming a little more tranquil. "But on the morning of the 23rd day of the 6th month, bring Otowa to the Jizo Temple on the outskirts of the village. If you do not, the people of this village will not survive!"

With these few words, the dragon flew up into the void and disappeared, the storm abated, and a blue sky could be seen between the clouds.

About two months passed, and the day stated by the dragon arrived.

"Otowa, please forgive me," the priest said. "This is something beyond my power." And embracing the young lady who had come to him in such mysterious circumstances, he shed big drops of tears.

"No, Your Holiness," Otowa replied. "I've stayed here far too long. I'll not forget your kindness for as long as I live."

Otowa also cried and cried, but at last got into the palanquin prepared for her. The palanquin then descended the long stone steps of the Chofukuji, and was followed by a line of villagers behind her.

At last they arrived at the Jizo Temple on the outskirts of the village. Otowa stepped down from the palanquin and bowed courteously to the crowd of people who had accompanied her.

"Now we must part," she said simply.

"Goodbye, Otowa." The priest grasped her hand, holding it tightly for a moment.

Just then, the sound of a horse's hooves could be heard approaching from the direction of Mount Myoken. Everyone turned to look and was amazed to see a handsome young man riding a pure white horse. The young man remained silent, but helped Otowa up onto the horse. In that moment, the young man, Otowa and the horse disappeared into a heavy mist.

The people of the village soon began to consider Otowa as the *nushi* of the pond, and to this day bring offerings to her there on the 23rd day of the 6th month.

Lake Otane

In Tottori Prefecture, there is an area famous for its sand dunes. The dunes look like hills of sugar and stretch as far as the eye can see. Sometimes, when the wind blows, the sands take on strange shapes.

In the center of these dunes is a large body of water called Lake Otane. This lake is always brimming with water, and in its very center there seem to float two small islands overgrown with trees.

Long ago, not far from this lake, there stood the house of a wealthy man who employed a maidservant by the name of Otane. Otane was kind and gentle, and when the other maids had to work late into the night, she would always bring them ripe persimmons to eat. Once they bit into these persimmons, they found them so sweet as to almost melt in their mouths, and the fatigue of their work simply faded away.

"Otane, these sweet persimmons seem to be in endless supply," one of the other maids said one day. "Where do you find them?"

Otane, however, just giggled and said nothing.

"There's not a single persimmon tree around this entire mansion," someone else said. "Where do you suppose she gets them?"

One day, one of the young servants decided to follow Otane to see where she was going. Otane was completely unaware of this, and when night fell, she slipped quietly out of the mansion. As always, she stepped quickly along the path, at last climbed up the sand dunes, and stood for a moment on the bank of the lake.

"Well, what is she going to do now?" the young servant wondered. But as he watched undetected, Otane leapt into the lake and then swam expertly among the water chestnuts that floated on the surface. Then, in what seemed like seconds, she reached one of the islands and began to climb easily up the persimmon trees that grew there.

"Otaneee!" the young man yelled as loudly as he could. But before his very eyes, Otane turned into a large snake.

The young man was so surprised that he fell down backwards, and then ran away in panic.

"It's all over," Otane thought. "He's seen my true form." And with that, she slithered into the lake and never came up again.

After Otane disappeared, sad and unfortunate events occurred one after another in the wealthy man's mansion. The people who worked there eventually all died or went away, and the house and fields were eventually sold to someone else.

The Catfish at Uso ga Fuchi

Many years ago, in the ancient province of Echizen, there was an extraordinarily deep pool called the Uso ga fuchi, close to the banks of the Asuwa River. A terrifying *nushi* of the river[3] lived in the pool, so people in the vicinity rarely came here to fish.

One day, however, the lord of the province, accompanied by a great number of samurai, passed by the pool. When the lord looked into the clear, transparent water of the pool, he saw thousands of fish swimming there.

"I've never seen so many fish!" he said. "Someone try to catch a few."

Despite their lord's order, no one stepped forward to obey his command.

Finally, one of the lord's retainers timidly approached him.

"My Lord," he said. "It has been said that since ancient times this pool is inhabited by a fearful *nushi*, and if one of even the tiniest fish is taken away, terrible disasters will follow. Because of this, even people in the nearby village will not fish here. Please, just this once, release us from your order."

But this only infuriated the lord.

"You fool!" he yelled. "I am the lord of this province! Every tree and every blade of grass is mine. How can there be a master greater than me? Can you really be afraid of the 'master' of some pool? Strike with anything you have—rifles or spears! It makes no difference to me!"

All the samurai shuddered before their lord's threatening face, and aiming carefully at the fish in the pool, fired their rifles and threw their spears.

At that very moment, the eastern sky suddenly grew dark, and with a horrible crash of thunder, countless lightning strikes fell from the void. And with eyes glaring like saucers and fire belching from its mouth, a huge catfish attacked the lord.

"Yaah!" the lord screamed. "Make way! Get me out of here!"

---

[3] See Otowa Pond, footnote 2.

The lord cowered in fear and ran away as fast as he could, while his samurai attendants followed after him, every man for himself.

Meanwhile, the Buddhist priest of a temple near the river was surprised by the sudden change in the weather and came outside to see what was happening.

What he saw was a giant catfish closing in on the lord, about to swallow him in one gulp.

"Look out!" the priest yelled.

Taking off his robe, the priest ran after the lord and threw it over the man's head.

And the catfish? It suddenly disappeared.

At length, the sky cleared and once again was cloudless and bright blue.

"I am deeply obliged to you, Your Holiness," the lord stammered, trying to contain his uncontrollable shaking. "Thanks to you, my life was saved."

After this incident, the priest's vestment was called the Demon-quelling Robe, and it is celebrated at the temple even today.

Gonzaburo the Flute Player

A long time ago in the ancient province of Kai, there lived a young man by the name of Gonzaburo, who had been very skilled at playing the flute from the time he was young. Because he carried his flute with him wherever he went, people called him Gonzaburo the Flute Player.

Gonzaburo was an extremely kind-hearted young man, and took excellent care of his aging mother.

One autumn, however, rains came down like never before, the river burst through the dikes and the entire area was flooded. In less time than it takes to tell, both their fields and their house were swept away, and the whereabouts of Gonzaburo's mother was unknown.

"My mother loved the sound of my flute," Gonzaburo reasoned. "If I walk around playing a familiar tune, I should be able to find her."

From the next day onward, Gonzaburo searched high and low for his mother, playing his flute without rest. But wherever he looked, he found only one muddy field after another.

"Could it be that she's down toward the river?" he wondered.

Gonzaburo walked along the bank of the river, but no matter how far he went, or how much he played his flute, he found no trace of his missing mother.

"Perhaps she's dead," he thought sadly to himself.

Completely downcast, Gonzaburo stood by the bank of the river, wondering why he had not been able to save his mother when the flood came. Concluding that there was no way he could go on living without her, he played one more melody on his flute, jumped into the river and drowned.

After a few days, however, a strange thing happened.

When night fell, the sound of the flute could be heard, coming from no place in particular, and the people who lived by the river started to feel that it was Gonzaburo's ghost, still walking back and forth looking for his mother.

This began to frighten them, so they built a grave marker for the flute player and had sutras read on his behalf. After that, the unsettling sound of the flute was no longer to be heard.

After some time, the river started to be called the Flute-playing

River, although no one really knew who it was that first came up with this name.

Now, there is a small shrine called the Gonzaburo Fudo[4] located on the riverbank, where the young man is celebrated to this day.

Botaro, the Man Who Turned into a Dragon

A long time ago, in the ancient province of Echigo, there stood a farmhouse in the village of Aoyanagi. The family that lived here consisted of a young man by the name of Botaro and his father and mother.

Botaro had loved to go fishing from the time he was a child. If there was ever the least bit of spare time, from the moment he woke up to the time he went to bed, off he would go to the nearby pond to fish. Even when he grew up to be an adult, he would go fishing as soon as his work was done in the fields.

"It's a bit shocking the way Botaro loves to fish," people said.

"Yes, it would have been better for him to have been a fisherman rather than a farmer," others commented.

But no matter what the people of the village said, Botaro would not give up his love of fishing.

One day, however, Botaro went out fishing as usual, but did not return home, even after it got dark.

"Could it be that Botaro has had some accident? Our only son?"

Botaro's parents were sick with worry, and almost as if they had lost their wits, searched the perimeter of the pond a number of times, and even waded into it hoping for a clue.

"Do you think he fell into the pond and drowned?" someone asked.

"No…. Perhaps he pestered the fish so many times that the *nushi* of the place got angry," another suggested.

All the people of the village went out as well and searched high

---

[4] An abbreviation of Fudo myo-o, an avatar of the Central Sun Buddha, known for his unstoppable flow of Buddha-consciousness. His statues and shrines are very often found at waterfalls or other moving bodies of water.

and low for their friend. But Botaro was nowhere to be found.

"I'm sure he's drowned," his mother wailed. And for many days thereafter, his parents gave him up for dead.

But then, one day....

"Hello! I'm home!" Botaro said gaily as he appeared at the front door.

"You ... you're alive!"

"Botaro!"

Botaro's parents jumped up in joy, and when the people of the village heard that he had returned, they rejoiced as though a member of their own family had suddenly come back.

Botaro continued with his fishing as usual, and would go off to the pond if he had any spare time, regardless of how much his parents protested. What's more, he never ever mentioned the reason he had not come home that day and caused everyone so much anxiety. Now his parents worried so much that the same thing would happen again, they lost the desire to go out to their work.

One day, however, when Botaro came back from the fields, he made no move to go fishing. And then he said something rather strange.

"Listen," he began. "I'm a little tired today, so I'm going to take a nap. Whatever you do, do not peep into where I'm sleeping."

So saying, he went into his room and shut the sliding paper doors.

"This is a bit odd, don't you think?" his father whispered to his mother. "What kind of thing is it telling us not to look into his room?"

His parents made as if they were going out to the fields to work, but then slipped stealthily around to the back of the house. From the outdoor kitchen, they could peep directly into his room.

And there on the floor, a dragon with two horns sprouting from its head lay outstretched, sound asleep. The room itself quickly became inundated with water, and the dragon began to snore in blasts that sounded like thunder.

"What ... what is this?" his parents cried as they looked at one another.

Hearing their cries, the dragon awoke and glared at the two of them with horrible menace. Suddenly, a violent wind arose and red flames belched from the dragon's mouth. Breaking through the ceiling, the dragon flew into the sky.

Everyone in the village was shocked when they heard this.

"Botaro fished so much that he was turned into the *nushi* of the pond," they said to each other.

And from that day forth, no one ever went to fish in that pond, much less threw a rock into it.

The pond is now called Bo ga ike, or Botaro's Pond, and you can visit it even today.

Oko's Song

In Yamanashi Prefecture, there is a large river called the Kamanashi-gawa. This river has always had splendid levees, and long ago the people of the village would gather together every summer to work on the levees.

Now, one summer, about two hundred years ago, work on the levees began as usual. This work consisted mostly of transporting large loads of earth to weak spots and pounding it down to make it solid. As this was a rather boring job, many of the workers soon got tired of it and would rest midway through, talking and laughing in small groups.

The village headmen noticed this and started to worry.

"The way things are going," one of them said, "the levees won't be completely repaired by the fall. What will we do when the typhoons come and the flooding begins?"

So the village headmen discussed the matter at some length and decided that they should call in an excellent singer by the name of Oko.

Oko was a young lady, the daughter of a poor family that lived in a nearby village. Although she was called "a young lady," she was, in a word, positively ugly. Her complexion, for example, was swarthy, her hair a frizzled mess, and everyone said that they had never seen such an uncomely woman, ever.

Nevertheless, Oko sang exceedingly well. Whenever anyone heard her beautiful voice, they were totally spellbound. When she opened her mouth to sing, even the clouds that passed over the mountains would seem to pause, and the fish swimming in the river would become motionless.

So the village headmen reasoned that if they could get Oko to sing at the construction site, the work would soon be completed.

"If my singing will be of some use to you," said Oko when the village headmen made their request, "I'll be glad to help out."

The next day she was brought to the construction site just as work was to begin.

"What? Why is that woman here?" one of the men asked.

"She's got a face like a monkey's," another added.

After a while, the young men got bored with the work as usual and began to amuse themselves by ridiculing Oko. But Oko merely took up a paddle for patting down the earth and began a song with a rhythmic beat. Her moving voice reverberated in the young men's hearts, and even those who had been in the midst of criticizing her, now opened their mouths in wonder.

Very soon the rhythm with which Oko both sang and pounded the earth caught on. Almost unconsciously, the young men took up their paddles, went back to their work places and began to pound the earth.

Oko's song continued without pause. And her voice, rather than becoming hoarse or raspy as she continued, only became more beautiful.

When the sun went down, Oko's song finally came to an end, but the young men, seemingly intoxicated with her voice, continued to work.

"All right, men! That's enough for today," one of the village headmen called out. "Tomorrow we'll ask you to carry on again."

Hearing this, the young men seemed to wake from their trance, put down their paddles and go home for the day. But when the headman inspected the site, he found that the work had advanced far more than usual. Bowing low, he happily thanked Oko with great respect.

From that day on, the young men worked with all they had, pounding away with the rhythm of Oko's song. Just hearing her voice, they felt their fatigue melt away, and whether engaged in transporting the earth or patting it down with paddles, not one of them fell idle.

Eventually, however, the reputation of Oko's voice spread throughout the land and this caused a problem. People came from all over, pushing and shoving just to hear her sing, and every day, it seemed, there was a mountain of unruly listeners lining the levees.

And in this way, the work started to slow down.

The village headmen were thoroughly perplexed and finally approached Oko.

"This is a terrible thing to ask," one of them said disconsolately, "but would you stop your singing?"

"Certainly," Oko responded cheerfully. "But if I can ever be of use to you again, please let me help." And with that, she returned home.

The next day, however, the work came to a sudden halt. Although the sightseers had all gone away, none of the young men even moved.

"If we can't hear Oko's song," one of them said, "you're going to have to count us out!"

"Who drove her away anyway?" yelled another.

The young men became angry and began to crowd in on the village headmen.

The headmen realized that they had no choice and hurried off to call Oko back. They were, however, to be disappointed. Unable to find her, they separated into search parties, but though they went through the entire village, Oko was never seen again.

Joren Falls

At the foot of Mount Amagi in the area of Izu, there is a large waterfall called the Joren[5] Falls. Descending some two hundred and fifty meters into a pool of blue-black water at the base of the falls, this waterfall's overall effect on visitors is to make them feel slightly ill at ease.

A long time ago, there was a young farmer by the name of Kanbe who lived not far from the waterfall. Every day he would till his fields while listening to the roar of the falling water nearby.

One day, Kanbe felt tired and decided to take a rest. Nestling into the large exposed root of a mulberry tree, he lit a pinch of tobacco in the bowl of his long narrow pipe. As he relaxed, a large silk spider[6] appeared out of nowhere and crawled up on top of Kanbe's foot. The spider attached its thread to Kanbe's big toe, crawled over to the pool at the base of the falls, and then came back again to wind the thread once more around Kanbe's toe.

"It's just like they say," Kanbe thought as he smoked his pipe and watched the spider with interest. "These spiders work hard."

In very little time at all, a number of threads had been woven between Kanbe's foot and the pool at the base of the falls and the spider had made a fine web.

Feeling that it was time to get back to work, Kanbe began to stand up and walk away, but it somehow seemed a shame to destroy the spider's web after all its hard work.

So gently unwinding the threads from his toe, he attached them to the mulberry tree against which he had been resting.

At that moment, the sky grew dark, the roar of the waterfall became even more deafening and the branches on the nearby trees began to sway violently.

As Kanbe let out a yell, the mulberry tree was ripped out by its roots and pulled towards the pond.

"This is that spider's doing, for sure," thought Kanbe in a panic. Turning pale, he watched as the mulberry tree was pulled into the pond,

---

[5] Literally, "Pure lotus."

[6] *Joro* means prostitute or courtesan. The *joro gumo*, or silk spider, is the *Nephila clavata*.

where it sank out of sight. "That was a close call. If I had hesitated to unloosen that spider's web for another moment, I'd be where that tree is now. What kind of silk spider was that?"

Kanbe rubbed his hand down his chest. His entire body had broken out in a cold sweat. There was no way he could work anymore today! Shouldering his hoe, he ran away as fast as he could, stopping only when he was safely inside his house.

The people of the village were astonished to hear Kanbe's story.

"The silk spider was probably the *nushi* of that pond," one man suggested.

After that, no one approached the waterfall, and Kanbe never went back to work in his mulberry orchard.

A number of years passed.

One day a woodcutter came by and was cutting down a cypress tree near the waterfall. He had come from another village, so had never heard the story of the silk spider. Distracted for just one moment, he unfortunately dropped the axe he had used for many years into the pool at the base of the falls.

"What do I do now?" he wondered.

Looking down into the blue-black water, he could make out a sort of eddy being sucked down to the depths of the pool.

"There's nothing else I can do," he thought. "I'll have to dive down after it."

The woodcutter had always been proud of his ability to swim. Taking off his clothes without hesitation, he jumped into the pool.

The water was so cold that for a moment he thought his heart would stop, but coming back up to the surface of the water, he took a deep breath and dove down again.

He was not sure how long he had been underwater, but when he surfaced again he found a beautiful woman standing in the shade of a rock projecting from the bottom of the pool. In her white, almost transparent hand she held the axe that was so important to him.

"I am a silk spider and the *nushi* of this pool," the woman said. "I'll be happy to return the axe you let fall down here. But in return, you must never tell anyone that this is where I live. If you speak to anyone about me, your life will be over."

The woman handed him the axe and, in an instant, sank to the bottom of the pool.

"That was horrible," the woodcutter thought to himself in shock. "What if I had been pulled down to the bottom by that spider?" And he began to shiver, more from fright than from the icy cold water.

When he returned to his lodging, the woodcutter immediately went to question the people of the village.

"What kind of *nushi* lives in that pool under the waterfall?" he asked.

The villagers then told him the story about how Kanbe had nearly been pulled into the pool by a silk spider.

"Ahh, I can imagine," the woodcutter responded.

"Why? Did something happen out there?" one of the villagers inquired.

"No, no, nothing at all." The woodcutter nervously stopped the conversation, knowing that if he mentioned anything about the woman he had seen that day, his life would be over. Giving a deceptive smile, he returned to his room.

That night, however, the woodcutter was drinking sake with some of the people of the village, and the latter were telling scary stories about the *nushi* of the pool.

"At any rate, the mulberry tree was ripped up by the roots and pulled into the pool," one of them related. "So don't forget yourself and go close to the place."

"That's right!" interjected another. "After his experience there, Kanbe's body got so weak that now he just lies around and can't go back to work."

"Yes, the whole affair was truly frightening!" said yet another.

Hearing these things, the woodcutter began to feel somewhat proud about having met the *nushi* of the pond.

"Well," he thought. "Not much can happen if I tell them just a little about it."

Drunk on sake, he suddenly stood up and looked down at the people around him.

"Hey!" he shouted out. "So what about a silk spider? I met her today and nothing happened."

"What?" they cried in unison, and stared at him in surprise.

"Yeah, and she was really pretty, too," he continued. He then related the entire story about dropping the axe in the pool.

"Heh! Unbelievable!" one of the villagers said.

"If she was that pretty, I'd like to meet her myself," said another man.

"Still," a third exclaimed, "how brave of you to dive into that pool!"

All of them were shocked and impressed at the same time, and none of them were ready to go home.

The woodcutter was now carried away by the alcohol, his own talk and the rapt attention of the others.

"Hah!" he shouted. "If she's going to take my life, let her try to take it now!"

Strangely, that very night the woodcutter suddenly passed away.

"She got him, after all," said one of the men who had been listening to his boasts.

"I never want to see another silk spider as long as I live," the man next to him quietly whispered.

After this happened, the village people became more and more afraid and never went close to the pool at the base of the waterfall again.

Miraculous Strength

不思議な力をめぐるお話

The Rich Man of Koyama

In Tottori Prefecture there is a large lake called Koyamaike.

A long time ago, there was a very wealthy man known as the Rich Man of Koyama who lived in this area. His house was as large as a castle, and inside it there was said to be a mountain of gold, silver and treasures of every kind. Every day, this man ate delicious meals, dressed in luxurious clothes and lived a life of doing exactly what he wanted. There was nothing in this world that a rich man might want that he could not have.

But early one summer, it was time for rice-planting, something even rich men could not avoid. Employing over a hundred servants and farmers from the surrounding area, the rich man had them working from early in the morning to late in the evening, planting the rice seedlings in the fields.[1] It was a crowded and bustling scene all day, with the traditional rice-planting songs floating over the fields, and the muddy fields themselves quickly taking on the color of the young green seedlings.

But the rich man's fields were broad and wide, and it appeared that even a great number of men working without rest would be unable to finish the task in a single day.

Now the sun would soon be sinking beneath the horizon, and there were still fields remaining where the rice-planting had not been completed.

The rice man surveyed the situation and was chagrined.

"If only the sun would stay up in the sky a little longer, they could finish this work," he thought.

Nevertheless, he had full faith that everything would go just the way he desired.

"It's likely that even the sun will listen to what I have to say," he mused.

---

[1] In Japan, rice seeds are sown in small restricted areas in early spring. Then, in early summer, the entire crop of seedlings is replanted in the rice paddies (or fields) to provide the plants the proper berth to grow. This is a labor-intensive job, to say the least, and Reischauer has noted that this would be equivalent to replanting the entire wheat crop of the United States.

Taking the folding fan he always had to hand, he opened it with a quick but noisy flourish and gestured toward the sun, which was even now beginning to sink behind the mountains in the west.

"Listen up!" he commanded. "It's still too early for you to go down. Do me the favor of doing so only after my rice-planting is finished!"

Then, wonder of wonders, the sun, which was already sinking fast, reversed its course and steadily climbed back into the sky.

"Hunh!" the rich man muttered. "Look at that! I can make the sun itself change course."

Quite impressed with himself, he ordered the rice-planting to continue.

The farmers and servants working in the fields were surprised, and began working again right away. Thanks to the rich man's tactic, they were able to complete rice-planting in every one of the fields that very day.

"Well, now," the rich man shouted. "You've all worked hard. Drink and eat your fill tonight."

That night, the servants and farmers sang and danced at the rich man's house, making merry until the break of day.

When the sun finally rose, the rich man was filled with a desire to see his broad and verdant fields and climbed up onto a platform that overlooked his lands.

What he saw, however, was not to his liking. Instead of green rice seedlings and paddies, all he could see was a lake, stretching far into the distance.

People say that after this event, the rich man's family slipped into a decline, and in the end, went entirely to ruin.

The Reincarnation of Sakuta

A long time ago, in the ancient province of Iyo, there lived a man in the village of Hotokemura by the name of Sakuta. Born a bit feeble-minded, he was made fun of by everyone.

When Sakuta grew up to be an adult, the men of the village would ask him questions, partly for their own amusement.

"Listen, Sakuta," one of them said. "You're going to be old enough to be taking a bride pretty soon. Who do you think you'll marry?"

"Me? Why I'm going to marry my little sister Otane," Sakuta responded, looking quite serious.

"You fool!" the man retorted. "Do you think you can take your own little sister for a bride?"

The men of the town were disgusted with that and lost all interest in him.

Then, one day, a man in the village found Sakuta standing next to the river, stamping his feet uncomfortably.

"What's the matter, Sakuta?" the man asked.

"I need to pee," Sakuta replied.

"Well, if you have to pee, why don't you go ahead and pee right there?" the man asked.

"If I pee in the river," said the fidgeting Sakuta, "it may annoy the people drinking from it downstream."

"I see," returned the man, half dumbfounded and half impressed.

Meanwhile, Sakuta could stand it no longer and ran off hurriedly in the direction of his home.

A man like this was really worthless for work either in the rice paddies or in the mountains. Every day, he would simply eat, then sleep, sleep, then eat.

One night, however, when Sakuta was sound asleep, the Buddha visited him in a dream.

"Listen, Sakuta," the Buddha said, "You have been born feeble-minded because of the sins of your ancestors. But if you pray to me with all your might from now on, you will become quite intelligent."

Sakuta was overjoyed, and the very next day walked around the village telling his dream to anyone who would listen. Knowing how feeble-minded he was, however, no one placed much faith in what he said.

Nevertheless, Sakuta promptly knelt down in front of the Buddhist altar and chanted the *nembutsu*[2] with everything he had.

"Hunh! Look at that. Sakuta's repeating the *nembutsu*!" someone said in amazement.

"Listen, they say he prays to the Buddha every spare moment of his day," another added.

The townspeople were half amused by the rumors spreading around about the suddenly changed Sakuta.

Decades passed by, and the feeble-minded Sakuta finally turned sixty. But his faith only became deeper and deeper, and he lived now only to pray to the Buddha.

Then one night, the Buddha appeared to him in a dream.

"Listen, Sakuta," the Buddha began. "You have prayed to me for a long, long time and your ancestors' sins have been cleaned away. When you are born into your next life, you will surely be happy. You can die now in peace."

And sure enough, the next day Sakuta became ill, quickly losing weight and color. When it was finally said that he was about to die, the villages came to visit him. Looking at the people who had gathered around his pillow, Sakuta spoke with complete conviction.

"It's necessary that I go and receive the greeting of the Buddha," he whispered. "When I am reborn, I will come back as the son of a very rich man. Please tell the others that this will be so."

The people of the village gave up completely.

"Just as you'd expect, Sakuta was a fool right up to his death," they thought, looking at his face with weary expressions.

But Sakuta quickly became serious.

---

[2] The practice of chanting the name of Amida Buddha over and over again.

"I'm sure that none of you believe what I'm saying," he now said in a low voice. "Fine. But please write 'Sakuta of Hotokemura' on my forehead. Then, when I am reborn, that name will be on my forehead again."

"There's nothing to be done," a man cut in. "Someone write down exactly what he has asked."

Again, half in amusement, the people of the village had Sakuta's name written on his forehead in black India ink. Sakuta smiled in pleasure and passed away as though he had gone to sleep.

Well then, three years after Sakuta died, a little boy was born into the house of a rich man in the capital of Kyoto. And strangely enough, he was born with some sort of black mark on his forehead. His parents were quite worried and called in a doctor to look at the boy, but the doctor said that it would go away on its own after a while and that they should just leave it alone.

But as the child grew bigger, the mark on his forehead became darker and darker. By the time he was five years old, the Chinese characters for 'Sakuta of Hotokemura' had become very distinct.

His parents were absolutely flabbergasted. Shaking in their fright, they took the child to the doctor, but the words would not be made to disappear regardless of the medicine he applied. When they visited the most famous doctor in the capital, he simply shook his head in wonder.

In desperation, they finally called in a soothsayer and had him divine the matter.

The soothsayer prayed and chanted with great intensity, then suddenly he glared at them as though possessed in a trance.

"To erase the characters on this child's forehead," the soothsayer uttered, "you must go to Hotokemura in the province of Iyo. There you will find the grave of a man by the name of Sakuta. If you wash the characters with dirt from the grave, they will surely disappear."

Hearing this, the child's parents quickly sent a messenger to Iyo and had him bring dirt from Sakuta's grave. When the messenger returned, they immediately rubbed the dirt on the child's forehead. Now the characters, which had been so black and distinct, faded away like a dream.

After these events, the child grew up to be a gentle and kind-hearted rich man, and lived his life quite happily. And the villagers of Hotokemura believe to this day that this happy and wealthy man was Sakuta's reincarnation.

The Fire in China

In Akita Prefecture, there is an old Buddhist temple called the Shoryoji, situated in the village of Yuzawa. A long, long time ago, an extraordinary priest by the name of Ryukoku Zenji lived at this temple.

One evening, the priest suddenly jumped up and yelled, "Fire!"

Startled by his shouts, all the monks also jumped up and ran out into the garden. There was, however, no smoke to be seen anywhere, and the priests thought that this was rather strange.

"Well, where's the fire?" one of them asked.

As they were all standing around with blank looks on their faces, Ryukoku Zenji came running up with two buckets of water.

"Why are you shillyshallying around?" he yelled. "Hurry up! Start throwing water on it!" And as he spoke, he started throwing water here and there in the garden.

"Honorable Ryukoku Zenji," a monk said stumblingly, "You're telling us to toss the water on the fire, but there's nothing here burning, is there?"

"No, of course not! This temple's not burning at all!" Ryukoku Zenji cried. "But the Chinshan Temple in China has caught on fire. Everybody, hurry, hurry!"

"What?" one of the monks sputtered. "The Chinshan Temple in China?"

The monks were dumbfounded to the point of being unable to say anything. Even if a temple in far-off China was burning, what was the point of throwing water on a temple in Japan?

"Stop complaining and get to work!" the great priest yelled.

Pushed into action, all the monks grabbed the water buckets, filled them to the brim and started throwing water over the rocks, trees and bushes in the garden.

"All right," Ryukoku Zenji finally said. "You've all worked hard. Thanks to you, the fire's been put out." And with a look of satisfaction, he went back to his room.

"That was absolutely crazy!" one of the monks complained. "Thanks to him, I've caught a cold."

"You know, Ryukoku Zenji may have become a little crazy," another added.

And they all returned to their own rooms, grumbling about one thing or another.

A number of days later, however, a letter arrived from the Chinshan Temple in China, politely thanking them for helping to put out the fire. As a token of gratitude, a large roll of brocade silk and a multicolored *hossu* accompanied the letter. A *hossu* is a high priest's horsehair whisk used for exorcisms or simply to keep away mosquitoes.

When the monks of the temple and the people of the village saw this, their mouths dropped open in surprise.

"This is something you might expect of a priest like Ryukoku Zenji," someone said. "Think about it! Putting out a fire in China from Japan!"

The roll of brocade and the *hossu* are still celebrated in the Shoryoji Temple in Yuzawa. People who have come on pilgrimages to the place, however, have over time plucked out nearly all of the horsehair from the *hossu* to have as talismans so that hardly any hair remains.

After this event, Ryukoku Zenji accomplished many feats, such as bringing rain during long droughts by praying to the dragons, and everyone revered him as nothing less than a Buddha.

The Dragon Palace Child

A long time ago, there was a poor flower seller in a place called Kuzu-maki. Every day the young man would come down from the mountain where he lived and pick flowers, but by the time he arrived at the village they were all broken and no one would buy them. As evening approached, he would walk down to the river and throw his remaining flowers into the water.

"Here, Oto-hime,"[3] he would say. "Take these flowers."

One day, when he came to the riverbank as usual, there had been a large flood and he was unable to cross to the other side.

"Well now, what a fix," he muttered to himself. "I won't be able to go home with the river like this."

As he stood there wondering what to do, a large turtle suddenly appeared at his feet, motioning for the young man to quickly get on its back. When he did so, the turtle began swimming with no trouble at all.

"Hey, hey!" the young man yelled nervously, striking the turtle on its shell. "Where are you taking me? The other bank is over there!"

"The truth is," the turtle replied, "I've received orders from Oto-hime to accompany you to the Dragon Palace. She wants to thank you for all of the flowers she's received from you."

So saying, the turtle plunged down into the water.

At length they arrived at the Dragon Palace. A feast was immediately brought before the young man and a young girl in a beautiful kimono danced before him. The delicious taste of what he was served was like nothing he had ever eaten before, and the beauty of the young girl was astonishing.

"I've heard about the Dragon Palace in stories," the young man mused, "and it really is as wonderful as they say."

The young man watched and ate as if in a dream.

After a while, Oto-hime arrived, accompanied by a great number of servants.

---

[3] The Princess of the Dragon Palace.

"Thank you for all the flowers," she began. "In thanks, I'm going to give you this child. Bring him up well and you will have whatever you desire."

And with this, she gave him a dirty, snotty-nosed little boy.

"Thank you very much," the flower seller said. I will take good care of him for sure. By the way, what is this child's name?"

"His name is Toho," she replied

That was a strange sort of name, he thought, but if the child was going to make all of his wishes come true, he would take him gladly.

The young man and Toho got onto the turtle's back and went home together.

When he returned from the beautiful Dragon Palace to his own broken-down home, he was aware of how dirty and cramped it was. He quickly took hold of Toho and made a request.

"Toho, I'm sorry to ask you this," he said apologetically, "but could you make this house into a large mansion?"

"Of course," responded the little boy. "That's easy."

Shutting his eyes tightly, Toho clapped three times and, miracle of miracles, the young man's dirty house turned immediately into a huge mansion.

"It's really true," the young man thought. "It's just like she said."

For his second request, the young man asked for some matting. Like before, Toho closed his eyes tightly and clapped his hands three times, and in the twinkling of an eye, a large section of beautiful matting was laid out before them.

The young man was now almost in a trance and one after another asked for things that he wanted.

"Well then," he said. "I guess there's nothing left that I need."

Feeling quite satisfied, the young man stepped into a room and looked around. But then, he remembered.

"Ah, how careless of me! Toho, sorry to trouble you again, but could you bring me some money?"

"How much would you like?" the child asked.

"Hmm," the young man considered. "A thousand *ryo*[4] ought to be enough."

"Is that all?" Toho smiled. "Nothing difficult about that."

---

[4] A unit of money used in ancient Japan.

As soon as Toho spoke, he once again clapped his hands and a thousand *ryo* appeared before his eyes.

With all his wealth, the young man became a moneylender, and was now one of the richest men in the province. Everyone called him "Sir."

And he became quite haughty.

The one thing that troubled him, however, was that no matter where he went, Toho had to go along with him. Moreover, the child always wore dirty clothes and had a runny nose.

"Toho," he would say, "how about blowing your nose?"

"No!" would come the response, and Toho's nose would remain just as before.

"Well, what about changing your clothes?"

"No!" was the inevitable reply.

No matter what was asked of him, the answer was always "No!"

Eventually, the young man became more and more tired of walking along with this little brat. Finally, one day, he spoke up.

"You have been a great help to me," he said, "but please get out of my house."

"Well, I've been at your side each and every day and I thought I'd given you everything you wanted," the boy said with some humility. "But if you're telling me to go, there's nothing I can do about it."

This said, Toho left the house immediately. But as soon as the young man gave a sigh of relief, the mansion and the warehouse both disappeared and he found himself sitting in his old broken-down house, the poor flower seller that he once was.

Kichiji-hime

Late one night, the emperor had a dream in which a god appeared to him.

"Take this painting and these shoes," the god intoned, "and travel around the entire country. If you do, you will be granted a young woman whose beauty is beyond compare in this world."

The god then vanished.

Startled, the emperor immediately awoke to find a painting and shoes near his pillow. He couldn't help but look at the picture in absolute rapture. The woman he saw looked just like a goddess with a wonderfully smiling face.

"What a beautiful woman!" he thought.

Right away, the emperor put the painting and the shoes in a portable shrine and set off around the country.

Whenever the shrine made its entrance into a new province, the emperor's retainers would yell, "In this portable shrine there is a painting and a pair of shoes. Both are blessed by the gods. Any woman who comes to bow in veneration to these articles will have great good fortune. Any woman is welcome, so please come quickly to pay your respects."

Hearing this, all the women in the area crowded in, each trying to be first.

As the emperor's retainers walked through the crowd of women, they looked avidly for anyone who resembled the lady in the painting. No matter which province they entered, however, no one appeared who looked exactly like her.

The emperor's procession finally arrived at the province of Izumo. From far away, they could see the dark forests of the Izumo Shrine. This was during the rice-planting season and the rice paddies were filled with crowds of people working hard at planting the young rice seedlings. The emperor's retainers could see that there were also a number of women working in the fields.

"In this portable shrine there is a painting and a pair of shoes," they once again shouted. "Both are blessed by the gods. Any woman who comes to bow in veneration to these articles will have great good fortune. Any woman is welcome, so please come quickly to pay your respects."

As soon as the women in the fields heard this, they all jumped from the rice paddies and gathered around the portable shrine, again each doing her best to be first.

There was, however, one young lady who remained working in the rice paddies.

The retainers thought this was strange, and one of them walked over to where she was bent over carefully planting each seedling in the muck.

"Well now," he said, "don't you want to have great good fortune, too?"

"Yes," she replied politely. "Even someone like me would like to have a fortunate life. But my station in life is to work and I cannot rest now."

The young lady's father had died early in her life and she had to work in rice paddies owned by other people in order to take care of her sick mother.

The retainer was impressed by this serious young lady, and drew close to her to get a better look at her face.

With a start, he realized that she looked exactly like the woman in the painting. Taking her quickly to the portable shrine, he had her try on the shoes, which, to his further amazement, fitted perfectly.

"Ahh, what a blessing," he sighed. "We have found her at last."

The emperor, of course, was overjoyed, and took the woman for his empress.

In time, the young woman took on the name Kichiji-hime and bore the emperor many children.

Even now, the graves of Kichiji-hime and the emperor are found in the province of Izumo.

The Thousand-league Eyes of Oto-hime

A long time ago in the ancient province of Echigo, in a village called Hojo, there was a goddess known as Oto-hime. She resided in a small shrine at the edge of town, but no one had ever seen her true form.

Now, this goddess had the strange power of being able to understand anything. No matter where, no matter who asked a question, an answer would come straight away. Regardless of what was being asked, if a person called upon her name she would tell them immediately what he or she wanted to know.

One time, a man called Gohei went out with his wife to work in the mountains. When they returned home that evening and were about to eat dinner, they discovered that the rice pot was empty.

"What's this?" Gohei complained. "I told you to prepare rice before we left this morning!"

"This can't be!" his wife exclaimed. "I cooked tonight's portion with this morning's and left it here in the pot."

"Don't be an old fool!" Gohei retorted.

But the woman once again protested that she wouldn't be mistaken about something like that, so they decided to call on Oto-hime.

"Oto-hime! Oto-hime!" they both intoned. "What happened to the rice in our pot?"

"Your next-door neighbor Gosaku stole it!" thundered a voice throughout the neighborhood.

When Gosaku heard this voice, he was astonished and quickly returned the rice he had stolen.

No one understood where Oto-hime actually was, but her thousand-league vision was considered valuable.

One day, a young woman had to leave her little baby at home and go out and harvest rice with the rest of her family. Even at midday, they were so busy that she could not be released from work.

"By now he's awake and crying," she thought nervously. But her bossy old mother-in-law never even suggested that she go back to the house and check on her little boy.

"Oto-hime! Oto-hime!" the young wife finally said quietly. "How is my baby?"

"Your baby has already woken up and is crying," the voice echoed over the rice fields.

At this, even the bothersome old mother-in-law could not remain quiet any more.

"Well go on," she croaked, giving the young wife permission to return. "Go back to the house and take care of the child."

And there was yet another event.

When the rice harvest was over, all the young men of the village gathered together and decided to have a celebration in thanks for the abundant harvest. Everyone brought rice, miso, daikon, potatoes and all sorts of delicious food for a real feast. But when everything was brought together, there weren't nearly enough bean-jam rice dumplings.

"Well, this is strange!" yelled Rokunosuke, who had been in charge of making the dumplings. "I carried all of them here for sure. Kichisa! I'll bet you're the one who took them!"

"It wasn't me!" Kichisa protested, glaring at Shohei. "It was Shohei who put them in the bowl! So, Shohei, it must have been you!"

"I … I didn't take the dumplings," said the weak-hearted Shohei.

"Liar!" Kichisa shouted. "You're a thief!"

"Give them back now," someone else demanded, "or you're going to get a beating!"

Everyone circled around Shohei and started to shove him, but the timid youth just shook his head and was unable to respond.

"It wasn't me. It wasn't me," he mumbled, and he looked as though he was ready to cry.

"Wait a minute!" interjected Kichisa, stopping the crowd of angry young men. "When Shohei went home a while ago, he must have taken the dumplings with him. He couldn't have eaten them just now. By this time, everyone in his family will have eaten them all up. Look, Shohei, I can forgive you. Just apologize to everyone."

But even with being coaxed in this way, Shohei only shed big tears and would not apologize.

"You idiot!' Kichisa yelled. "We were ready to forgive you, if you only said you were sorry. You're nothing but a stubborn mule!"

"We can't forgive him now," someone else said. "Let's give him a good beating!"

But just as Rokunosuke raised his fist and was ready to strike, Shinji, one of the youths who had said nothing up to this point, stood up.

"Wait just a minute," he said. 'Is there any proof that Shohei stole the dumplings?"

Everyone stopped for a moment and looked at Shinji.

"I'm going to ask Oto-hime if he took them or not," the young man continued.

"Why ask Oto-hime?" Kichisa said nervously. "We all know Shohei did it."

"No, I'm going to ask her anyway," said Shinji. "Oto-hime! Oto-hime! Please tell us who took the dumplings."

"The one who took the dumplings was not Shohei," Oto-hime's voice rang out. "It was Kichisa! He has wrapped them in a large bundle and hidden them under his floor."

When everyone ran to Kichisa's house and looked under the floor, sure enough, there were the dumplings, wrapped in a large bundle, just as Oto-hime said.

"Kichisa! You were the one after all!" everyone yelled and gave him a sound beating.

"Forgive me! I've done a horrible thing!" Kichisa cried and ran away holding the bumps on his head.

Well, thanks to Oto-hime, after a while no one told a lie or did anything bad in this village again. Everyone knew that if they did, Oto-hime could be asked to make the matter public right away.

By and by, the reputation of this honest village became widely known, and people from other places came here to seek brides and bridegrooms.

"This is thanks to Oto-hime," the villagers remarked among themselves.

"Yes, and if we don't treat her well, something bad may happen," others said.

So saying, whenever anyone prepared good food to eat, they always took some portion of it to offer at Oto-hime's shrine.

One autumn, however, rabbits and badgers laid waste to some fields close by the shrine. The owner of those fields, a man by the name of Rokuzo, made a trap, and baited it with fried tofu. And one evening....

"Help! Please help!" yelled Oto-hime's voice. "It hurts! It hurts!"

Utagawa Kunisada. "O-iwa's Ghost." The ghost of murdered wife O-iwa, subject of one of Japan's oldest and most famous ghost stories. n.d. (*Art Institute of Chicago*)

Tsukioka Yoshitoshi. "The Ghost of Seigen Haunting Sakura Hime." Princess Sakura Hime is visited by the spirit of the monk Seigen, whose infatuation with her survives past death. 1889. (*Los Angeles County Museum of Art*)

Utagawa Kuniyoshi. "Minamoto no Yorimitsu-ko no Yakata ni Tsuchigu-mo Yokai o Nasu Zu." The legendary hero Minamoto no Yorimitsu reclines on his sick bed as the earth spider conjures demons to torment him. c. 1843. (*Wikimedia Commons*)

Utagawa Kuniyoshi. "Kisokaidō Rokujūkyū Tsugi no Uchi Fukaya Yuriwaka Daijin." The warrior Yuriwaka Daijin fires his bow at Fukaya-shuku station along the Nakasendō highway. 1852. (*Wikimedia Commons*)

Tsukioka Yoshitoshi. "Sangoku Tarō Kneeling before Demon and Warrior." Sangoku Tarō is visited by a demon during his travels. From the series "Handsome Heroes of the Water Margin." 1866. (*Wikimedia Commons*)

Utagawa Kuniyoshi. "Keyamura Rokusuke Struggling with Three Kappa." Model for the idea samurai, Keyamura Rokusuke, battles a group of kappa. c. 1850s. (*Wikimedia Commons*)

Utagawa Kuniyoshi. "Takagi Toranosuke Capturing a Kappa." Takagi Toranosuke battles a kappa underwater at the Tamura River in Sagami Province. n.d. (*Wikimedia Commons*)

Utagawa Toyokuni. "Tokaido Yotsuya Kaidan." The ghost of O-iwa appears to enact revenge upon her murderous husband. 1812. (*Metropolitan Museum of Art*)

Utagawa Kuniyoshi. "The Poet Dainagon Sees an Apparition." A towering ghost recites a poem as the poet Dainagon Tsunenobu works in his study at night. 1860. (*Wikimedia Commons*)

Kawanabe Kyōsai. "Enma To Jigoku-dayu-zu." Enma, the king of Hell. Japanese children were often told by parents that Enma would pull out their tongues if they misbehaved. c. 1800s. (*Wikimedia Commons*)

Utagawa Hiroshige. "Ushiwakamaru Benkei at Gojo Bridge Guimet." The warrior-monk Benkei duels with the young Minamoto no Yoshitsune (Ushiwaka) at Gojo Bridge in Kyoto. c. 1834-35. (*Wikimedia Commons*)

Utagawa Hiroshige. "Ushiwakamaru Taught Martial Arts." The legendary samurai Minamoto no Yoshitsune (Ushiwaka) is instructed in martial arts by tengu on Mount Kurama. 1823-24. (*Wikimedia Commons*)

Utagawa Kuniyoshi. "Watanabe no Tsuna Fighting a Demon." Watanabe no Tsuna battles a demon at the old Rashomon gate in Kyoto. n.d. (*Wikimedia Commons*)

Tsukioka Yoshitoshi. "The Wrestler Onogawa Kisaburo Blowing Smoke at a One-Eyed Monster." The legendary sumo wrestler Onogawa Kisaburo is visited by a monster and nonchalantly blows smoke into its face from his pipe. 1865. (*Los Angeles County Museum of Art*)

Utagawa Hirokage. "Edo Meisho Dōke Zukushi, Ryōgoku no Yūdachi."
A demon climbs from the Sumida River up the Ryōgoku Bridge in Edo
(Tokyo). 1859. (*Wikimedia Commons*)

月百姿

源氏
夕顔巻

Tsukioka Yoshitoshi. "Genji Yugao Maki." A scene from the novel *The Tale of Genji*, the ghost of Genji's lover Yugoa stands alone surrounded by vines. From the series One Hundred Aspects of the Moon. 1886. (*Wikimedia Commons*)

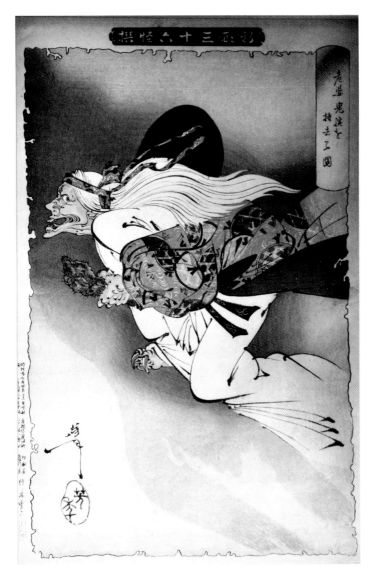

Tsukioka Yoshitoshi. "The Flying Demon." A demon with flowing white hair flies through the sky. From the series *New Forms of Thirty-six Ghosts*. 1889. (*Wikimedia Commons*)

The villagers jumped up and ran in the direction the voice had come from. And there, in the trap, was the dead body of a large white fox.

"Oto-hime's true form was a white fox!" they all exclaimed.

With great sorrow, the villagers performed a funeral for the fox and built a new shrine in its honor.

And this shrine remains in Hojo village to this day.

Pure Hearts

美しい心をめぐるお話

The Heavenly Feathered Robe

Long ago in the ancient province of Suruga, in the village of Miho no matsubara, there lived a fisherman by the name of Hakuryo. One day, as he was walking along the beach, he was aware of a lovely fragrance coming from somewhere.

"Well now," he wondered, "where could this be coming from?"

When Hakuryo looked around, he saw a beautiful robe hanging from the branch of a pine tree nearby. Every time a breeze arose, it looked exactly as if a white bird had perched on the branch.

Hakuryo quickly climbed the pine tree and took hold of the robe. It was as soft as feathers and sparkled in the light of the sun.

"I've heard stories about things like this," Hakuryo thought to himself. "Could this be a robe of one of the heavenly beings?"

Hakuryo tucked the robe under his arm and climbed down from the tree. He could not even think any more about fishing that day, and so started to walk away from the beach and return home.

"Excuse me," a woman's voice came from behind him. "Would you wait just a moment, please?"

When Hakuryo looked around, there stood a woman so beautiful that it seemed as though he was waking from a dream.

"That is my robe," she said with a troubled look. "Would you please return it to me?"

"No," replied Hakuryo, "this is something I just found."

"Please don't say that," the woman continued politely. "The scenery here is so beautiful that I just had to take off my robe and hang it on that branch for a moment and walk along the beach. Without my robe, I cannot return to heaven."

"So you are, in fact, a heavenly being?" said Hakuryo, tucking the robe under his arm even more securely. "Now that I know it's the robe of a heavenly being, I'll never give it back. Whether it's yours or not, it's something that I found on my own and I'm going to make it a family heirloom."

"But this robe is of no use to human beings," the woman said on the verge of tears. "Please, please return it to me. Can't you see that I'm begging you?"

"No, I'm not giving it back," Hakuryo stated stubbornly. "This is mine."

At this, the heavenly being's eyes filled with tears and she covered her face with her hands.

"Ohh, what can I do?" she moaned. "Without my feathered robe, I cannot return to heaven. Nor can I live in this place. All I can do is die!"

With this, the heavenly being cried so hard that her shoulders shook.

Gazing upon the sobbing figure of the heavenly being, Hakuryo, as hardened a man as he was, began to feel sorry for her.

"I understand," he began. "I'll give the robe back to you. When I see you like this, my chest wells up with pain."

When she heard these words from Hakuryo, the heavenly being suddenly took her hands from her face almost as if in shock.

"Will you really do that?" she exclaimed. "Then I'll be able to return to heaven with no trouble at all." And her face shone almost in laughter for the first time.

"But in return, I have one request," Hakuryo added. "I have heard that the dance of heavenly beings is beyond compare. Would you then, at least demonstrate this dance for me?"

"That is easily done," the heavenly being replied. "But first, the robe...."

"No, no," said Hakuryo, holding the robe behind his back. "First things first. If I give you this robe, you'll just go back to heaven without showing me your dance."

"That is not true," the heavenly being retorted with a grim, almost frightening expression. "There are no lies in the world of heavenly beings. Suspicion and lies belong only with human beings."

Hakuryo immediately felt ashamed and nervously handed the robe over to the heavenly being.

The heavenly being then put on the robe and began to dance with astonishing tranquility. Each time she moved, a fragrance filled the air, and the feathered robe sparkled in the sunlight. Hakuryo meanwhile lost all memory of where he was and what he was doing. He could only gaze at this beautiful dance as if in a daze.

As the heavenly being danced, she gradually rose into the sky, until she had ascended beyond the pine branches. Then she disappeared completely into the mist.

Yoro Falls

Many years ago in the ancient province of Mino, there lived a very kind-hearted young man and his aged father. They were extremely poor and there was often no money to buy a day's provision of rice.

Now, the young man's father loved drinking sake, but on the days when they couldn't even afford to buy rice, how were they going to have enough money to buy sake?

"Please forgive me, Father," the young man would say. "Tomorrow I'll work even harder and go out to get you some sake."

So saying, the young man would go out every day to gather firewood, but the money he earned from this came to almost nothing. Thinking of how happy his father looked when drinking sake, he became very sad.

"I work so hard," he thought to himself one day, "why am I unable to buy just a little sake?" Crestfallen, he returned home.

"Don't worry about it," his father said. "I'm just fine as I am. Going without sake is not so important, you know."

But when these words fell on the young man's ears, he became even more despondent.

"All right!" he said to himself. "Tomorrow I'm going to buy my father some sake, no matter what!"

The next morning, the young man got up while it was still dark and went off to the mountain. Working right up until evening and taking no rest, he was able to gather much more firewood than usual.

"With all this, I should be able to buy at least a little sake," he thought.

The young man loaded the firewood on his back and began to hurry down the mountain path. He was so anxious to return home, however, that his feet slipped on something and he tumbled down into the valley below the path. Although he lost consciousness for a short while, he suddenly came to, aware of the sound of water not far away. Looking around, he saw a delicate waterfall falling off a nearby ledge.

"What a beautiful waterfall," the young man said to himself.

As thirsty as he was, he scooped up a handful of water and put it to his mouth.

"What's this?" he wondered in surprise, inclining his head to one side. For a moment, thoroughly flustered, he quickly drank another mouthful.

"This … this water tastes like sake!" And no matter how many mouthfuls he drank, sure enough it tasted just like sake. Not only that, it had the taste of the very finest quality.

"This is wonderful!" he shouted. "If I can take this water home, my father will surely be overjoyed!"

Taking the gourd he carried at his waist, the young man filled it with this sake-water and returned home in high spirits.

As the young man was late in coming home, his father was quite worried.

"What happened?" he said anxiously as soon as he saw his son's face. "You're way too late, aren't you?"

"I'm sorry to have made you worry," the young man replied. "To make up for it, I've brought you a rather wonderful present."

Taking the gourd from his waist, he showed it to his father.

"Take just a mouthful," he offered.

The young man took a sake cup from the shelf and filled it with the sake-water he had carried home. His father took the cup with an amused smile and raised it to his lips. Suddenly his eyes started to blink.

"Why, this is wonderful!" he almost shouted. "Where did you get such a high-class sake as this?"

And so the young man told his father of the day's events, leaving out no detail.

"Is that so?" the old man said with tears flowing from his eyes. "This is surely a reward from the gods for your tender-heartedness. What a blessing!"

Thanks to this delicious sake, the bent-over back of the young man's father straightened up a bit and he was much more at ease in his old age.

This story was eventually told to the lord of Mino Province.

"What an impressive fellow," the lord proclaimed, sending the young man a number of rewards, and in the end making him a samurai.

After this, the local people began to call this waterfall the Yoro[1] Falls.

Ikoma-hime of Saku

In the north central area of Japan known as Shinshu, there is an area of grazing land called the Mochizuki[2] Pasture in the locality of Saku, a place famous for excellent horses since times past.

One year, a long time ago, a beautiful princess was born to the lord who owned this pasture. On the same day, it happened that a cream-tinted dapple-gray colt was born out in the pasture. Such horses are said to have the added luster of red tea. After this colt was born, it very soon stood up and ran around the pasture in the direction of the evening sun. The colt ran like the wind, its luxuriant mane glittering like gold. The lord witnessed this and was overjoyed.

---

[1] Yoro (養老), literally, taking care of the aged. Interestingly, the great Edo-period physician Kaibara Ekiken recommended a little sake in the morning and evening to stimulate one's circulation.

[2] Mochizuki (望月), literally, "gazing at the moon," but meaning a full moon.

"What a splendid horse this is," he exclaimed. "Having been born on the same day as the princess, I'm sure it must be a gentle-hearted thing."

So saying, he named his daughter Ikoma-hime.[3]

As the days passed, the princess became increasingly beautiful, while the colt grew more and more robust. When she was still a small girl, nothing pleased the princess more than riding this horse. Whether she went picking flowers in the spring, playing in the water during the summer or gathering chestnuts in the fall, she could not be separated from the cream-tinted dapple-gray horse.

At length, the princess grew into a beautiful young lady, and when the young men of the area saw her riding about on her beautiful horse, every one of them wanted to have her as his bride.

Rumors of Ikoma-hime eventually reached the capital, and became known to the emperor himself.

"I would like to have such a beautiful young lady as my own wife," the emperor thought, and very soon ordered his retainers to call upon the lord of the pasture and to bring the princess back to the capital.

"What?" the lord asked. "The emperor would like me to give him Ikoma-hime? What a blessing this is!"

The lord immediately gave his consent to the emperor's request. When he thought about having his own child as the emperor's wife, he felt as if he was ascending to heaven. Thus, he decided to have Ikoma-hime accompanied to the capital right away.

From the day of Ikoma-hime's departure for the capital, however, the cream-tinted dapple-gray horse began to lose its vigor and indeed very quickly became ill.

"Such a splendid horse as this will not come around twice in a lifetime," the lord said in alarm. "By all means, do not let this horse die."

At the lord's command, a famous doctor was called in and the horse was given medicines so expensive that human beings would be unable to afford them.

Yet, the cream-tinted dapple-gray horse gradually became more and more emaciated and its once abundant gold-colored mane lost all its luster.

---

[3] Ikoma (生駒), literally, "giving birth to a colt." Thus, the princess's title becomes something like the "Colt-born Princess."

At this point, a famous master of incantations was called in to see what he could do.

The master of incantations took one look at the horse and fell back in shock.

"This is quite serious," he said. "As is the custom with horses, this horse loves the princess quite deeply."

"Don't be foolish," the lord retorted.

"No," the man rejoined. "If you think this is foolishness, have the horse given some feed by the hand of the princess herself."

Ikoma-hime was quickly called back and she fed the cream-tinted dapple-gray horse some grass. Then and there, the horse that had been on the verge of death and unable even to move, quickly stood up, looked in the direction of Ikoma-hime and whinnied in a coquettish way.

As the princess watched this, her eyes filled with tears.

"This may be but a horse," she sobbed, "but I don't know how I can abandon it and go off to the capital. This horse thinks so much of me. Please make me its bride."

"You have been summoned by the emperor!" her father yelled. "To go off with a horse is absolutely crazy!"

But no matter how angry he got, or how sweetly he coaxed her, Ikoma-hime would not comply with the lord's demand, and he was totally nonplussed.

He thereupon consulted his retainers.

"If this horse can gallop around the circumference of this province

three times in two hours," he explained, "I'll let it have the princess."
He reasoned that no horse, however swift it might be, would be able
to go around his wide province three times in just two hours.

So at length, the cream-tinted dapple-gray horse was taken out
into the garden. Its black eyes glittering, it looked fixedly at Ikoma-hime. When the signal bell was struck with a resounding "gonnng,"
the horse whinnied once and shot off like an arrow.

Crossing the fields, going over the mountains and splashing through
the rivers, the cream-tinted dapple-gray horse ran without stopping,
following the circumference of the province once, and then twice.

The lord turned pale.

"This is no ordinary horse," he gasped. "At this rate, it won't take
even two hours. All right, I'll just ring the bell before the time is up."

So before the promised time, his retainer rang the bell.

The deep sound was lifted by the wind and carried far away.

At that moment, the cream-tinted dapple-gray horse was running
along the ridge of the last crag before the finish line. Wheeling about,
it leapt head first into the deep river below.

And, it is said, from that moment on, Ikoma-hime wasted completely away.

The Rice-planting Jizo

In Gumma Prefecture there is a place called Oai, where a fine old
Buddhist temple, the Zenjo-In Kudoku-ji, is located. In this temple is
seated a Buddha image, which is celebrated by the people of the village,
who call it the rice-planting Jizo.[4]

One summer a long time ago, rice-planting had begun in the
village and every household was extraordinarily busy. At this time of
year, everyone, from children to the elderly, worked hard in the rice

---

[4] Jizo (地蔵). Sanskrit, *Ksitigarbha*; Chinese, *Ti-tsang*. Devoted to saving all sentient
beings between the Nirvana of Shakyamuni and the advent of Maitreya, he travels
through the Six Realms of Existence preaching the Buddha-dharma. He is particularly
known as the bodhisattva of children, travelers and animals.

paddies. There was, however, a farmer in the village whose only helper in this work was ill.

"Now I'm in a real fix," he thought. "I wonder if there is someone around who can help me out."

The farmer looked everywhere, but at this busy time there was no one who could offer any assistance. Doing rice-planting by oneself is a grave situation.

Just when he was at a loss as to what to do, a complete stranger came up to him and offered to give him a hand.

"What? Really?" the farmer said in joyful surprise. "That would be a true blessing!" And the two of them immediately set off for the rice paddies.

Well, how this man could work! He was as quick and efficient as a machine, and planted the seedlings in perfect rows. The farmer doubted that they would be able to finish the work in a single day but, in fact, all the paddies had been filled with seedlings before night fell.

"I don't know how to thank you," the farmer said. "I know this is probably not sufficient, but please accept it as your wages today."

But as the farmer tried to give the stranger some money, the latter just waved his hand and said, "Not at all. I don't need anything like that." And he quickly left.

The following day, and the day after that, this man worked with other households who were without help and thus in trouble with the rice-planting. And just as before, when the people tried to offer him money in return for his labor, he would refuse.

"This is strange," one man said. "Who can this fellow be?"

"He seems to be a real Buddha," exclaimed another.

"Hey, let's follow him tomorrow night and see where he goes," suggested still another.

So the following day after the rice-planting had been completed, the young men of the village stealthily followed the man to find out where he had come from. But the man walked quickly, even as he gazed out over the green rice paddies with an expression of pleasure, and when he got as far as the Kudoku-ji, he seemed to evaporate like smoke.

"Now this is really strange," one of the young men said. "Could we have been fooled by a *tanuki*?"

"No, not at all," replied one of the others. "There's no reason to think that a *tanuki* would have helped us with the rice-planting."

Still, the young men felt as though they had been bewitched by a fox, and finally returned home.

When the abbot of the Kudoku-ji heard the story that night, he, too, thought it rather strange, and made a careful round of the temple himself. Yet, as far as he could see, nobody had been there at all.

The next morning, however, he thought he might intone one of the sutras, and went in to the main hall of the edifice. Looking up at the Buddha's face, he was suddenly aware that it was splattered with mud. Not only that, there was mud on its hands and knees as well.

"Well, well," he thought to himself. "It must have been the Buddha who helped with the rice-planting."

Astonished at this conclusion, the abbot put the palms of his hands together in prayer, thanked the Buddha over and over for his benevolent action, and spoke of how overjoyed the village people would be when they understood what had happened.

Indeed, the people of the village were overwhelmed by the Buddha's kindness, presented it with offerings and prayed to it with deep reverence.

And sometime after these events, although no one is sure when, people began to worship this Buddha as the Rice-planting Jizo.

The Kudzu Leaf Fox

A long time ago, in the ancient province of Settsu, there lived a samurai by the name of Abe no Yasuna in the village of Abeno. One year during the autumn, Yasuna, accompanied by five or six retainers, went off to visit the shrine of a local deity in the Shinoda Forest. The forest was filled with color. Bush clover and Chinese bellflowers were everywhere, and the flowers of fall were out in profusion. The men looked at this scene in amazement.

"What a beautiful view!" Yasuna exclaimed. "Should we stop here and drink some sake?"

Yasuna ordered his men to stop, and they quickly prepared for some merrymaking. Soon, they were gazing at the bright red autumn leaves and draining their cups of sake.

Suddenly, there was a clamor and a white fox leapt in among them and hid under the sleeve of Yasuna's robe. Without a sound, it rubbed its head against Yasuna, seemingly in supplication.

"All right," Yasuna assured the frightened animal, "don't worry." He then took the container box that had been placed behind him and hid the fox inside.

Soon after, some men carrying bows and arrows approached Yasuna and his men as they sat drinking.

"Did a white fox go running through here just now?" they asked.

"No," Yasuna replied firmly. "We haven't seen anything like a white fox here."

"That can't be," said the man who appeared to be the group's leader. "It should have come through here for sure. Everyone! Spread out and flush it out!"

The men noisily trampled over the carpet that Yasuna's retainers had set down and began to search the area. Yasuna sprang to his feet.

"This is outrageous!" he shouted. "How dare you disturb our drinking party? Men, send them packing!"

"What?" the intruders' leader cried. "You're nothing but a hayseed samurai!"

"You'll see about that!" yelled Yasuna. "Cut them down!"

Yasuna's retainers unsheathed their swords, not one of them showing any sign of weakness. The so-called leader fled on the spot, while his followers nearly fell over each other trying to keep up with him.

Yasuna then let the white fox out of the box. "It's all right now," he said gently. "Go quickly!"

The white fox quickly fled deep into Shinoda Forest, but not before turning to look back several times with an extremely happy look.

But just as Yasuna and his retainers were finishing up their drinking party and getting ready to return, the men who had previously intruded on them returned, this time accompanied by about a hundred samurai.

"My name is Ishikawa Tsunehei," said their leader. "You dared to shame me a while ago. Now, my fellows, seize them!"

No matter how strong Yasuna's retainers were, there was only so much that the five or six of them could do. Soon, they and Yasuna were all bound and made to kneel before Tsunehei.

"Cut off their heads!" Tsunehei commanded. His samurai had just raised their swords in the air when a voice declared:

"Goodness! Just a moment, please!"

Looking behind them, they saw a Buddhist priest with pure white eyebrows and a pure white beard. He walked in through the crowd and came to a stop in front of Yasuna.

"I am the abbot of the Fujii Temple," he said in a strong but quiet voice.

"Ahh! The abbot!" murmured Tsunehei's men.

Completely flustered, Tsunehei knelt down before the old priest. The Fujii Temple was where his ancestors' graves were located, and it was the old priest who would read the sutras on appropriate days before their mortuary tablets. There was no way that Tsunehei could stand up to him.

"Master Tsunehei," the priest said. "What sort of thing is it to cut down men out viewing the autumn leaves? As a Buddhist priest, I can't permit this."

"Yes, Sir. Of course," came the reply.

Tsunehei signaled his men with a look to leave right away, then he himself hurried off.

"Thank you for saving us from this dangerous situation," Yasuna said, and bowed deeply. But when he looked up, the priest was nowhere to be found. Only a white fox was seen running into the undergrowth.

"Well," he said to his retainers, "that white fox transformed itself into the priest and saved our lives." He and his retainers then straightened their robes and gave thanks to the fox.

The day was now dark, and their small group made its way hurriedly down the rough mountain path. They could not dilly-dally along the way, as there was a chance that Ishikawa Tsunehei and his men might chase after them. They had all been wounded in the fracas earlier on, however, and were terribly thirsty.

"There must be water somewhere around here," Yasuna mumbled to himself.

Somehow, Yasuna got separated from his retainers as he searched for a stream or pond to slake his thirst, and suddenly found himself completely alone. After walking along the mountain path for a while, however, he spied a small stream running through the ravine below.

"Ahh, water," he sighed. "Thank goodness."

Yasuna climbed down into the ravine, guided by the sound of the water. When he reached the stream, however, he was surprised to find a young lady by the bank washing her clothes. The young lady saw that Yasuna was badly wounded and quickly ran up to him.

"Lord samurai," she said in alarm. "You have some terrible wounds and should have them treated right away. If you don't mind its shabbiness, please come to my house and let me attend to them.

After drinking some water from the mountain stream, Yasuna allowed himself to be guided to the young woman's house. His wounds were deeper than he had thought, however, and with every movement, they began to bleed again.

The kind young woman was up all night treating Yasuna's wounds. But thanks to her, after two or three days he was finally able to get up and walk around a little.

"I've been saved, thanks to you," Yasuna said quietly, pressing his palms to the ground and bowing deeply. "There is absolutely nothing I can say that will express my gratitude. But will you at least tell me your name?"

"Yes," she replied shyly. "I am called Kudzu Leaf."

"Kudzu Leaf! What a fine name," Yasuna said, almost to himself.

So saying, Yasuna got ready to return home, but somehow, he found it too painful to leave this kind young lady.

"I have a request," he suddenly stammered. "Would you care to become my wife? I've grown tired of this life of swordfights and battles and would like to live in this house in peace."

"Lord samurai!" the young woman blurted out, and her eyes filled with tears of joy.

In this way, the two of them became man and wife. Kudzu Leaf was truly a tender-hearted young woman, and Yasuna spent every day happily, soon forgetting the time he had spent as a samurai.

In no time at all, three years passed, and Kudzu Leaf gave birth to a dear baby boy. Yasuna named the child Abe no doji, or "the child of Abe Forest," and before they knew it, the child had reached his seventh year.

One day, however, the child came in from playing outdoors and found his mother asleep, her head resting on the loom where she had been weaving. But what was this? Wasn't that a white tail sticking out from the hem of her robe?

"Mommy! You're growing a tail!" the little boy called out.

At the sound of her child's voice, Kudzu Leaf suddenly woke up, and horribly flustered tried to hide her tail. But it was too late.

"Mommy has a tail! Mommy has a tail!" the little boy shouted as he ran out to the field where Yasuna was working.

"Ahh, it's all over," Kudzu Leaf thought to herself. Now she could do nothing but cry. But at length she stood up and took out her writing box. With the brush dipped in ink, she wrote a quick poem on the nearby sliding paper door.

> *If you long for me,*
> *please come and ask,*
> *deep in the Shinoda Forest*
> *of bitter kudzu leaves*
> *at Izumi Spring.*

The poem meant that Kudzu Leaf was the white fox of Shinoda Forest, and if Yasuna and their son wanted to see her, they would have to come to that place.

As soon as she had finished writing the poem, Kudzu Leaf was transformed into a beautiful white fox and leapt outside. By the time Yasuna and the little boy reached home, she was nowhere to be seen.

"So you were that white fox of so many years ago," muttered Yasuna to himself.

And finding the poem on the sliding paper door, he let out a deep sigh.

"Where's Mommy?" The little boy who had just been making such a fuss about the tail, now began searching the house for his mother.

"Please listen," Yasuna said tenderly. "Your mother has gone to a faraway place. From now on, it will be just the two of us living here."

"No!" the little boy cried. "I want Mommy! I want Mommy!"

"All right then," Yasuna agreed. "Let's go and find her."

Carrying the little boy on his back, Yasuna walked to the Shinoda Forest. As the two shouted out Kudzu Leaf's name, a white fox suddenly appeared. Moving close to them, it presented Yasuna with a charm and a hand box that contained a quartz jewel.

"I am the white fox you saved long ago," it said. "Once having returned to this form, I can no longer take human shape again. If you carry this charm, no matter what kind of problems you encounter in this world, you will understand them quickly. And if you place this quartz jewel to your ear, you will understand the words of birds and beasts. When this child grows up, please pass these things on to him. Please take care of him well."

And with that, the white fox trotted into the Shinoda Forest, looking back time and time again until it disappeared from sight.

Thanks to the charm and quartz jewel bequeathed to him by his mother, the young boy eventually grew up to become the famous scholar of divination, Abe Haruakira, who often gave advice to the emperor.

The Akoya Pine

The events in this story took place a long time ago, when the city of Nara was the capital of Japan, and Fujiwara Toyomitsu was the minister who governed the ancient province of Uzen. Toyomitsu had a daughter who gave birth to a beautiful child whom they called Akoya-hime.

One autumn evening when the moon was quite bright, Akoya-hime sat alone playing the *koto*. After a while, she was aware of the sound of a flute, which seemed to be coming out of nowhere, and that the *koto* and flute were in perfect harmony.

"Goodness," she wondered. "How beautifully this flute is being played. Who could be playing it so well?"

The princess stopped playing the *koto* for a moment and looked around the garden. There stood a handsome young man, in the light of the moon. The young man saw the princess and smiled, then disappeared into nothing.

"What a handsome young man!" the princess thought to herself. Hoping to see him a second time, she again sat playing her *koto* the following night. By and by, just as she thought that she heard the sound of the flute, the young man appeared.

"How wonderfully your highness plays the *koto*," he said, speaking for the first time. "I don't believe I've ever heard one played so well."

"No, no," she replied bashfully. "But the sound of your flute is beyond compare!"

In this way, the two began playing together every night, and before long had fallen in love.

One night, however, the young man looked intently at the princess's face and appeared to be quite sad.

"My name is Natori Taro and I live in the foothills of Mount Chitose," the young man finally sighed. "It has been such a pleasure to have got along so well with your highness, but tonight we must part."

"Why are you saying such an unhappy thing?" the princess sobbed through her tears, clinging to the young man's chest. "I would much rather die than part from you!"

"There could be nothing more painful for me either," the young man replied. "But my life comes to an end today." And he gently pulled himself away and started to leave.

"Wait!" the princess cried. "Please take me with you!"

But as she tried to hold on to the young man's sleeve, he disappeared completely, leaving what seemed to be the shadow of a pine tree.

"It must be that he is the spirit of a pine tree," she half-whispered to herself. "But how sad for even a pine tree to have its life taken away."

The princess stared at the shadow of the pine tree and sighed deeply.

Around that time, a bridge that spanned the nearby Natori River had been washed away by a flood, and it had been decided to cut down a huge and very old pine tree that grew on Mount Chitose as material for a new bridge. No matter how the woodsmen chopped away and tried to pull it down, however, the tree would not budge.

"There's something strange about this," one of the woodsmen said suspiciously.

"Well," said another, "let's try pulling it down once more."

A thick straw rope was tied around the pine tree and a great number of woodsmen pulled with all their strength, but the tree did not budge.

The princess heard about the woodsmen's problem and knew that this tree must surely be the young man she loved so much. Immediately going up Mount Chitose, she stood next to the old pine.

"I will never forget you," she said, once again in tears, "even if they cut you down. Please know that I will never take any man as a husband."

So saying, she softly touched the tree. And the tree, which up until now had stood as unwavering as a boulder, fell over with perfect ease and was carried to the bridge's construction site.

After this event, the princess had a hut constructed next to the pine tree's stump, and she cut her hair and became a Buddhist nun. There she prayed for the soul of the pine tree until the day she died.

Strong Samurai

強いさむらいをめぐるお話

Ushiwakamaru and Benkei

Long ago, there was a temple on Mount Hiei outside of Kyoto called the Musashibo. There lived an extraordinarily boisterous monk by the name of Benkei.

When Benkei was a child, he was given the name Oniwaka, or Young Demon, and as his name implied, he was possessed of astonishing strength. Indeed, by the time he was seven, no grown man was a match for him.

"This child is as disorderly as any demon I've ever heard of," his father lamented to the boy's mother. "There's nothing we can do but make an acolyte out of him. He might improve at least a little that way."

Thus, his parents entrusted him to the monks on Mount Hiei.

But Oniwaka's outrageous behavior did not stop after being sent to the temple. If anyone ran afoul of him, he would give his perceived adversary a good beating, and even turn over the Buddhist altars.

Nobody knew what to do with him.

Nevertheless, as Oniwaka grew older, he became a monk at the Musashibo Temple and changed his name to Benkei. But, one day....

"Ahh, what a narrow and boring world this mountain temple is," he sighed to himself. "I think I'll go down to Kyoto and collect a hundred swords for myself."

So Benkei went off to the capital. The very first night he covered his face with a white hood and stood brandishing a large halberd at the Gojo Bridge. This bridge was, and still is, quite famous in Kyoto, and in Benkei's time it was passed over by several thousand people every day.

"I suppose any number of samurai will pass by here," Benkei figured with a grin, and he stood resolutely in the middle of the bridge with both arms spread wide.

In this way, if a samurai came by with a sword in his sash, Benkei would immediately initiate a fight and take the man's sword. With his extraordinary strength, no samurai could stand against him.

Within a few days, Benkei had collected nine hundred and ninety-nine swords from the samurai who had had the bad luck of encountering him. He lacked only one more sword. However, the rumor that

a giant of a priest stood at Gojo Bridge every night had spread around Kyoto, and when night fell no one dared cross the bridge.

"What a bunch of cowards!" Benkei grumbled. "Isn't there anyone in the whole capital who would dare to be my opponent?"

As he paced back and forth in irritation across the bridge, he suddenly heard the beautiful sound of a flute. Then, in the moonlight, he could see a young man wearing a light cloth over his head walking in his direction.

"What's this?" Benkei asked himself. "A child?"

Then he looked at what hung from the young man's waist and spied an absolutely splendid sword. It was a beautiful piece of work fashioned with gold filigree, and quite clearly surpassed any of the swords he had taken by force up until now.

"Hand over the sword you wear at your waist!" Benkei demanded as he stood directly in front of the young man, stretching both arms out wide.

But the young man barely glanced at the huge priest and serenely passed him by.

"Why, you cheeky little brat!"

Benkei took up his halberd and swiftly swept it down at the young man's feet. To his surprise, however, the young man had *already* jumped fifteen or twenty feet past him. Adjusting his stance, the priest then took aim at the young man's head and brought his weapon down with full force.

Thunk!

Benkei had used way too much force and his halberd split the heavy wooden plank of the bridge as though it had been a battle axe.

By now the young man was standing on the bridge's balustrade, beckoning the priest to come and get him.

"This time I'll split you in two!" Benkei yelled, as he raised his halberd over his head. But suddenly, a folding fan hit him squarely on the forehead, and as he closed his eyes for a moment the young man had struck the weapon out of his hands. Adding to this indignity, when he tried to pick it up, he felt someone resolutely kicking his rear end from behind.

Benkei fell forward and collapsed onto the bridge. Immediately, the young man jumped onto his back and locked the priest's neck in his arm.

The young man was unbelievable strong.

"I ... I give up," Benkei groaned.

So even Benkei surrendered in the end. When he finally stood up, he pressed his palms together in supplication.

"Never have I known anyone as strong as you," he wheezed. "Would you please tell me your name?"

"I am called Ushiwakamaru," the young man replied, his eyes glittering brightly.

"Then I humbly request to become your retainer," Benkei said with great courtesy.

"I would like that," the young man returned. "But right now, I am in the custody of a temple. In due course I will become a samurai and will come looking for you. I hope you will become my retainer then."

At the time of this event, Ushiwakamaru was only fifteen years old. Later, when he grew older, he changed his name to Minamoto Yoshitsune, became a general of the Minamoto Clan and defeated the Taira Clan's armies with great finesse.

For his part, Benkei was always at Yoshitsune's side, and brought down any number of his master's enemies with his famous halberd.

Defeat of the Ogre at Hime Shrine

In Nagano Prefecture there is a small shrine called the Hime no miya, located in the village of Kamisato. Long ago, a horrible ogre resided in this shrine. On the morning before the festival celebrated at the shrine, an arrow fletched with white feathers would be found stuck to the roof of a house in which a young lady lived. The young lady of this unfortunate household was then put in a plain wooden box, which was placed as an offering before the shrine. Had this not been done, disasters like droughts or floods would occur that year, and the people of the village would not be able to harvest their grains or other produce of the fields.

"Whose house will be struck by the arrow this year?" the villagers all wondered. Each year as the festival approached, the families in which there were young women, worried so much that they never got a good night's sleep.

One year, the arrow landed on the roof of a rich man who had only one daughter. This was a disaster. Everyone in the household gathered and discussed the matter, but there was really nothing they could do.

"Ahhh!" the rich man wailed. "I'd rather die than have my only daughter taken away!"

He and his wife embraced the girl and shed bitter tears.

At that time, a samurai on a journey passed through the village.

"I'm just passing through on a journey," he said, "but what is going on here?"

"The truth is," the rich man cried, "our only daughter has been chosen to be offered to this god." And through his tears, the man explained the situation.

"There's no reason why a god would do such an outrageous thing," the samurai said flatly. "This surely has to be the work of some ogre. Listen, I'm going to show you this ogre's true form."

So saying, he decided to rescue the young lady.

At length, the midnight of the fatal day arrived. The forest around the shrine had returned to total silence.

The samurai, who had got into the box in place of the young lady, gripped his sword and waited for the ogre to come.

"Any time now, any time now," he imagined.

Just then, the samurai could hear the sound of thudding footsteps approaching, and he knew that the monster was almost upon him. Inside the box, he held onto his sword.

"Hee, hee, hee, hee, hee!" An uncanny laughter pierced the air, and instantaneously the lid of the box was ripped off.

"Now!"

The samurai leapt from the box, and in the same breath took aim and brought his sword down upon the black form before him. The monster let out a hair-raising scream, but the samurai was on it immediately and there was no way of escaping.

"Did you think I'd be beaten by something like you?" the samurai yelled, as he slashed down, slashed down, and slashed down again.

Eventually, the monster was somehow able to flee, and screaming its high-pitched sounds, ran deep into the forest surrounding the shrine.

The following morning, the villagers and the samurai went back to the scene to see what they could find, and discovered traces of bright red blood leading into the shrine. Frightened though they were, they followed the drops of blood, only to find a cavernous hole in the floor. There in the hole was the gorilla-like form of a dog-faced baboon, covered in blood and quite dead.

"This is the true form of your monster," the samurai said matter-of-factly, showing no emotion from his terrific battle the night before.

"Thanks to you, we've been saved!" the villagers shouted with great joy, and bowed low to the samurai.

You probably know the rest of the story. This strong samurai was the famous swordsman Iwami Jutaro, and thanks to him the villagers were able to live in peace for the rest of their days.

Yuriwaka, the State Minister

Long ago, in the ancient prefecture of Bungo, situated on the great island of Kyushu, there lived a great archer by the name of Yuriwaka, the State Minister, who could comfortably draw a six-foot iron bow and sink a ship with a single arrow.

At the time of these events, the enemy's ships had arrived at Kyushu and were sailing about as they pleased, wreaking havoc wherever they went. Thus, the emperor commanded Yuriwaka to shoot at the ships.

At around that time, Yuriwaka had married a beautiful princess by the name of Kasuga-hime.

"I must go now to destroy the enemy," said Yuriwaka to his new wife, "but I will return to you without fail."

Thinking longingly of his wife, Yuriwaka set sail, taking with him a great company of retainers.

But the battles waged day after day for three years. The enemy, as strong as they were, could not match Yuriwaka's powerful bow. Their ships were sunk one after another, until they finally fled altogether.

Yuriwaka had defeated the enemy and survived unscathed, and now decided to return to the princess so dear to his heart.

"Tomorrow I'll at last return home," he thought happily to himself, "but today I'll rest a bit on land."

On their return trip, Yuriwaka and his retainers landed on a small island called Genkai-jima. All of them were happy about their imminent return and celebrated with sake and song. Tired from his long battles and unused to drinking sake for some time, Yuriwaka fell into a deep sleep when night finally came. But then, something dreadful happened.

Two of his retainers, the brothers Beppu Sadasumi and Sadatsura, had wanted to become state ministers for some time, and now, while Yuriwaka slept, they sailed off leaving him on the island alone. In time, the brother Sadasumi, who eventually was chosen to rule Kyushu in Yuriwaka's place, began to want the beautiful Kasuga-hime as his own wife.

"Lord Yuriwaka was struck by an enemy arrow and died," Sadasumi lied. "There is no use in waiting for the dead. Why don't you become my wife now?"

"No," she replied adamantly, "no matter what has happened to Lord Yuriwaka, he is still my husband. It would be outrageous for me to become your wife."

And no matter how many times he begged her, the princess would not accept his offer.

Finally, Sadasumi became angry and threw the princess into a prison in the middle of the mountains.

"If Lord Yuriwaka is no longer alive," Kasuga-hime thought, "I would rather die myself." And she wound her sash around her neck.

At that very moment, a hawk flew in through the prison window. When the princess looked at it carefully, she realized that it was Yuriwaka's favorite hawk, the one he called Midorimaru.

"It's ... it's Midorimaru!" the princess cried, and as she held the hawk to her breast she noticed a piece of cloth attached to its leg. On the cloth, Yuriwaka's name was written in blood.

"Can he still be alive?" she wondered in joy, and tying a brush, ink stick and small ink stone to the hawk's leg, she released it into the sky. The hawk circled the prison roof, then disappeared high into the heavens.

With the heavy weight of its load, however, the hawk tired within sight of Genkai-jima and fell into the sea.

When his hawk did not return, Yuriwaka became more and more uneasy. Every day he walked along the shoreline, waiting to see a boat that could help. Then, one day he was rescued by a passing fisherman and was able to return to his own province.

At that time, Sadasumi had ordered a great archery rally to be held in the Bungo, and Yuriwaka was able to disguise himself in order to take part in the contest.

When the moment came for him to step forward, he broke the bow that had been handed to him and asked for a stronger one.

"What?" yelled Sadasumi. "Here, then. Try fitting an arrow to Yuriwaka's old iron bow! If you can't do it, I'll have your head!"

Yuriwaka nodded calmly and grasped his beloved bow. Fitting it with an arrow, he drew the bow to the shape of a full moon. Then, he turned around and faced his enemy.

"Beppu Sadasumi," he yelled aloud. "Have you forgotten Yuri-waka?" And released the arrow.

With a hum, the arrow pierced Sadasumi's breast. Instantly fitting another arrow in the bow, he released this one into the back of the fleeing Sadatsura.

Kasuga-hime was soon released and ran into Yuriwakas's embrace.

Once more, Yuriwaka became the minister of Bungo province, and lived happily together with the princess until they both passed away.

The Chinese Bridge at Seta

Many years ago, in the ancient province of Omi, there lived a man named Tawara no Touta who was famous for his archery skills. One day, when Touta was crossing the Chinese Bridge at Seta, which spans a section of Lake Biwa, he encountered a huge serpent, perhaps the length of five human beings, stretched across the center of his path. The serpent's eyes glittered with fiery light and flames burst from between its fangs. It was a truly frightening sight.

An ordinary person would have been petrified with fear, but Touta was, as you might imagine, a strong samurai.

"What a nuisance," he grumbled, "sprawling around in a place like this!" He stepped nonchalantly over the serpent's back.

But then…. "Excuse me," a voice came from behind.

"What's this?" Touta thought to himself. "Is this serpent about to complain?"

Turning around, however, he found a beautiful woman in the place where the huge serpent had been.

"Do you have some business with me?" Touta asked curtly.

"The truth is that I have a favor to ask of you," the woman replied courteously.

"A favor?" Touta repeated.

"Yes," she replied. "I am, in fact, a dragon that lives under this bridge. I had heard you were a powerful samurai and so I transformed myself into the huge serpent you found asleep here. And just as rumor has it, you are a fearless man."

"So?" Touta responded, still showing little patience with the situation.

"Please listen to my story," the woman continued, even more courteously. "There is a giant centipede living on Mount Mikami just visible over there. This centipede comes here to the lake and abducts many of my kind. If this goes on for long, our entire family of dragons will be wiped out. Our enemy the centipede is long enough to wrap itself around Mount Mikami seven and a half times, so he is too big for us to fight. Please, would you kill this horrible beast?"

And the woman, who was, in fact, a dragon, put the palms of her hands together in supplication.

"All right," Touta said matter of factly, "If this centipede is that much of a problem, I'll get rid of it for you."

Touta then followed the woman, and in a short while could see the Dragon Palace off in the distance. The main hall was sprinkled with gold and silver and was beautiful enough to make one's eyes open wide.

"So this is the Dragon Palace," pondered Touta, as he gazed at it as though in a trance. "And it's just like they say."

"Please, please, come this way." Just then, the dragon king, accompanied by his retainers, came out to greet him.

Touta was shown to his room, a spacious hall carpeted with crystals. On the trays set before him were mountains of delicious foods laid side by side and golden turtle shells filled with sake. At length, a number of beautiful women appeared and began to dance to the harmonious sounds of flutes and bells.

Touta, looking on in rapture and completely forgetting the passage of time, felt as though he was in Heaven.

Suddenly, the spacious hall turned dark.

"Lord Touta!" said the dragon king in a quavering voice. "The centipede has come!"

"Good!" replied the great archer. "Everyone hide!"

Touta stood up, grasping his bow and arrows. The sky over Mount Mikami quickly turned red, and simultaneously hundreds of fireballs flew here and there, closing in on the palace of the dragons.

"Those must be the centipede's eyes!" Touta notched an arrow in his bow, aimed right between the two brightest fireballs and released the bowstring. But as the arrow hit its target, it made a sound as though it had struck a solid rock wall.

"I'm in for it now," Touta muttered. Quickly sending a second arrow from his bow, he heard the same dull thud as it ricocheted off the centipede just like the first.

Only a single arrow now remained and he could hear the centipede's bellowing as it came closer and closer.

"Ahh," moaned the dragon king at Touta's side, "what can we do?"

"Why, yes! I nearly forgot!" mumbled Touta to himself, taking the point of the third arrow and applying it with a good bit of his own spit.

Centipedes loath human spit more than anything else in the world. Fitting the third arrow to his bow, Touta resolutely took aim.

"Eat this!" he yelled. Released from the bowstring, the arrow raised a groaning sound as it flew towards its target.

"Yahh!" the centipede screamed as the arrow neatly perforated its forehead.

The hundreds of fireballs vanished at once, a huge spray of water rose over them, and the dragon palace shook as though there had been an earthquake. Yells went up from the dragons as they all held their heads in their hands and fell to the palace floor. At last, the shaking stopped and the great hall was as brightly lit as before.

Looking up, they saw that the water of the lake was turning bright red. In the middle of the lake itself, the corpse of the giant centipede with an arrow in its forehead was slowly pitching and rolling back and forth.

"Thank you so much," the dragon king sighed, bowing his head in gratitude. "Now we can live in peace."

He then ordered his retainers to bring one straw rice bag, one roll of silk and a hanging bell.

"This is but a token of our gratitude," he said humbly. "Please take them with you on your return."

"This is more than kind of you," Touta replied. "That delicious meal was quite sufficient, you know."

Strangely enough, the rice bag Touta received from the dragon king never became empty, no matter how much rice was taken from it, and the roll of silk never came to an end. As a result, Touta eventually became a very wealthy man.

Touta donated the hanging bell to the nearby Buddhist temple, the Miidera, and its rich and beautiful tones could be heard from one end of Omi to the other.

Unfortunate People

かわいそうな人をめぐるお話

The Mirror of Matsuyama

Long ago, in the ancient province of Echigo in a place called Matsuyama, there lived a man and his wife and their daughter.

Although the woman was ill, her husband was ordered by the emperor to go to the capital. When the morning of his departure finally came, he called his daughter to his room.

"When your mother is no longer ill," he said quietly, "I will come back to you. But until then, please take good care of her."

"Father, please," the young girl cried. "I want to go to the capital, too!"

"Now, now," her father consoled her. "Take good care of your mother so that you both can come to the capital soon."

So saying, the man left for the capital.

Years passed by and the girl's mother became increasingly ill. Her father, however, was terribly busy at his duties and was unable to return home. Then one day, her mother called her to her bedside.

"I'm afraid I'm not going to live much longer," the woman said in a weak voice. "When I'm gone, please take good care of your father."

Having said this, she reached underneath her pillow and took out a pale copper mirror wrapped in cloth.

"Your father bought this mirror for me a long time ago," she whispered. "If you want to see me after I've passed on, take out this mirror and look into it. I will always be right there."

"No, Mother!" the girl wailed. "I don't want you to die!"

The girl held her mother's pale thin hand and cried and cried. But after a short while, her mother passed away.

The young girl now lived completely alone, and thinking of her mother every day she did nothing but shed tears. Then, one day she missed her mother so much that she took out the mirror, unwrapped the cloth and looked into it. There, in the very center, was her mother's face.

"Oh, Mother!" she said aloud.

The young girl was beside herself, and broke into a smile. In the mirror, her mother did the same.

In this way, the girl lived from day to day, and when she became inconsolably sad, she would take out the mirror and look at her mother's face.

At long last, the girl's father heard about his wife's death and returned from the capital, bringing with him a new wife.

"How painful your life must have been," he said, embracing his daughter and spilling many tears. "Please forgive me."

The girl buried her face in her father's breast and cried in long soft sobs. How many years had she longed for him? The sorrow she had had to bear for so long rose to the surface again and again.

"I'm not leaving you alone ever again," her father said softly while stroking her face. "This time, I'm taking you back to the capital with me. And this is your new mother!"

With that, he turned around and faced the woman seated behind him.

But in an instant the young girl pushed her father away and jumped to her feet.

"No!" she yelled adamantly. "I don't want to do anything like going to the capital!" And saying nothing else, she ran to her room.

Soon it would be time for her father to return to the capital, but no matter how he scolded or cajoled, the girl made no attempt to get along with his new wife. Confounded, he finally consulted his new wife.

"What in the world am I going to do?" he asked in despair. "Don't you have any good ideas?"

"Well, it's clear that she doesn't like me at all," his wife grumbled. "But we can't just let things go along like this. I'm going to let her know that right now!"

His new wife would hear nothing to the contrary, and went straight to the young girl's room.

"What are you doing in here every day?" she demanded.

"Nothing," the girl replied, and nervously hid the mirror behind her back.

"If you're not doing anything, why don't you come out then?" the new wife continued, glaring at the girl. "Don't you like me?"

"No … it's not that…," the girl replied hesitantly.

Just then, her father came in and spied the mirror she was hiding behind her.

"Why," he said with an angry look, "isn't that the mirror I gave to your mother? What are you doing with it?"

The girl then broke down in tears.

"I was visiting with my mother," she sobbed. "Just before she died, she told me that if I wanted to see her, all I had to do was to look in this mirror!"

"Ah, I see." He now looked at her with a different expression, for his daughter's face was exactly like that of his dead wife's. The girl had looked into the mirror, seen her own face, and truly thought it was her mother's. When he considered the tender heart of his first wife, his breast filled with emotion.

"There's nothing more I can do," he thought. "I'll just have to leave things as they are for a while…." And he quietly left the room.

When his new wife heard this, however, she got angrier than before.

"I refuse to let her look into that mirror again!" she shouted, and with that forcibly took the mirror from the girl's hand.

Without the mirror, the young girl could no longer see her mother. And how could she call a woman who had taken such an important thing away from her, her "mother?" If she could not meet her real mother, she would rather die.

Quietly slipping out of the house, the young girl went down to the edge of the nearby pond. The surface of the pond was as cold and clear as a mirror. There she could see her mother's face perfectly reflected.

"Oh, Mother," she whispered softly. Then, without a second thought, she leapt into the pond.

It is said that from that time, it has been known as Mirror Pond.

The Motoshichi-kuroshichi Bird

Deep in the mountains around Aizu, in Fukushima Prefecture, there is a bird called the Motoshichi-kuroshichi. One wing of this bird is white while the other is black. On autumn evenings, it flies around the forest crying plaintively.

A very long time ago, there lived a hunter in this forest. His wife had died young and left him with two sons, one called Motoshichi, the other Kuroshichi.

When he was young, this hunter was so famous that his name was known to everyone in the vicinity. He could shoot a large wild boar with a single arrow, or take down ten to twenty rabbits in a single day.

But now his health was beginning to fail him and when returning from the mountains, all he wanted to do was to sit and drink sake. His only joy was in watching his two sons grow daily into true hunters.

After a number of years had passed, his sons had grown sufficiently to go hunting by themselves.

"Listen, Father," the eldest brother Motoshichi said. "Just watch how many rabbits I'll bring home today."

"I can pull a bow, too, you know," the younger brother Kuroshichi added, not to be outdone.

"All right then," their father replied. "Let's all three of us go out today." And picking up his old bow for the first time in a long time, he led his two sons out into the mountain.

Now these boys were, after all, their famous father's sons. And not to be outdone by him, they took in plenty of game that day.

"Well, I can rest easy now," the hunter said happily, as he rubbed his worn-out feet.

At this, his two robust young hunters went quickly deeper into the mountain, despite their father's protests. And suddenly he realized they were nowhere to be seen.

"Hey! Motoshichi! Kuroshichi!" he called as loudly as he could. But there was no answer.

Soon night fell and the forest was completely dark.

"Maybe they went home ahead of me," the hunter reasoned, and quickly returned to their house. But no one was there and the house was quiet and empty.

The hunter decided to wait a little while longer, but his sons did not return. Increasingly anxious, he finally went out in the pitch-black night and went back to the mountain again.

"Motoshichi! Kuroshichi!" he yelled repeatedly, walking back and forth through the mountains. But his sons did not reply.

Half out of his wits, the hunter searched again and again through the dark mountains, stumbling over tree stumps and scratched by thorn bushes until his face, hands and feet were covered with blood. Nevertheless, he walked in circles the entire night, calling out the names of his sons repeatedly.

The next morning, some of the villagers who had come out to the mountain to gather firewood found the hunter collapsed under a white birch tree. They hurriedly tried to revive him, but his body was already cold.

Just then, they saw a bird that had perched on the branch of a nearby tree. One wing of the bird was white, while the other was black. Soon, it began to cry plaintively.

"Motoshichi! Kuroshichi!" it called, as it flapped its wings and circled over the men below.

Ever since then, whenever people have sighted this feathered creature, they have called it the Motoshichi-kuroshichi Bird. But no one ever knew what happened to the two brothers.

Anju and Chushiou

On a lonely road on the outskirts of a village, four people – an elder sister by the name of Anju, a younger brother, Chushiou, their mother and an old maidservant – walked on.

"Mother," pleaded Anju, who was now walking with a limp. "How much longer do we have to walk?"

"We still have a long way to go," her mother patiently replied.

"But will we really be able to meet our father?" asked Chushiou, nearly in tears. Although the boy had started out robustly and in high spirits, he now had to walk with the aid of a stick.

All of them had become terribly thin, their faces had been burnt by the sun and their eyes stared straight ahead. How many mountains had they walked over by now? How many rivers had they forded? The rain had beaten down on them, and the wind had blown them about, and now they were clearly tottering on their feet.

The children's father had been deceived by some evil person and had been taken away to the far-off land of Tsukushi. The four of them were walking to the place where their father might be. Anju, the eldest of the two, was fourteen years old. Chushiou, her younger brother, was only twelve.

Now, as the four of them sat beneath a bridge and ate their cold rice balls, a man came up to them and spoke.

"I am a sailor by the name of Yamaoka Daiyu," he said kindly. "Why don't you stay at my house tonight? It's warm and I can give you some hot gruel."

The four travelers were delighted and agreed to his generous offer.

The next day, Yamaoka Daiyu accompanied them to a nearby beach.

"Well, you can set your minds at ease now," he assured them. "My friend's boat is going from here to Tsukushi. If you'd like to get on board, you won't have to walk any farther."

"You've really saved us," the mother cried, bowing over and over again. The sea was wide and a deep blue-green, and in the far distance was covered in mist.

"Once we've crossed the water," the children both thought, "we'll be in Tsukushi where our father is!" and their breasts beat within them.

There were two boats docked there at a cliff and in each was a strong-looking man at the helm.

"If you don't mind, the children should go in one boat and the adults in the other," Yamaoka Daiyu explained. "We'll put your belongings in yet another."

So saying, he helped Anju and Chushiou into one boat and their mother and the maidservant into the other.

"Will the boats be going together?" the maidservant asked anxiously.

"Everything will be fine," Yamaoka Daiyu said with a smile. "Now, be careful!"

At length, the boats moved offshore, but when they got out into the deep sea, one boat suddenly went to the right while the other went to the left. The four passengers turned pale and cried out, but the two boats were soon far apart.

"Please, turn the boat around!" their mother pleaded, clutching at the man at the helm.

"Huh!" the man scowled. "So you've finally understood what's going on? We're taking you to two different provinces to sell you as slaves!"

The children called out plaintively for their mother and maidservant, but the boats gradually drew farther apart until their voices could no longer be heard. The two adults also called out desperately and leaned so far out of their boat that they nearly fell into the sea.

"Anju!" their mother cried out with her remaining strength. "Hold fast to your amulet of Jizo! Chushiou! Take good care of the knife your father left you!"

Who would have known that the kindly Yamaoka Daiyu was nothing but a dastardly kidnapper!

Now, in the province of Tango, there lived a very wealthy man by the name of Sansho Daiyu. He had bought a number of slaves from all over and set them to work while paying them nothing. Sadly, Anju and Chushiou were also brought to this man and sold to him.

"From this day forth, you are my property," the man said, as he stroked the scraggly beard on his red face. "Anju, you are to go to the seashore every day and draw water. Chushiou, you are to go to the mountains and collect firewood. And I will not stand for any laziness!"

The very next day, the two children were put to work. Chushiou went off to the mountains to collect firewood, but did not really understand how to use his sickle, and in no time at all had cut most of his fingers. Anju, of course, went off to the sea to draw water into a bucket, but the bucket was so heavy that she spilled most of the water on the way back.

"It's because you're so careless!" Sansho Daiyu yelled, and had his retainers beat the two children and give them no food.

That night Anju and Chushiou held each other and cried in their small dirty hut. They talked about wanting to escape and to see their mother again. But Sansho Daiyu's guards overheard them and quickly brought them before him as he sat drinking sake before a brightly burning hearth.

"What! You want to run away?" he growled. "I'll brand the both of you!"

With that, he took a red-hot tong from the hearth, stuck it firmly to Anju's forehead, and watched with satisfaction as the girl cried out and collapsed. Chushiou immediately leapt at Sansho Daiyu, but he was just a child and could in no way defeat the larger man.

"I'll fix this little brat!" Sansho Daiyu exploded.

Grabbing Chushiou, Sansho Daiyu pressed the tong against the boy's forehead. Both children now screamed in pain, their eyes rolling back into their heads.

Then they both woke from what must have been a terrible dream.

"Ahh, that was so frightening!" cried Chushiou.

"But it was only a dream," his sister consoled him.

As Anju was squeezing her trembling brother's hand, something fell down to her lap from the breast of her robe. Looking down, she saw that it was the tiny amulet of Jizo.

When had she put it there, she wondered. And then, there it was – the brand from a fire tong clearly impressed on Jizo's forehead!

Jizo had saved them from a horrible fate.

The two pressed their palms together in prayer and gave thanks to the bodhisattva with all their hearts.

The next day, Anju got up while it was still dark. Pulling her little brother by the hand, she climbed up the mountain behind Sansho Daiyu's mansion as fast as they could go.

"Listen, Chushiou," she whispered. "Soon we will have made our escape. Go to that temple you see facing the forest."

"Aren't you going with me?" Chushiou asked fearfully.

"No," Anju replied. "If we're together, we'll be more easily found. Take this amulet of Jizo and think of it as your elder sister."

"All right," said Chushiou. "I'll meet up with you later for sure!" He then squeezed his elder sister's hand tightly and ran towards the temple, tears flooding from his eyes.

Chushiou was able to escape to the temple without trouble. The kindly priest cleverly deceived Sansho Daiyu's retainers, who had come to capture the children, and sent them back none the wiser. He then sent the boy to Kyoto, which was where the emperor resided at that time.

Chushiou thereupon went to the home of a high-positioned

retainer of the emperor, and told him all about his father, mother and elder sister.

The retainer was shocked.

"This has been a dreadful experience for you," the retainer declared. "I will help find your father right away."

And this he tried to do. The children's father, however, had succumbed to an illness by this time and had already passed away.

Many years passed. Chushiou grew up to be a fine adult and was commanded by the emperor to become the lord of the province of Tamba. (You may recall that Tamba was where the terrible Sansho Daiyu lived.)

Chushiou then set out to rescue his elder sister, but tragically the poor thing had already died.

"Ahh, if only I had come for her a little sooner," cried Chushiou to himself, shedding bitter tears. But he then took Sansho Daiyu into custody and released all the people who had been kidnapped by the man.

Chushiou lamented the deaths of his father and elder sister, but then wondered if his mother and her maidservant had possibly survived. Severely questioning Sansho Daiyu's retainers, he learned that the two women had been kidnapped as well and sent to the province of Sado. And there he went immediately.

He found, however, that no one there knew anything of the two, and thought that they, too, must have died.

But one day, as he was walking along forlornly, he came upon a dilapidated house in the middle of a wide field. In the garden was a blind old lady drying chestnuts. As she sang in a small weak voice, she tried to chase away the sparrows that came to eat the chestnuts:

> *My darling little Anju, ho yare ho!*
> *My darling little Chushiou, ho yare ho!"*

Hearing this song, Chushiou was taken aback and stood stock still. Then he looked carefully at the old lady's face.

"Ahh, Mother! Mother!" he cried aloud. "It's me, Chushiou!"

Chushiou ran as fast as he could to the old lady, who he now knew was his mother.

Taking the talisman of Jizo from the breast of his robe, he pressed it to the woman's eyes. In a moment, his blind mother's eyes were opened and flowed with tears.

"Ahh, Chushiou!" she wept.

"Mother!" Chushiou cried.

And the two embraced in a flood of tears.

⮜

Otome Pass

There is a section of an old path crossing Hakone in Kanagawa Prefecture called the Otome Pass. Long ago, it took hours to cross this pass. Recently, however, a fine road has been constructed and the traveler can cross it in about ten minutes.

Many years ago, there was a young woman named Otome who lived in a farmhouse quite near this place. Her father was ill, but she remained good-natured and was beautiful besides. Moreover, she was popular with the young men of the village and received numerous proposals to make her a bride.

Otome, however, would slip out of the house in the middle of the night and go off somewhere unbeknown to anyone.

Her sick father wondered where she went every night and became quite worried. He said nothing about his concern, however, and Otome continued going out every night, sometimes not returning until dawn. Yet, when he heard a rumor that his daughter had found a boyfriend and was going out to see him every night, he could no longer keep silent.

One snowy night, when Otome had quietly left the house, her father got up from his bed and secretly followed her. Otome's footprints left clear traces in the snow, but as the snow continued to fall harder and harder, her father found it difficult , even painful, to walk. As angry as he was, however, he simply ground his teeth and kept climbing the path, step by step.

Following his daughter's footsteps, he finally arrived at the top of the pass. There at the side of the road, someone had fallen into a hole in the snow and was struggling to get out. Looking carefully, he could see that it was his daughter Otome. Instinctively, he drew near to help her, but suddenly thought the better of it.

"No, wait a moment," he said to himself. "This is probably divine retribution for having deceived her father and done some bad thing."

Thus, he passed by her with a look of indifference.

Reasoning that she was on her way back from the direction in which he was going, he crossed over the pass and continued down the other side. At the bottom, he found that her footsteps stopped in front of a small temple dedicated to the bodhisattva Jizo.

"What in the world was she doing here?" Otome's father wondered, and woke up the old man who lived at the temple. Surely, he would know.

"Ah, yes, that young lady," the old man began. "I saw her just a little while ago. And what an admirable young lady she is! Every night she comes here and prays that her sick father will get well again. Despite rain or wind, she hasn't missed a single day. Tonight is exactly the one hundredth time she's come here to pray."

The old man talked on and on about what a praiseworthy young lady Otome was.

"Can this be so?" her father said quietly to himself. "What a fool I was to believe the villagers' rumor!"

Running back in panic to the place where he had last seen Otome, he found that she had been buried in the falling snow. With all his strength, he pulled her from the hole but it was too late. She was already dead.

"Otome!" he cried. "Please forgive me!" Holding his daughter's cold body to his breast, he shed tears that never seemed to end.

The villagers deeply regretted having spread such an irresponsible rumor, and from that time on called this place Otome Pass.

~~⊃

Chujo-hime

These events occurred long ago, when Nara was still the capital of Japan.

Among the retainers of the emperor, there was a minister of state by the name of Fujiwara Toyonari. This minister had one daughter named Nagatani-hime, whose mother had died when she was only three years old.

"This will be a tragic situation," the minister thought, "as long the child has no mother."

Thus, when the child was seven years old, he married a woman called Teruhi no mae and she became his daughter's new mother.

This new mother was very beautiful, but her heart was crooked and she was quite ill-tempered. Needless to say, she hated Nagatani-hime, who everyone else loved and considered to be gentle and adorable. Even if Nagatani-hime addressed her as "Mother," Teruhi no mae would look the other way and ignore her. If the girl was just a little slow in completing the work her new mother had set for her, the woman would raise her voice and yell at the little girl in front of everyone. Still, the gentle-hearted Nagatani-hime would never complain, but instead work even harder for her new mother.

When Nagatani-hime was thirteen years old, the emperor became very ill. There was a river that ran before his palace, and the noise of this rushing stream made it impossible for him to sleep. No one, however, was able to do anything to lessen this disturbance. Thus, the sweet-tempered Nagatani-hime composed a poem for him, which she proposed as a sort of prayer.

The emperor immediately called for Nagatani hime, and had her read the poem before him.

Never mind the waves, may the Tatsuta River fall silent;
May all the emperor's sufferings refrain and wash away.

What do you suppose happened then? The river that had roared so furiously up until then, suddenly became placid.

The emperor was overjoyed. Complimenting both Nagatani-hime and her poem, he elevated her to the rank of *chujo*.[1] After that, everyone began to call her Chujo-hime.

When the girl's new mother found out about this, she hated Chujo-hime all the more.

"What was so wonderful about that poem?" she complained. "Even I could compose one better than that!"

Obsessed with her own evil thoughts, she began to slander Chujo-hime, and eventually conceived the idea of killing her.

"If only she were dead," she grumbled, "I would be the most popular woman in the palace."

Finally, she commanded one of her retainers to take Chujo-hime to Mount Hibari, a lonely and isolated area between the ancient provinces of Yamato and Kii, and kill her.

The retainer cleverly deceived Chujo-hime and took her to Mount Hibari, but once there he had no heart to kill her. Instead, he bowed with both palms on the ground, and explained the situation.

"The truth is," he said frankly, "that I was commanded by your mother to take you here and kill you. But why should I do that to someone who has done no crime at all?"

"Thank you for being so forthright," she replied, sadly lowering her eyes. "But somehow I am guilty of having made my mother so angry. I can stay here on this mountain and live alone, so please go back to my mother and tell her that you have done your duty."

"No," the retainer replied, "I cannot just leave you in such a place and go home. My wife and I together will serve you here."

So saying, the retainer quickly cut down some of the nearby trees and, thatching a roof, made a small hut for her there. He then returned to the capital, gathered together the princess's personal belongings and his wife, and went back to the mountain. There, the three of them lived a lonely life far away from the capital.

---

[1] A middle court rank.

The retainer and his wife gathered firewood every day and picked flowers which they sold in the village at the foot of the mountain. With the little money they earned, they were able to buy just enough rice for her and themselves.

"How sad this is for her," the retainer lamented. "If she were in the capital, she would never be so much in want."

"How true, how true," his wife agreed. "What a horrible person her mother must be."

The retainer and his wife exchanged glances, their eyes heavy with tears.

"Please don't be so sad," she said softly. "Thanks to the two of you, I can live here like this with no troubles at all."

So saying, Chujo-hime gathered firewood with hands unaccustomed to hard work, and brought water from the valley stream. If she had any leisure at all, she sat quietly alone and recited the sutras.

As for the minister, he finally returned home after a long absence due to his heavy responsibilities of state. On the night of his return, he was confronted by Teruhi no mae.

"What a horrible woman Chujo-hime turned out to be," she lied. "She's run off with some strange man."

Hearing this, the minister was outraged.

"Such a loose woman is no daughter of mine!" he fumed. "You may have her expelled!"

In her heart, however, Teruhi no mae knew that she had already accomplished this.

"The fact is," she said with an affectionate air, "I ordered one of my retainers to get rid of her."

"That's fine," the minister replied, utterly deceived by Teruhi no mae. "I never want to see her again."

However, one day the minister went out with his retainers to hunt at Mount Hibari. Riding about the mountain with his bow to hand, he suddenly noticed a small hut.

"Can someone be living out here in the mountains like this?" he wondered. Thinking this to be quite strange, he peeked inside the hut, only to see a beautiful woman reciting a sutra with all of her heart.

"What? It's you?" he instinctively called out.

"Father!" Chujo-hime cried. "How I've grieved for you!"

She fell on her father's breast, and while he, too, wanted to embrace her, in his confusion he suddenly thrust her away.

"No!" he stuttered. "You're disgusting! You ... you're no longer my daughter!"

"But why?" she pleaded.

"You ... you...," the minister hesitated. He then recounted the story he had been told by Teruhi no mae.

"Oh, that's just terrible!" Chujo-hime cried as she covered her face with her hands. "How could she say such things? Do you, my own father, believe that I am such a woman?"

Just then, the retainer and his wife returned to the hut and recounted the entire history of events to the minister.

"Is that so?" he muttered. "Daughter, please forgive me!"

This time the minister embraced his daughter tightly, wiping her cheeks (and his own) of tears time and again.

Chujo-hime now returned to the capital and her home with the minister, but did not want to meet her new mother ever again. Further, she decided to shave her head and become a nun.

"I want to become a disciple of the Buddha," she explained, "and to see my long-departed mother."

And no matter how the minister opposed this idea, she would not take no for an answer.

Thus, Chujo-hime went to the Taima-dera, a temple just outside of Kyoto, and became a nun.

"Please, let me see my mother," she prayed. "Let me see the Buddha's Pure Land."

For three years, Chujo-hime prayed and recited the sutras with great fervor. Then, one day, two nuns appeared, seemingly out of nowhere.

"You must gather enough lotus stalks to put on the backs of a hundred horses," they said in calm religious tones.

Chujo-hime asked her father, the minister, for help, and quickly gathered the lotus stalks. The two nuns then spun thread from the stalks and rinsed it in the spring water in front of the temple. The thread immediately began to shine with a dazzling glare and become imbued with the five colors.[2]

The two nuns had the thread carried into the main hall and soon began to weave it into a beautiful cloth. At length, the inside of the hall began to shine with the brilliance of the dawn, and suddenly the nuns disappeared.

Chujo-hime let out a gasp. The cloth left by the nuns caught the morning sun and shone like a brocade of gems and jewels. On the cloth itself was a profusion of red and white lotus blossoms, and celestial goddesses played upon flutes and danced above the clouds. Among them was the unmistakable face of her real mother.

Chujo-hime stared at the cloth as if in a trance for what must have seemed to others to be a long, long time. At some point she heard the voices of the two nuns.

"This is the Buddha's Pure Land that you desired to see," they seemed to say in a whisper. "And among the celestial goddesses, you have surely recognized your mother."

"Thank you, thank you!" Chujo-hime said so quietly that no one else would have heard. She then began to recite the sutra again with all her heart.

This cloth woven from the thread of lotus stalks is now called the Chujo-hime Mandala, and today is still in the possession of the Taima-dera.

---

[2] The five colors—blue, yellow, red, black and white—which, according to Buddhist tradition, represent meditation, memory, zeal, wisdom and faith, respectively.

The Stone That Cried at Night

Long, long ago, in the ancient province of Totomi, in a place called Sayo, located in the middle of the mountains, there lived a young woman by the name of O-ishi.[3] One day, O-ishi was requested by someone to go to a place called Kanaya and bring back a loan. As she approached the mountain pass on her return home, the day turned dark and she thought she had better hurry. Just as she was about to descend the mountain on the other side of the pass, a man appeared bearing an unsheathed sword.

"You there, lady!" he yelled brusquely. "Put down the money you're carrying inside your robe!"

"Please leave me alone!" she pleaded, with her palms together in supplication. "This money belongs to someone else who is in terrible need of it!"

"Don't make excuses to me!" the man continued. "Just hand it over."

The man thereupon grabbed O-ishi and thrust his hand into the pocket of her robe.

O-ishi screamed for help, wrestled out of the man's grasp and tried to run away. In an instant, the man brandished his sword and slashed O-ishi across the back. O-ishi groaned and fell, the man took the money from the breast pocket of her robe and quickly off down the mountain.

At the time, O-ishi was a full nine months pregnant. Clinging to a large stone next to her, she writhed in pain but was able to give birth to a baby boy. She had no strength, however, to pick up the crying baby and quickly passed away. The baby, too, having just been born, could not cry loudly enough to attract anyone's attention.

At that moment, however, the stone that O-ishi had clung to, somehow felt the tragedy of the baby's situation and cried out in a loud voice. The priest at the nearby Kuenji, a Buddhist temple, heard the cry and rushed to the scene. There, he was horrified to find a dead woman covered with blood, with a naked newborn baby at her side.

"This is terrible! Terrible!" he muttered.

---

[3] O-ishi (お石), literally, Honorable (or Miss) Stone.

The priest quickly picked up the baby and brought it back to the temple. He then called on a number of people to help carry O-ishi's body back.

"You poor thing," he thought. "Well, I'll take care of your baby. Be at peace and go to the Buddha."

Thus, the priest buried O-ishi in a simple grave and intoned a sutra for her sake.

The priest, however, was quite poor, and was reduced to making millet jelly candies and selling them in order to have enough money to bring up the child. He named the boy Otohachi.

Thanks to the priest, Otohachi grew rapidly and soon reached the age of thirteen.

Strange to tell, from the time O-ishi was murdered, when night drew near, the stone would cry aloud in a pitiful voice.

"It's that stone that cries at night," the people in the village murmured to one another. "There's no doubt about it. It's possessed by that murdered woman's soul."

To put her soul at peace, the people offered flowers to the stone and the priest intoned the sutras, but every night the same sad cries issued forth from that tragic place.

One day, Otohachi approached the priest with a serious expression.

"The people of the village tell me that the voice coming from the stone that cries at night is my mother's," he said bluntly. "Why is that?"

"It could certainly be," the priest replied sympathetically. "The fact of the matter is that your mother ... well, she was murdered by a highwayman there." He then told Otohachi the story, leaving out no detail.

"But, listen," the priest continued, "You've already grown up to be a fine young man. There's no need to be discouraged, no matter what has happened. You should study hard and become a great priest."

Hearing this, Otohachi's eyes brimmed with tears and he pressed his palms together in thanks.

"I understand everything you've said to me," he said tearfully. "But from now on, every time I even think I hear the stone that cries at night, my heart is going to break. So I'm going to the capital to study to become a swordsmith."

Though the priest tried his hardest to persuade Otohachi to stay, the young man was stubborn and would hear none of it.

"If you're that determined," the priest said at last, "then you should become a swordsmith. If you do, please become the best swordsmith in all of Japan."

"I will," replied Otohachi gratefully. "And I will never forget what I owe you for taking care of me for so long."

The next day, Otohachi was seen off by the priest and left on his journey to the capital. In his heart, he was absolutely resolved.

"No matter what happens," he thought calmly to himself, "I am going to cut down my mother's killer."

Years passed. After a time, Otohachi became a first-rate swordsmith, and was employed at the workshop of Minamoto Goro in the province of Yamato. One day, as he was working alone, a traveler came in with a request.

"I'd like you to repair and sharpen this sword," he said, handing over his sheathed weapon. Otohachi removed the blade from its scabbard and could see that it was nicked badly in one or two places.

"What happened here?" he inquired.

"The truth is," the man laughed, "I cut a woman down at a pass, seventeen or eighteen years ago. But in doing so, my sword struck the large stone next to her."

"This has to be the man," Otohachi thought, stifling the anger that was boiling up inside him.

"Huh, a woman, you say?" he continued with an indifferent look. "What did you kill her for?"

Thinking that the swordsmith was interested in his story, the man told him everything, as though it was something he was proud of.

"There's no doubt about it," Otohachi was now convinced. "This is the man who killed my mother."

Otohachi grasped the man's sword with a firm grip.

"Listen well," he said, showing none of the emotion that filled his breast. "The little boy that was born that night was me. You are my mother's killer. Prepare to die."

Immediately, he struck the man. The man tried in vain to flee, but this time Otohachi cut him squarely through the back. The traveler fell where he was and died.

Strangely enough, after that event the stone was never heard to cry again. But the marks nicked on it by the killer's sword remain there today.

Book Two:
Strange Tales

Man-eating
Demons and Yamanba

The Two Children and the Yamanba

A long time ago in a certain place, there were two children, an elder sister and a younger brother, named Hanako and Jiro. One year, the persimmon tree in their garden was laden with bright red fruit and their mother called the two children to her.

"Take these persimmons to your grandmother," she said.

"Yay!" the children yelled. "We get to see our grandmother!"

The two were overjoyed. They divided the persimmons into two piles and put them into their packs.

"But don't dally along the way," their mother warned. "You could meet a *yamanba*."[1]

"Don't worry about a thing!" Hanako laughed.

"Just leave it to us!" her little brother added with a grin.

The two shouldered their packs and set off in high spirits. Their grandmother's house was on the other side of the mountain. They held hands and started up the mountain path.

After a short while, an old woman appeared from the opposite direction.

"Well, well!" she asked kindly. "Now where are the two of you going?"

"We're taking persimmons to our grandmother's house!" Hanako answered gaily.

"Well, this is a piece of good luck," the old lady said with a smile. "I'm your grandmother, you know."

"That's not true!" Jiro interjected. "Our grandmother has a mole on her cheek."

"Oh, I put a little rice powder on to cover that mole just a little while ago," the old lady said quickly. "I'll go wash it off right now."

The old lady ran off in a hurry but came back shortly. This time,

---

[1] *Yamanba*, or *yama uba* (山姥), literally, an old lady of the mountains. The term is often translated as "mountain witch," but the image of a witch in the West has perhaps been too much influenced by Walt Disney movies or *The Wizard of Oz*. The *yamanba* is often pictured as a slightly chubby lady who can transform into an evil-looking apparition, but is not the skinny, long-nosed woman we think of from the books and movies of our own childhood.

sure enough, there was a mole on her cheek.

"You *are* our grandmother! You really are!" the two children shouted, running up to the old lady, who smiled and embraced them warmly.

"You two have really become big!" she said happily. "Why, in a little while I wouldn't have recognized you." And she noisily crunched the persimmons one after another as they walked along the path.

"Were Grandma's teeth always that strong?" Jiro whispered to Hanako.

"No, but she has that mole for sure," Hanako answered under her breath.

Although the two children thought that something was a little strange, they went with the old lady to her house on the other side of the mountain.

When they arrived, the old lady immediately made a fine dinner for the two of them. Being very hungry, they ate until their stomachs were full.

Then the old lady put them on her lap and spoke kind-heartedly to them.

"Well now," she asked gently, "Which one of you would like to sleep with me tonight?"

"I do!" yelled Hanako.

"No! Me! Me!" yelled Jiro, not to be left out.

Neither of the children wanted to give in. Finally, the old lady had to make the decision herself.

"Now, now!" she said soothingly. "Tonight, let our chubby little Hanako go first." And she led Hanako off to her bedroom.

There was nothing that Jiro could do, so he curled up to sleep by himself in the next room.

Just about midnight, however, Jiro suddenly woke up to a crunching, munching sound, as though something was being chewed and eaten in the old lady's room.

"Ah ha! Grandma is eating her persimmons," Jiro thought, and suddenly became hungry for a persimmon himself.

"Grandma!" he called. "Let me have one, too."

Instantly, the old lady threw something through his door. But when he got up to get it, Jiro saw that it was his sister's blood-spattered arm.

"Yaah!" he screamed and leapt outside, nearly falling down as he went. The old lady they had thought was their grandmother had turned out to be a terrifying *yamanba*, and he knew without a doubt that she had eaten his sister Hanako.

Jiro ran away in a panic, hardly knowing where his footsteps led.

"Wait!" the *yamanba* yelled as she ran after him.

Jiro had no idea what to do, but suddenly he saw a large tree in front of him. Quickly climbing up the tree, he took off his clothes and fastened them to a branch. He then leapt out of the tree and ran off without looking back, as naked as the day he was born.

When the *yamanba* reached the tree, she looked up and saw Jiro's clothes.

"Hunh!" she grinned, standing under the tree. "You can't run any farther now. It's too bad you can't do anything as long as you're up there!"

The near-sighted old *yamanba* stood staring at Jiro's clothes, thinking the boy was too afraid to move.

"You know, it would be a shame to eat you all by myself," she chuckled. "Wait right there and I'll go and get some of my friends." She quickly ran off, soon returning with her companions.

But when they were finally able to grab hold of Jiro's clothing, they found there was nothing inside, and they had only an empty shell. The *yamanba*'s friends were furious, and with yells and curses condemning her as a liar, killed her on the spot.

The Woman Who Did Not Eat

A long time ago in a certain place, there was a man who was extraordinarily stingy. As time went by, his friends began to worry because he would not take a wife.

"Don't you think you're taking this too far?" asked one of his friends. "Isn't it time you got married?"

"I don't mind having a wife," the man replied testily, "just find me one that won't eat." Of course, he knew full well that there isn't a person who doesn't eat.

"You know, your miserliness is second to none," the friend replied. And after that, he gave up and never mentioned the subject again.

But one evening, a pretty young woman knocked on the man's door.

"I'm on a journey," she said hesitantly, "but the sun has gone down and I find myself with nowhere to spend the night. May I stay here tonight?"

"I don't mind if you stay overnight," the man said indifferently, "but I have no food to serve you."

"Actually, I don't eat," the woman went on. "It will be sufficient if I can just stay the night."

"What?" the man stammered. "That's quite surprising. You really don't eat at all?"

"No, up to now, I've never eaten anything," was the reply.

"I see," the man said, still taken aback. "I imagine one could get along quite well that way."

And in this way, the man allowed the young lady to stay overnight.

The next morning, however, the woman did not appear to be ready to move on. On the contrary, she prepared the man's breakfast for him and even cleaned his house. The following day, she did the same and the day after that as well, but never once did she eat anything although she worked quite hard.

"Well now," the man thought to himself, "I've found an excellent wife." And, overjoyed at this good fortune, he took the woman to be his bride.

Soon after, he called on his friend.

"I've finally found a wife who doesn't eat," he said full of pride.

"If your wife doesn't eat," the friend said suspiciously, "she's not a human being. If you don't come to your senses, you're going to meet with disaster!"

"I don't know what you're talking about," the man broke in angrily. "My wife is pretty, too, so you're just jealous, I suppose." And he quickly returned home.

But soon, a strange rumor began to circulate. The man's wife, it was said, was a demon who had taken human form. Thus, his friend, once again, came to visit him.

"Get rid of this woman right away," he warned the man. "She's not a human being and you're the only one who doesn't realize it."

His friend spoke with great seriousness, so the man, as satisfied as he was with his situation, began to worry, too. And in this state of mind, he made a plan.

"I'm going off to town," he said to his wife one day. "But I won't be back before dark."

With this, he left the house, but very quickly returned and hid behind a rafter in the ceiling. His wife, of course, did not know this, and as soon as she thought she was alone, began to wash some rice. After that, she boiled the rice in a large pot, made thirty-three rice balls, took three mackerel from the kitchen, and grilled them over the fire.

"Is she going to eat all of that?" the man wondered from his perch.

The man was appalled, but continued looking. The woman then untied her hair and let it fall loose around her shoulders. Parting the hair on top of her head, she exposed a wide mouth, gaping in anticipation. Finally, sitting down heavily in the kitchen, she threw the rice balls and mackerel into the open mouth at the top of her head.

"She ... she's a demon, after all," the man nearly blurted out. Climbing down silently through a high window in the ceiling, he fled to his friend's house.

"You see?" his friend said, as he looked at the man's pale and frightened expression. "This is why I couldn't remain silent. But you'll have to go home today and act as though you don't know anything. If she senses you've seen her true form, the worst could happen. I'll take care of her for you later."

When night fell, the man nervously returned home. His wife, however, told him that she had a headache and went straight to bed.

"That will never do," the man said with an innocent look. "You should try to take some medicine."

"No," she replied. "I can't stand medicine!"

"Well then, I'll go and have a curative charm made for you," the man suggested and went to call for his friend.

The friend came disguised as a conjurer and examined the woman's head.

"Your headache is divine punishment for eating thirty-three rice balls!" he suddenly yelled. "It's divine punishment for eating three mackerel!"

"So you saw me!" the woman screamed as she leapt up. In an instant, her eyes slanted upward and her mouth widened from ear to ear.

"Oh, no! A man-eating demon!" the friend cried out.

But the words were no longer out of his mouth than the demon jumped on him and ate him up in gulps, from his head down.

The husband tried to run away but was so terrified that he could not move.

When the demon had finished eating his friend, she grabbed the man by his neck and put him on her head. She then ran off to the mountain behind the village.

"Oh, you gods!" the man prayed with all his might, while riding along on the demon's head. "Please save me!"

Going up and over the mountain, the demon crossed a plain and entered a forest. Just then, the man saw a large tree in front of him, with a branch extending from it.

"That's it!" the man thought and grabbed hold of the branch.

The demon, meanwhile, did not realize what had happened and kept on running. Just as the man got down from the branch, however, he saw that the demon had returned. Shaking with fear, he hid in a thicket of mugwort and irises.

The demon walked over and stood before the thicket.

"Don't try to escape!" she growled

Luckily, at that moment the man remembered that demons hate mugwort and irises more than anything. Just by the touch of these plants, their bodies will decompose immediately. Ripping some from the ground, the man threw them at the demon and hit his mark.

"Yaah," the demon screamed. "If it weren't for these damned weeds, I would have eaten you complete...."

But before it could finish cursing, it died and rotted away.

～

The Woman Who Disappeared Behind a Tree

A long time ago, there were three ladies who were employed in the palace of the emperor. The three got along wonderfully well, and wherever they went, they went together.

One night, when the moon was shining brilliantly, the three ladies were taking a pleasant walk in the direction of the palace when they came to a large pine tree.

"Excuse me," they heard a voice say, "I'd like to talk with you for a moment."

A man appeared from behind the tree and beckoned to one of the ladies.

"What do you want?" the lady asked, and she went around to the other side of the pine tree.

The other two ladies, however, became concerned when their friend did not reappear, even though they waited a long time.

"What do you suppose has happened?" one of them said anxiously.

"Do you think she was carried off by that man?" replied the other, with a worried look.

The two ladies became quite uneasy and went around to the back of the tree. But the man and woman were not there.

"Where could they have gone?" they both wondered.

As the two looked around the circumference of the tree, something white fell from above.

"What's this?" one of them asked.

The two bent down and picked up the white object. Instantly, they screamed and threw it down. For this "something" was the torn-off arm of a woman.

"Someone ... someone come quickly!" one cried, and they both ran to the palace guards, stumbling as they went.

"Mur ... murder!" screamed the other lady. And with this, the two fainted dead away.

All the guards came running out of the palace, their swords drawn. But when they approached the pine tree, they found only the parts of a woman's hands and feet scattered about, and no sign of her body or even a heart or liver.

Soon, the people in the palace heard the disturbance and gathered at the pine tree.

"What kind of person would have done this?" one asked incredulously.

"What a horrible thing to have done," another offered.

Startled and scared, they looked at each other and discussed the matter at length. Finally, an old man came out from among them with a knowing look.

"You know," he started. "A long, long time ago, a woman was eaten under this very tree. People said it was the act of a man-eating demon, a demon that takes human shape and calls women to him."

When they heard this, everyone shivered.

"If a woman goes to some lonely place," they whispered one to another, "she should not go off with some stranger, even if he asks her to."

And with this, they all went back to their rooms.

The Azure Hood

A long time ago, there was a very clever priest by the name of Kai'an. Now, one year Kai'an was traveling through the northern part of Japan on a journey of Buddhist self-discipline and austerities, and as he arrived at the village of Tomita in the ancient province of Shimotsuke, the sun began to set. Looking around for some place to spend the night, he spied a farmhouse that appeared to be owned by a very rich man.

"Good," he thought, "perhaps they'll let me stay here."

Just as he was considering this, and had walked up to the front of the farmhouse, the men who had finished their work in the fields began to return to the farmhouse as well. When the men saw the priest, they stopped in their tracks and stared fixedly at him with eyes that seemed full of fear.

"The mountain demon has come!" yelled one of the men as loud as he could. "Everyone, get over here!"

In an instant, the entire village was in an uproar. The women and children cried and shrieked, trying to hide themselves in the cellars and attics, while others were so frightened they could not move. Very quickly, the men came running up with mattocks and long poles and made straight for the priest to give him a beating.

"What ... what's going on here?" shouted the priest, while confusedly dodging their blows as well as he could.

In the scuffle, his azure hood fell from his head, exposing his face.

"Wait!" one of the men commanded. "We've made a mistake!" And the attackers again stopped in their tracks.

"What in the world is this all about?" the priest demanded with an angry expression.

At that moment, the master of the farmhouse stepped forward and gave a low bow.

"Please forgive us," he pleaded. "We have done you a terrible discourtesy."

"I'm just a priest traveling the provinces in Buddhist austerities," the priest addressed him. "I came here because I thought I might ask for a place to stay the night. Surely there is nothing suspicious about that."

"I understand," the master replied humbly. "Please make your lodging here for the night." And with that, he dismissed the village men and took the priest inside his house.

The priest wondered why he had nearly been beaten and could hardly wait to ask the master of the house the reason for his poor treatment. After the evening meal, he could wait no longer. "If you wouldn't mind," he began, "would you please tell me why I was attacked by the villagers today?"

"Of course," the master replied. "The truth is that there is a temple situated in a nearby mountain and we mistook you for the abbot that resides there."

"Well," the priest inquired, "just before the fracas today, someone yelled, 'The mountain demon has come!' Does this demon sometimes transform himself into an abbot?"

"No, not at all," the master continued. "The abbot himself has become a demon."

For a moment, the master of the house knotted his brows with a troubled expression, but then went on with his story.

"This abbot was quite a scholar and a man of the finest virtue. But last year, while he was summoned to a temple in some other province to conduct a memorial service, he met a beautiful young boy and brought him back here.

"Well, the boy was so good-looking that his face appeared to be that of a beautiful young girl and the abbot treated him exactly as if he were his own child. He would not let the boy be away from his side for even a moment day and night, and because of that, the services at the temple and the funerals for the villagers were totally neglected.

"This April, however, the young boy suddenly took ill and died. The abbot was so grief-stricken that it seemed he had gone insane. And rather than give the boy a funeral, he acted as though the child were still alive, hugging him and even carrying him on his back.

"In the meanwhile, the boy's body began to decompose and to give off a terrible smell, but still the abbot would not let go of him. In the end, the old man wound up eating the boy's flesh and even his bones."

As the master related this tale, he turned pale, and his whole body began to shake.

"This is just horrible," the priest muttered to himself, involuntarily turning away.

But the master was not finished with his story.

"The abbot went completely crazy, and in the end became a demon that eats human flesh. After that, he comes to the village almost every night, digs up the graves of those who have recently passed away and eats their flesh.

"For this reason, the villagers have become so frightened that they lock their doors at night and will not go outside until dawn. Recently, this story has gone around the province and nobody even passes through here anymore.

"Those people who tried to beat you earlier today mistook you for this abbot that now feeds upon human flesh. Please understand what they have been through."

Having gone this far in his story, the master let out a deep sigh.

"When you find that even a fine abbot like this can do such horrible things," the priest said, wiping his eyes and putting the palms of his hands together, "you have to think that the human being is a very sad animal indeed. But if we brace ourselves and put our faith in the Buddha, we should be able to bring him back to his former human self."

"All right!" he then declared, "I'm going to visit the abbot and try to make his mind anew."

"Thank you so much," the master said softly. "If you can do that, everyone here will be overjoyed."

The next evening, the priest walked up to the mountain temple. Although it had once been a quite stately place, the walls had now fallen in, the floor boards were coming apart and it had the look of having been haunted for some time.

The priest stood in front of the main hall.

"I am a priest on a journey," he announced, "and would like to stay here for just one night."

But there was no answer.

After calling out a number of times, however, a thin, emaciated man tottered out and stared at him.

"As you can see," he said in a hoarse, unsettling voice, "this temple is nearly in ruins. I have no rice or bedding, so go somewhere else."

As he said this, he glared at the priest, looking him up and down.

"Well, I need neither rice nor bedding," the priest replied. "Just let me lie down in a corner of the main hall and that will be sufficient."

"If that's so, go and lie down wherever you like," the abbot cackled and went back inside.

With that, the priest stepped up into the hall without saying a word and purposely sat down at the abbot's side. He was, however, completely ignored, and the two stayed there silently, sitting next to each other for a long time. After a while, the night turned quite dark and the moon came up over the horizon.

Finally, the abbot got up and disappeared into the next room. It was completely silent. Not a sound could be heard. The priest sat peacefully with perfect posture and stared straight ahead.

At last, the abbot suddenly came out into the room and looked around, glaring into every corner.

"That stinking priest," he mumbled crossly, "where did he disappear to? He was here just a while ago."

Although the priest was sitting right before the old man's eyes, the latter leapt into the garden cursing and yelling and started running around the grounds, going this way and that. Then, just as suddenly, he stepped back up into the main hall and ran right past the priest.

The priest kept silent and watched as the scene unfolded. The abbot then began to dance as though he had lost his wits, finally falling down in a heap.

By this time, the eastern sky had become brighter and the morning light began to penetrate the room. The old man sat up abruptly and looked around as though he had suddenly sobered up from being drunk on sake. At length, he noticed the priest still sitting in the center of the hall. He squatted down unsteadily and let out a deep sigh.

"How are you?" the priest asked. "If you're hungry, you can eat some of my flesh."

"Were you sitting here all night?" the abbot asked in disbelief.

"Yes," came the reply. "I just sat here and watched you carefully."

At this point, the abbot collapsed into a flood of tears.

"Ahh, I've shown you a despicable sight!" he groaned.

As the old man cried, he made fists of both hands and repeatedly struck himself on the head. Finally, his tears came to an end and he pressed his palms together in supplication before the priest.

"I am someone who eats human flesh," he said in a whisper, "but I have never eaten the flesh of a fine priest like you. Despite that, you may wonder why I couldn't see you at all last night. It's probably because I've come to see with the demon's eyes – eyes that only see those who have died."

And tears once again fell from the old man's eyes.

"Isn't it true that you go to the village at night and eat people from their very graves?" the priest demanded, staring at the old man with an awful glare.

"Please forgive me!" the abbot pleaded. "Somehow, I cared too much for that child, and after he died I began to eat human flesh. Can't you help me, please?"

"All right," the priest went on. "Will you straighten up and listen to me carefully?"

"If a human heart can come back to itself, I'll do anything you say," the abbot said submissively.

"Well then," the priest continued, "come and sit down right here."

The priest had the old man sit down on a large rock in front of the veranda and put his own azure hood over the man's head.

"If you will sit on this rock and intone the sutras with all of your heart, at some point you should return to your former human self," the priest instructed him. "Until then, do not move no matter what happens."

So saying, the priest departed.

After that, the old abbot did not appear in the village again, but whether he returned to his former self or not, nobody knew. Everyone was still afraid, and no one ever visited or even passed through the vicinity of the temple.

A year went by, and the priest, continuing on his journey of the northern provinces, happened by the village again. Stopping by the master's house, he inquired into what had occurred since he was there last.

"Thanks to you," the master explained, "that flesh-eating old man has not come to our village at all and everyone is overjoyed. The village itself is now like it used to be and we have many visitors. But we don't know if the old abbot is alive or dead. Everyone is still very fearful of him and no one will climb up to the temple."

So the next day, the priest went up to the temple. The temple buildings were in a greater state of ruin than before and the rank weeds had grown as tall as a man's shoulders. The roof of the main hall leaned so much to the side that it seemed as though it would fall over any moment.

The priest pushed his way through the weeds and stood looking at the main hall. And there, on the now moss-covered rock, sat the emaciated abbot, now almost nothing but skin and bones. The abbot's eyes were sunk deep into his head and the long hair on his head and beard looked like dead autumn grasses. In a voice that sounded like the faint buzz of a mosquito, he intoned the *nembutsu*.[2]

"What!" the priest cried. "You've still not regained a human heart? You stupid old man!"

---

[2] The repetition of the Buddha Amida's name in prayer. In Japanese, it goes *Namu Amida Butsu*.

At that, the priest raised his staff and with a shout struck the old abbot's head.

The abbot's body then shattered like ice, and all that remained was the azure hood and a few white bones.

After these events, the villagers rebuilt the ruined temple and had this wonderful priest take up residence there. The temple itself is now called the Taiheizan Daichuji, and people go there to pray nearly every day.

The Younger Brother Who Turned into a Demon

Long ago there was a frightful structure called the Agi Bridge, spanning a waterway in the ancient province of Omi. On or under this bridge there lived a demon that ate human flesh, and people were so frightened by this that no one ever crossed the river here.

Now, once there were a number of samurai drinking sake at their lord's residence and the subject of conversation turned to this bridge.

One of the men got rather drunk.

"Ahh, you're all spineless," he called out. "If someone would loan me a fawn-colored horse, I'd cross that bridge for you!"

The "fawn-colored horse" referred to their lord's horse, which was a splendid one indeed, and very fleet of foot.

"That would be interesting," one of his companions shot back. "If you would do us the favor of crossing the bridge even once, we could find out if the rumor is true or not."

Others also spurred him on and the man got more and more carried away.

"Listen up!" the drunken man went on. "I'll cross that bridge for you! Someone go and borrow the lord's horse!"

Just then, their lord walked in on them.

"Well then," he interjected, "what's all this fuss about?"

The samurai explained to their lord what they had been talking about and asked him to loan them his horse.

"Fine!" the lord responded. "If this man has courage enough to cross the bridge, I'll be glad to let him borrow my horse."

At which point, the man began to hesitate.

"No, no," he squirmed. "That was just a joke. It would be quite unseemly for me to borrow the lord's splendid horse."

"You coward!" one of the men yelled. "It's a little too late for that!"

"Did you think you could make fools of us?" another added. And they all stared at him with very severe looks.

The man was now in a difficult situation.

"No," he stammered. "It's not that I'm afraid to cross the bridge. But to borrow the lord's horse would be inexcusable."

"No need to worry about that," the lord cut in. "I hereby loan you my horse."

Once the lord had said that, there was no longer any reason to refuse.

"Ahh, I've said something really stupid," the man thought to himself and he sobered up immediately despite the amount of sake he had drunk.

So the fawn-colored horse was led up from the stable right away. The man smeared its hindquarters with plenty of oil and made sure that the saddle was securely cinched around the horse's belly. Then, making sure his own clothing and belongings were as light as possible, he mounted.

"Do your best!" the men encouraged him as he departed.

As the man approached Agi Bridge, the surrounding area seemed gloomy and dark. It was as quiet as death and not even a stray dog passed by.

"This is really unpleasant," he said to himself. "And scary enough…." He began to nervously cross the bridge.

It was, however, a rather long bridge, and to make matters worse he could see that someone was standing right in the middle of it.

Thinking it must surely be the flesh-eating demon, he brought his horse to an abrupt halt. When he looked carefully, however, he saw that it was a young lady dressed in a purple coat and red skirt-pants.

"A woman?" he wondered.

Heaving a sigh of relief, he brought his horse up next to the woman. She was rather beautiful and seemed to be truly in trouble. She was just asking him to help her by letting her onto the horse.

"But, wait! Wait!" he thought, as he was about to pull her up behind him. "This may be the demon transformed into a woman's shape." And with that thought, he made as if to silently ride past her.

"Please wait!" the woman pleaded, obviously quite upset. "Why are you running away? Please let me ride with you. My feet hurt terribly and I don't know what to do."

The man was now completely confused. But if this really was the flesh-eating demon, he would be in real trouble. When he considered that possibility, he suddenly became frightened and whipped his horse into action.

"Wait! Wait, please," the woman yelled. In that instant she reached out for the horse's tail. The man had saturated the tail in oil as well, however, and as it slipped through her fingers she fell down onto the wooden planks of the bridge.

"This is it!" the man said to himself, and applying the whip, the horse galloped away with terrific speed.

"Yaaah!" the woman screamed.

When the man looked back over his shoulder, he could see that she had instantaneously been transformed into a flesh-eating demon.

"Waaait! Waaait!" it screamed, with a voice that sent a shiver up the man's spine.

And it seemed to be coming closer and closer.

In absolute fear, the man involuntarily looked back again. The demon's head was deep red and it had only one eye. It was at least nine feet tall and had three fingers on each hand. Its nails were sharp and looked to be made of iron.

"Oh, Honored Kannon!" the man stammered. "Please save me!"

The man intoned the *nembutsu* with everything he had as he whipped his horse. Perhaps thanks to his prayer, he was able to cross the bridge and escape to a place where he found lodging.

"Yaah!" the demon shrieked in vexation from behind. "Someday I'll get you!" And in that moment, vanished like thin smoke.

The next day, the man took the long way around and finally returned to his lord's mansion. Seeing him approach, everyone ran out and gathered around him.

"What happened?" someone asked breathlessly. "Did you meet up with the demon?"

"Thank the gods, you've made it back safely," another added.

Questions and yells of congratulations went from mouth to mouth, but the man had turned completely pale and could only shake, sitting silently in the saddle.

At length, the lord himself came out, and when the man had finally regained his composure, he related the story to the lord.

"You're lucky to have come back alive," the lord said. "This is what can happen when you say something mindlessly. What would you have done if the demon had got a hold of you?"

The lord thoroughly scolded the man, but also praised him for his courage and, as a reward, presented him with the fawn-colored horse.

In that moment, pride entered his heart.

"Hunh!" he later sneered at his companions. "What do you think? Is there any one of you who would cross that bridge? If there is, I'll loan him my horse!"

But no one gave him one word of reply.

"So, just as we thought," one of the men said, "the rumor was true!"

"You won't see *me* crossing that bridge," whispered another.

And they all walked away in dejection.

A little while after these events, however, unpleasant things began to happen one after another at the man's residence. The entire family would become sick, or someone would sustain some injury, and nothing really good would happen to them at all. It was generally felt that they were receiving some sort of divine punishment.

The man was eventually disturbed by these developments and sought out a soothsayer.

"This is, indeed, a divine punishment," the soothsayer announced. "And after two more days, something terrible is going to happen. On that date, you must lock yourself in the house and not let anyone enter it from the outside."

The man was shocked and quickly ran home.

When the day arrived, the man tightly locked all the doors and gates to the house and strictly ordered his servants not to let anyone in, no matter who it was.

As it happened, however, the man's only younger brother, who had gone off with their mother to the northern provinces, returned that day after many years absence.

Younger brother he may have been, but he was not allowed entrance into the house.

"If I let someone into the house today, something disastrous may happen," the man yelled from inside the house. "Tomorrow, I'll definitely come out to greet you, but I can't let you stay here tonight."

"That makes things difficult," the brother shouted back. "If I were just by myself, I could go stay somewhere else, but I have a large group of servants accompanying me. Is there no way you can let us in? On top of that, our mother…."

"What?" the man cried. "Is our mother there with you?

"No, no," came the reply. "Our mother became ill and passed away. But I've brought her ashes here with me."

Hearing that, the man couldn't help but shed tears. For a long time he had wanted to see his mother and now she was dead.

"Well then, it's all right," he sobbed. "Someone open the gate."

When the gate was opened, his younger brother rushed in as though he could wait no longer and grasped the man by the hand.

"Elder Brother," he sighed. "It's been quite a while."

"Ah, you look well," the man replied happily. "Come in, come in."

The man brought his younger brother into the sitting room and took the container of his mother's ashes in both hands.

"You must be hungry," he said affectionately. "I'll have dinner prepared for you right away."

The man ordered his own wife to bring in the meal and, unable to wait for his younger brother to finish eating, asked him a number of questions about their deceased mother.

"Our mother wanted to see you so much," his younger brother informed him.

Hearing this, the man could not help but think about how tender-hearted his mother had been, and shed tears enough to wet his sleeves. In the next room, his wife began to cry as well.

But after the two men talked for a while, they started to argue, and suddenly stood up and started to fight. They grappled fiercely, first one on top, and then the other.

The man's wife was horrified and ran into the room.

"Stop!" she yelled. "The two of you, stop!"

After they had tumbled about in the room for a minute or two, the man was finally able to pin his brother down.

"Quick!" the man shouted desperately. "Get me my sword over there!"

"What ... what are you saying," his wife said disbelievingly. "Have you gone mad?"

"Quick! Hand it to me right now!" he bellowed.

"I will not!" was the adamant reply.

"Are you telling me to die?" he cried out.

Just as he said this, his younger brother was able to once again get on top, and in that instant bit through the man's throat.

The man groaned, was quickly spattered with blood and died in seconds.

"Who ... who are you?" the man's wife screamed as the younger brother turned into the demon right before her eyes.

"Thanks to you, I'm alive!" the demon cackled as it looked the man's wife up and down.

Then, just like that, it fled.

So, sadly, the man was finally killed by the demon. And later, when the matter was investigated, it was found that the "large group of servants" was nothing but human bones.

"That was really frightening," one of the man's companions remarked.

"He said something mindlessly, crossed the bridge and paid for it with his life," another added.

Soon the matter became known to everyone, and unkind words about the man spread from mouth to mouth.

After this mishap, people prayed that the demon might never be seen again, and sure enough, at least at Agi Bridge, it seemed to have disappeared forever.

People Who Were Cursed

The Pale, Thin Soul

Long ago, in the ancient province of Totomi, there was a very rich man by the name of Ogane, who lived in a place called Yokosuka. Ogane possessed many rice paddies and vegetable fields and lived in a mansion as fine as any provincial lord's.

But for some reason no one was able to understand, the people of his household became sick and died one after the other. At length, only his old grandmother remained.

"That house is under some divine punishment for sure," some people said.

"No one will even work there anymore," said others.

Thus, everyone took their leave of the mansion and no one was left to take care of the old lady.

There was nothing she could do, so the old lady just lived there by herself. By and by, she also took sick and passed away.

With this, the relatives came rushing in, and even before the funeral was over, divided up all the land and assets. After that, no one bothered to even visit her gravesite.

One night, not long after the old lady had passed away, a light rain fell just like in the rainy season, even though summer had already begun. One of the relatives was passing by the rice paddies when he thought he saw a pale light like one that might come from a paper lantern. Suddenly, the light began to flit back and forth in front of him.

"This is my rice paddy," it whispered. "That is my rice paddy, too."

The relative was startled half out of his wits and ran back to his house through the rain, slipping and sliding as he went.

"That *had* to be the old lady's soul,"[1] he said to himself. "She must be resentful because we took her fields."

He was now so frightened that he lacked the strength to go out and work in the rice paddies.

---

[1] Soul (魂), *kon*. This is slightly complicated by the fact that the people of the Far East believe that the human being has two souls, one the *kon*, which is received from Heaven, is a yang element and eventually returns to Heaven after death, and the 魄, *haku*, which is received from the Earth, is the yin element and eventually returns to earth.

Now, the human soul is something that remains after death. It shines with a pale thin, light and flits around in the dark.

Unfortunately, after this event, on nights when rain fell or when there was no moon, this soul was certain to appear, and to flit back and forth over the fields and paddies. Soon, the other relatives who had snatched up all the assets of the mansion began to feel uneasy as well. Those who had taken the rice paddies and fields abandoned them completely.

Eventually, the pale, thin soul began to appear, even when unrelated villagers passed by.

"This is my rice paddy," it whispered as it flitted over the fields. "That is my rice paddy, too."

"Just as you'd think, bad deeds do not go unpunished," some people said.

"It's because they didn't take care of her at all, but rushed in and grabbed all the property," others declared.

Such words passed from mouth to mouth in the village.

This soul, however, never committed anything evil or untoward. After flitting around for a while, it would always return to its own grave. And for some reason, if someone yelled, "Old lady Ogane is far, far away," it would quickly approach. On the contrary, if "The old lady is close by, close by," was shouted, the soul would depart right away.

In this way, if the children of this village spied a pale light at night, they would shout, "Old lady Ogane is close by, close by," and try to send it away.

Even today, when chasing butterflies, they, like all children, sing, "Come, fire, fire, fireflies! The water there is bitter, and the water here is sweet!" But they never forget to add, "Old lady Ogane is close by, close by," and to look carefully at what they have caught.

O-iwa's Curse

About three hundred and twenty years ago, there was a samurai by the name of Tamiya Iemon who lived in the Yotsuya samon-cho section of Edo. Iemon had an only daughter named O-iwa, who was a rather pitiable young woman. At the age of three, her mother had passed away, and when she was five, she contracted smallpox, a terrible disease which causes unsightly pockmarks on one's face. Thus, when O-iwa turned twenty-one, no one wanted to take her as a bride. By this time, too, her father Iemon had become ill.

"As long as I'm alive," he thought, "I've got to search for a husband for O-iwa."

Iemon asked his friends and acquaintances to do their best and find a husband for his daughter.

Finally, a thirty-one year old penniless *ronin*[2] from the province of Settsu was found. Having no money, he thought he might do well to marry the young woman, despite her unsightly face. Regardless of the circumstances, both Iemon and O-iwa were overjoyed.

The man was soon brought to Edo and a marriage ceremony was performed.

From the start, this *ronin* was very helpful to Iemon and he treated O-iwa quite well.

"We've been provided with a good husband," Iemon said to himself. "I can put my mind at ease."

But though he now felt happy and at peace, Iemon died not long after. His son-in-law thereupon changed his own name to Iemon and became master of the Tamiya household.

This new Iemon had now progressed from the status of a *ronin* to that of a samurai with an official position, and he worked seriously so as not to bring shame to his father-in-law's good name. He also treated his unsightly wife well. As a consequence, he became very popular with his superiors.

"This is a truly fine man," they said. "He should soon become a great samurai."

---

[2] A masterless samurai.

Among his superiors was a man by the name of Ito Sezaemon, who treated him quite well and often invited him to his home to relax and enjoy himself. But at this man's house was a lovely young lady called O-koto, and after meeting her a number of times, Iemon fell in love. To make matters worse, O-koto also fell in love with this serious and manly samurai.

Iemon, however, was married to O-iwa and was unable to meet privately with O-koto. And if he separated from O-iwa, he would have to become a *ronin* once again.

"What an ugly face," he began to think.

As he compared O-iwa's unsightliness with the beautiful O-koto, he became less and less pleased with her. Soon, he could no longer bear to look at her. Even returning home now became unpleasant, and Iemon began distracting himself by drinking sake.

By passing the sake shop every night, his money began to run out and Iemon began selling off his household effects one after another. Eventually, he was shirking the duties of his office.

"Please! Return to yourself as a serious samurai," his wife cried. "I'll do anything you ask!"

O-iwa pleaded with him to reform himself, but he would not listen to her at all.

"Shut up, you old witch!" he yelled, hitting and kicking her. "I don't even want to look at you!" And off he went to Sezaemon's house to discuss his situation with him.

However, Sezaemon was fundamentally not a good man. He had grown weary of O-koto, the daughter he had once doted upon, and had intentionally planned to have the two young people fall in love. His true desire was to have Iemon drive O-iwa away and marry O-koto as soon as possible.

"You are at in a difficult position, Iemon," Sezaemon said frankly. "If you continue like this, you'll be released from your official duties. Why don't you resign yourself to having O-iwa leave your house for a while? Let her understand that you'll bring her back once you've got back on your feet again."

The good-hearted O-iwa had no idea that this was simply a scheme to get rid of her and readily agreed.

"I won't come back to the house until you can change," she said lovingly and went off to become a maid at a faraway samurai's house.

"A ha!" Iemon exclaimed. "That went off well."

And far from being chagrined, he was overjoyed. Now he could live with O-koto without any constraint at all.

"O-iwa has left me so I must find a new wife," he explained.

So saying, he soon had a wedding ceremony to marry O-koto. And when he compared his new wife with the unsightly O-iwa, she seemed to have the beauty of a bright shining jewel.

"Ahh, what a lucky man I am," he mused. "I've managed to inherit the Tamiya house and drive O-iwa away."

Soon after, O-koto gave birth to a child, and Iemon began once again to work responsibly at his official duties. O-iwa, however, knew none of this and worked hard as a maid, waiting for the happy day when Iemon would come to take her back. Yet, he never came.

But one day, a tobacco seller by the name of Mosuke dropped by the mansion where O-iwa was working. He had often gone to sell tobacco at the house where she had grown up and knew her face well. She immediately asked how Iemon was doing.

"What? Well, uh...." Mosuke answered, completely taken off guard. "Why, everyone says that you became disgusted with Iemon and left him, you know. He has a new wife and a child now and they are living quite happily together."

"What are you saying?" O-iwa cried. "Can that be true?"

"Why, yes, for sure," Mosuke continued. "Why, I've seen it with my own eyes."

"That damned man!" she screamed. "I'll teach him to deceive me!"

O-iwa turned deathly pale and ran out of the front gate still barefoot. Completely unnerved, Mosuke chased after her but soon lost sight of her. Sometime later, someone saw O-iwa, looking as though she had gone insane, walking near Iemon's mansion, but in the end, no one knew where she had gone.

Strange to say, however, from that time on, untoward things began to occur at Iemon's residence. O-iwa would suddenly appear in the room where Iemon and O-koto were sleeping. Her pockmarked face had become even more horribly disfigured, and the long hair on her head dangled down like drooping snakes.

"You tenacious old witch!" Iemon yelled. "Why don't you let go?"

Grasping his sword, he swung repeatedly at the woman but there was nothing there. And no matter how many times he tried to cut her down, O-iwa's ghost came every night and glared horribly at Iemon and his new wife.

Iemon now seemed to have gone totally insane, and even when he looked at his beautiful wife, her face appeared just like O-iwa's. Sadly, soon after these events began, their child suddenly took sick and died.

"This is O-iwa's curse, for sure," O-koto sobbed. And when night fell, she would wonder around the house, bereft of her senses, begging for O-iwa's forgiveness.

Finally, O-koto died, too.

In the end, Iemon's face was filled with pockmarks just like O-iwa's and, frothing at the mouth, he passed into the next world.

After the destruction of Iemon's household, Ito Sezaemon's family, too, one after another were killed by O-iwa's curse. But her curse did not stop there, for anyone who lived in Iemon's mansion after these events also died of unknown causes.

In the end, someone built an Inari[3] shrine dedicated to O-iwa over the ruins of the mansion, and prayed that her curse would be no more. Because of this, it is said, her ghost was never seen again.

Long Black Hair

Long ago in the ancient province of Iwaki, there was a tofu seller who lived in the town of Koori. This tofu seller had an only daughter, a beautiful young woman by the name of O-fuku.

Now, on New Year's Day of her seventeenth year, O-fuku tied up her long black hair, put on a holiday kimono and went off to a friend's house for the day's amusements. When she arrived, there were already a number of other young ladies there, happily playing the New Year card games. O-fuku joined them right away, eating holiday delicacies, drinking sake and amusing herself so that she forgot all about the time.

---

[3] The deity of plentitude and good harvest. The deity's messenger is the fox, statues of which appear at Inari's shrines, and which are often conflated with the deity him—or herself.

Ordinarily, O-fuku rarely drank sake, but by evening she was completely drunk. Finally tottering home, she crawled under the *kotatsu*[4] without changing out of her kimono and fell asleep. The sleeve of her kimono, however, soon caught fire from the flame beneath the *kotatsu*, and the fire began to spread. In her drunken sleep, O-fuku was unconscious and completely unaware of the danger she was in.

Suddenly, she jumped up with a scream, for not only was her kimono now in flames but also her long black hair.

"Somebody ... somebody, help!" she cried out.

O-fuku ran wildly about the room as though she had lost her mind, but there was nothing she could do. In total panic, she bolted out of the house and into the garden and leapt into the pond.

The people of the household hurried to where she was, but by this time her entire body had been terribly burned and the skin of her once beautiful face was peeled in strips, revealing peach-colored flesh beneath.

A doctor was summoned immediately and he treated her as well as he could, but there was not much he could do.

The next morning, O-fuku's friends heard about the calamity and came to visit her one after another. When they saw that her entire body was wrapped in bandages, however, they were at a loss of words and hardly knew how to comfort her.

---

[4] A low table with a heater underneath and covered by a quilt. Traditionally, the heater was filled with charcoal or some other fuel, but nowadays an electric heat unit is used.

After a while, O-fuku opened her eyes and glanced at the long black hair of the friend sitting next to her pillow.

"How nice," she muttered. "You have such beautiful hair…," and she closed her eyes again as tears ran down her cheeks.

"What are you saying?" one of her friends replied. "After you've recovered from your burns, you'll have beautiful hair just as you did before."

"No," O-fuku said in a weak voice, shutting her eyes tightly. "I'm not going to live for long."

"Don't say such a thing!" the friend next to her said quickly. "Be positive and you'll get well soon."

"What's a little burn?" another added, trying to cheer her up.

But O-fuku only spoke in a delirium, repeating over and over that she was going to die.

Gradually, her friends began to feel uncomfortable and, one by one returned to their homes. After that, no one came to ask after her.

In two or three days, the story of O-fuku's misfortune had circulated around the town, and was finally repeated to the wife of the priest who lived at the Koori-dera, the local Buddhist temple.

"How sad!" the woman thought as she worked away in the kitchen. "She was so pretty. And she used to come to the temple quite often…."

Just then, she heard the footsteps of someone coming from the direction of the temple gate. The footsteps stopped in front of the main hall, as though someone were praying to the Buddha there.

"Well, my husband must have come back," she said to herself.

With that thought in mind, the priest's wife began washing some rice in preparation to cook a meal when the kitchen door opened, and there stood O-fuku.

"My goodness, it's O-fuku," the woman stammered in surprise, looking the girl over from head to toe.

O-fuku's long black hair was tied up and beautifully arranged, she wore a tidy kimono and her skin did not seem to be burned at all.

"I … I heard that you had been burned," the woman said, trying to compose herself.

"Yes, I was," O-fuku replied with a polite laugh. "But I've completely recovered."

"This is quite strange," the priest's wife mused, shaking her head in disbelief. "Just a while ago, I heard that she was close to death."

Nevertheless, here was O-fuku, right before her eyes, looking like a healthy young woman.

"That's wonderful!" the priest's wife said. "I'm going to make some tea, so why don't you go and wait in the sitting room?"

"Thank you, I will!" came O-fuku's reply, in her usual cheerful way.

"Rumors!" muttered the priest's wife. "You just can't rely on them at all!"

Having prepared the tea, the priest's wife went to the sitting room but O-fuku was nowhere to be seen.

"That's strange," she pondered. "I wonder where she went?"

Putting down the tea, she searched here and there around the temple but found no one. She then returned to the sitting room and waited for a while, but O-fuku did not come back.

As she waited there, the priest's wife began to feel a strange sensation.

"Could that have been O-fuku's ghost?" she thought, and in the same instant a cold shiver went up and down her entire body.

Just at that moment, someone from the town ran up to the temple.

"The tofu seller's daughter has just passed away," he yelled. "They're going to have a wake, so I've come for the priest!"

"Hunh? What?" the priest's wife shouted involuntarily, turning completely pale.

"Well, please let the priest know," the man replied, somewhat shocked at the woman's expression. He then quickly left the temple.

The following day, a funeral was conducted and O-fuku's corpse was buried in a grave behind the Koori-dera.

But that night, one of O-fuku's friends was talking at home with her mother about O-fuku's sad story when suddenly she felt a cold breeze come through the room. In that instant, the string that tied up her long black hair was somehow cut and her hair fell in front of her face, just like a ghost.

"That's dreadful!" her mother exclaimed and nervously bound her daughter's hair up from her face.

"Mother! I'm afraid!" the daughter cried, holding on to her mother as they both began to tremble.

Much later that night, the priest and his wife heard a terrifying scream and quickly jumped up out of their bedding. Someone, it seemed, was running around noisily inside the main hall. The two of them hurried over to the main hall and nervously peeped inside.

And there was O-fuku, who was supposed to be buried in her grave, screaming and running around inside the hall as though she had lost her wits.

The priest and his wife were so frightened that they could do nothing but squat down in a heap right where they were and yell hoarsely for help. After a moment, however, the priest got a hold on himself and began to intone a sutra for all he was worth.

With that, O-fuku quickly calmed down, and at some point, disappeared altogether.

"Oh, how frightening!" the priest's wife whispered in a still shaky voice. "That was O-fuku's ghost for sure!"

For seven days after that,[5] O-fuku's ghost would loosen her friends' long black hair and run around inside the main hall. And each time this occurred, the priest would intone the sutra with all his heart. Thanks to that, on the evening of the eighth day, the young ladies' hair was no longer disturbed and O-fuku's ghost no longer appeared.

But even today, you can see that a small piece of the railing on the Buddhist altar was broken when O-fuku's ghost ran into it in her panic and fear.

The O-matsu Jizo

In the ancient province of Ugo, in a place called Oodate, there was a famous swordsman by the name of Nagayama Budaiyu. This man was so famous for his sword technique that hundreds of disciples always gathered at his *dojo* (道場).[6]

Budaiyu, however, was troubled by one thing, though he told no one: his only daughter, Misao, who had turned one year old, had never spoken a word. The rumor that she was a mute spread throughout the

---

[5] Seven days is the period that some Buddhists believe is required for a person's soul to transmigrate.

[6] The place where a martial art is practiced. Usually a hall with a plain wood floor. The word (道場) itself means "a place where the Way (the Way of swordsmanship, karate, judo, etc.) is practiced

village and Budaiyu was so chagrined he could hardly bear it. He had had various doctors look at her but they only shook their heads.

"The poor thing," he lamented. "I wonder how she could have been born a mute." And every time he looked at Misao's face, tears would fall down his cheeks.

Even so, Misao quickly grew to be a sweet little girl.

One spring day, the maid, O-matsu, hoisted Misao on her back and took her to a warm place in the garden to play. In a corner of the garden there was a spring-fed well and the surface of the water was as clear as a mirror.

O-matsu, with Misao on her back, stole a glance down the well. There, in the cool shadows of the well, was a young woman's face. Her complexion was white, her eyes large and she looked just like the goddess of spring.

"It looks just like my face," O-matsu thought happily as she affected a slightly prim expression.

The face on the surface of the water also smiled.

Then, suddenly, Misao let out a happy little laugh.

"Goodness!" O-matsu thought, "Misao has said something." And in her surprise, she thought she would try to make Misao speak again.

"Here, sweet thing," she cooed, "look, look!"

But the instant she leaned forward, Misao slipped off her back and fell into the well with a splash.

"Oh, no!" she cried, and panicking tried to save the child. But she was only a weak young lady and there was nothing she could do.

As O-matsu screamed for someone to come, Budaiyu and his disciples ran into the garden. One of the disciples then jumped into the well fully clothed and pulled Misao out. But Misao was no longer breathing.

Budaiyu held Misao's cold body and cried loudly. After a while, however, he suddenly stood up and glared at O-matsu.

"O-matsu!" he yelled. "How dare you kill my darling little girl!" And he struck O-matsu with all his might.

As the blows rained down on her, O-matsu cried and tried to apologize. But Budaiyu was so angry that he seemed to have gone insane. After he had stomped and kicked her, he picked her up by the scruff of the neck and threw her into the well. Then he lifted up a large stone and dropped it into the well on top of her.

O-matsu's screams rose up from the well but Budaiyu stormed back to his house and locked himself in his room.

"Never mind!" he shouted as he left. "Leave her there!"

The night after O-matsu was killed, however, something strange happened in the *dojo*. Just as everyone thought they heard screams coming from the well, all of the lights went out and a blood-stained woman suddenly appeared. Budaiyu immediately unsheathed his sword and struck at the woman, but the sword seemed to go through thin air.

No matter how famous a swordsman might be, he cannot cut down a ghost.

Meanwhile, it seemed as though O-matsu's ghost was going to come into the *dojō*. Terrified, Budaiyu's disciples ran out the place so quickly they nearly tumbled out of the door, until not one was left.

Then, one evening not long after, Budaiyu's mansion caught fire and Budaiyu and everyone there was burned to death.

Even today, there is a small statue of Jizo standing in the middle of the mansion's ruins, placed there to console O-matsu's ghost. Next to it is a large rock someone pulled out of the well.

⤳

O-kiku's Curse

A long time ago, in a place called Numata in the ancient area of Joshu, there was a samurai by the name of Obata Kazusa no suke. Kazusa no suke was a deeply suspicious man, and short-tempered as well, and did nothing more than yell at his retainers.

In the samurai's mansion was a pretty maid by the name of O-kiku. She was really the only member of his household that he liked, and he had her take care of all his personal affairs. In fact, he left almost everything up to her.

One morning, however, when he was about to eat his breakfast, which was served to him by O-kiku, he noticed something shining in the middle of his rice. When he picked it out with his chopsticks and looked to see what it was, he found that it was a small sewing needle.

Kazusa no suke's face turned pale and his body shook with anger.

"You ungrateful wench!" he yelled angrily. "How dare you try to kill me? Speak! Why have you done this?"

O-kiku wilted under her master's outburst and all she could do was tremble. Clinging on the straw matting, she only hung her head.

"Speak! Speak up!" Kazusa no suke screamed, kicking over the dishes and beating O-kiku in a rage.

But O-kiku was completely stunned.

"Please forgive me," she pleaded. "I had no idea there was a needle in your rice."

"What? You still don't confess?" Kazusa no suke fumed, holding down O-kiku's head with his foot.

Just at this moment, Kazusa no suke's wife entered the room. When she saw her husband forcing down O-kiku's head with his foot, she laughed out loud.

"This woman was born with a twisted disposition and she's stubborn as well," she sneered. "She'll never confess, with a light inquiry like this. Why don't you give her the 'snake treatment'?"

"All right!" he commanded. "Strip her right down to her skin!"

Kasusa no suke ordered his retainers to take off O-kiku's clothes, and he himself threw her into a bathtub filled with snakes. Then he put the lid on top of the tub.

"Well," he called out, "how about a confession now?"

But O-kiku had committed no crime, so what was she to confess?

At length, the tub was filled with water and the connecting furnace was ignited. The water became hotter and hotter, until it was about to boil. The snakes began to panic in their excruciating pain and bit down O-kiku's body without letting go. Each time she was bitten, O-kiku let out a horrific scream.

Hardened as he was, Kazusa no suke felt a twinge of fear, and was ready to take the lid off of the tub. His wife, however, pushed it back down with a thud.

"This frightful woman tried to kill you," she exclaimed. "It's better to kill her before she tries again."

There was nothing Kazusa no suke could do, so he let the torture continue.

Finally, O-kiku was near her end.

"Only a demon kills innocent people!" she shrieked. "But my

hatred will make you pay!"

And with that, she died.

The next day, Kazusa no suke's wife suddenly became ill. Her body burned with a high fever and she felt as though she was being stuck all over with needles. A doctor was called immediately but he could find no cause for her illness. And even though she took a medicine so expensive it would make one's eyes pop out, the fever did not abate in the least.

"O-kiku, forgive me!" his wife mumbled over and over as she writhed in pain and ground her teeth. "I've done wrong!"

On the seventh night of her affliction, she confessed to her husband.

"O… O-kiku's ghost … please help me," she murmured. "I was the one who put the needle in your rice." And she breathed her last.

Now Kazusa no suke understood that it was his wife who had tried to kill him, and realized that she had been jealous because of his special treatment of his maidservant. Moreover, she had dragged him into this crime.

"So that's it," he said to himself and turned pale. "I've done a horrible thing."

But even if he repented now, it would not bring O-kiku back to life.

After his wife died, a ghost started appearing every night from O-kiku's room. Its entire body was wrapped in snakes, its hair fell down in disheveled confusion, and it was fearsome enough to make one gasp in horror. The retainers and maids of the household were terrified and left one by one until Kazusa no suke was the only person there.

O-kiku's ghost now appeared before Kazusa no suke both day and night, threatening to kill him in an eerie voice. Then she would disappear.

Kazusa no suke, the samurai, was now almost insane with fear.

At this point, the lord who Kazusa no suke served decided to move his entire entourage to another castle in a place called Matsushiro.

"Now I can escape O-kiku's ghost!" he thought, and completely overjoyed he abandoned his mansion and moved to Matsushiro.

When the lord's entourage reached Matsushiro, however, there was something unaccountable. Upon their arrival, there was one more palanquin in the retinue than there had been when they set off.

"This is strange, isn't it," the lord asked the palanquin bearers. "Who was riding in that palanquin?"

"It was a beautiful young woman," one of the bearers offered. "But she was not in good condition and was deathly pale."

When Kazusa no suke heard this, his blood ran cold and he collapsed on the ground.

"This has to be O-kiku's ghost," he shuddered.

And just as he thought, O-kiku's ghost began to appear at his new mansion in Matsushiro. Soon, Kazusa no suke went insane and died.

After Kazusa no suke passed away, however, unhappy events began to occur, one after another, at his relatives' households.

"This must be O-kiku's curse," many of them thought. "If we don't do something, she's going to kill us all."

Thus, the people of the Obata clan gathered together and built a shrine to O-kiku next to Kazusa no suke's mansion. There they venerated O-kiku and prayed for everything they were worth.

After that, O-kiku's ghost no longer appeared and the curse vanished as though it had been nothing more than a bad dream.

⌒⌒つ

The Curse of the Giant Eel

A long time ago, in the city of Edo, there was a wall plasterer who had an almost morbid dislike of eel.[7] At work, if broiled eel was served, just looking at it would make him feel queasy.

"I went to the trouble to make a good meal," someone once said angrily, "and this conceited wall plasterer wouldn't touch it."

But the man didn't like eel and there was nothing to be done about that.

Still, it was strange that he didn't like broiled eel, which is so delicious. But there was a reason why he not only disliked eel but was also a little afraid of it.

---

[7] *Unagi* (鰻), considered a delicacy in Japan where it is eaten during the summer to revive one's vitality.

This plasterer had originally been born into a samurai household. When he was young, he left the house and tried his hand at various jobs, but in the end became a wall plasterer. This story, however, takes place before he became a wall plasterer, when he was the son-in-law of the master of an eel restaurant.

One day, this man went out to buy eels with his father-in-law. They picked out the most vigorous looking eels, put them in a container and carried them back to the restaurant. At the very moment his father-in-law was about to put the eels into the bamboo weir,[8] he realized that among the eels they had bought, there were two way beyond the normal size.

"That's strange," he called to his son-in-law. "I don't remember these eels being there when I bought the rest."

"That *is* strange," the man replied, shaking his head. "There were certainly no eels of this size there. But that's all right, isn't it? There's a really rich customer who comes here often asking for large eels, you know. Shall I put them aside so he can take a look at them?"

"Yes, please do," his father-in-law agreed. "That man won't complain no matter how big or expensive an eel is."

Sure enough, the next day, the rich man came to the restaurant and brought along a friend. The master of the shop nearly leapt out in his eagerness to greet them and told them the story of the eels. The rich man was overjoyed.

"This is a rare treat!" he exclaimed. "Broil an eel right away!"

The master of the shop then went down to the stream in which he had placed the bamboo weir and grabbed one of the giant eels. For some reason, however, he was unable to stick the pick into the eel's head.[9] He had been preparing eel cuisine for decades and this was the first time he was unable to pierce the head properly. Just when he thought he had finally succeeded, he had instead pierced his own left hand.

---

[8] *Ikesu*, a bamboo basket or container that is set down into a stream in order to keep the eels alive. The bamboo strips are far enough apart to let water in but close enough that the eels cannot escape.

[9] An eel is prepared for broiling by pinning its head to a plank with a sort of ice pick, and when the head is secure pulling the length of its body down the plank with one hand and splitting it down the middle with a knife in the other. Mark Twain once witnessed this preparation while walking through a fish market and asked the fishmonger if this was not painful for the eel. "Oh, yes, sir, just a little," came the reply. "But they get used to it."

There was nothing else he could do, so he called his son-in-law to take over, pressed his left hand to stop the bleeding and retreated into the interior of the shop

"It's awfully strange that my father-in-law would get hurt pinning down an eel," the man thought, and went about butchering the eel as he had always done in the past.

Nevertheless, he, too, was unable to do the job successfully.

"I can see this is a tough one," he concluded.

As he pushed the eel down in vain, the eel quickly wrapped itself around his left hand and held on with surprising strength. The man's hand suddenly went numb and he let go of the eel.

It was clear that he was not going to be able to prepare this eel by himself, but at the same time he knew that if he asked someone for help he would be laughed at and lose everyone's respect. He was totally at a loss.

"Look," he finally addressed the eel in desperation. "No matter how you wriggle and squirm, you're going to end up as somebody's meal. I'm begging you to let me prepare you for broiling, and if you will I'll leave this shop and never engage in this business again."

Oddly, the eel, which had been struggling as tenaciously as it could, now suddenly quietened down. In that instant, the man pinned its head with the pick and split it down the middle.

Soon, a huge broiled eel was carried in to the rich man, who was barely able to sit down as he waited. His friend, however, almost immediately turned down the offer of a portion, and the rich man, after eating only a little, quickly felt unwell and even threw up what he had eaten. It wasn't that it tasted bad, there was just something unsettling about it.

That night, a little after midnight, an unusual cry came from the bamboo tank in the stream behind the shop. Wondering what it might be, the man got out of bed, went to take a look but found nothing unusual. Even the lid of the bamboo weir was securely fastened. Nevertheless, just to make sure, he opened the lid and looked in.

With a scream, he leapt backward. There, in the weir, were hundreds of eels, their heads raised like snakes, glaring directly at him. Yelling for help, he fainted dead away.

The shop assistants who heard his cry came running, but they, too, turned pale and could do little but tremble in their fright. And what

Toyohara Kunichika. "O-kiku." The tormented ghost of the murdered servant girl O-kiku emerges to take vengeance upon her killer. n.d. (*Wikimedia Commons*)

Tsukioka Yoshitoshi. "The Enlightenment." A group of ghosts visit the former courtesan Jigoku-dayū to show her the errors of her ways. From the *Thirty-six Ghosts* series. 1890. (*Wikimedia Commons*)

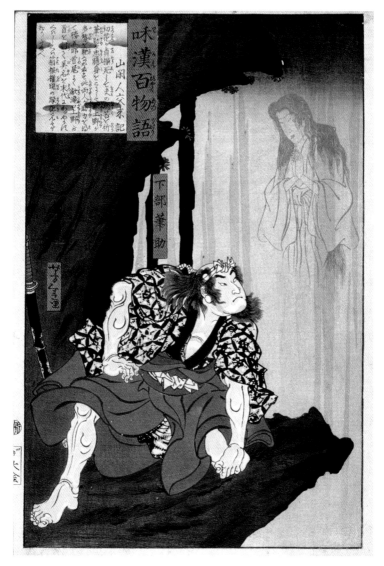

Tsukioka Yoshitoshi. "Shimobe Fudesuke and the Ghost of the Woman in the Waterfall." The spirit of Shimobe Fudesuke's wife appears in a waterfall in this print from the series *One Hundred Ghost Tales of Japan and China*. 1865. (*Los Angeles County Museum of Art*)

Katsushika, Hokusai. "The Laughing Demon." A terrifying demon laughs while holding the severed head of a child. 1830. (*Library of Congress*)

Tsukioka Yoshitoshi. "Kusunoki Tamonmaru Masayuki Surprising a Fox Ghost." Kusunoki Tamonmaru Masayuki, general of Nanchō, is surprised by a fox ghost in this print from the series *One Hundred Ghost Tales of Japan and China*. 1865. (*Los Angeles County Museum of Art*)

Tsukioka Yoshitoshi. "Kodembō no Shōshichi, an Osaka Thief, Tormented by Ghosts." A common thief on the streets of Osaka is set upon by a group of ghosts as he attempts to fight back. 1875. (*Los Angeles County Museum of Art*)

Tsukioka Yoshitoshi. "Lord Sadanobu Threatens a Demon in the Palace at Night." Matsaudaira Sabanodu, a daimyō of the Tokugawa shogunate, attempts to intimidate a demon. 1889. (*Los Angeles County Museum of Art*)

Tsukioka Yoshitoshi. "Minamoto no Yorimitsu Cuts at the Earth Spider."
The hero Minamoto no Yorimitsu attacks the infamous Earth Spider
in this print from the series *New Forms of Thirty-six Ghosts*. 1892. (*Los
Angeles County Museum of Art*)

Tsukioka Yoshitoshi. "Driving Away the Demons." The samurai Min-amoto no Tametomo engages with demons in this print from the *Thir-ty-six Ghosts* series. 1890. (*Wikimedia Commons*)

Tsukioka Yoshitoshi. "Ōya Tarō Mitsukune Watching Skeletons." The warrior Ōya Tarō Mitsukune watches as a group of skeletons fight. From the series *One Hundred Ghost Tales of Japan and China*. 1865. (*Wikimedia Commons*)

Utagawa Kuniyoshi. "Taira no Koreshige Attacked by a Demon." The female demon Kijo and samurai Taira no Koreshige fight to the death. n.d. (*Wikimedia Commons*)

Utagawa Kuniyoshi. "Shimotsuke no Kuni Nasu no Hara Kinmo Haku-men Kyubi no Akko Taiji no Ga." Warriors Miuranosuke Tsunetane and Kazusanosuke Hirotsune attack the nine-tailed demon fox of Nasu Moor. c. 1834. (*Wikimedia Commons*)

Tsukioka Yoshitoshi. "Shirafuji Genta Watching Kappa Wrestle." Sumo wrestler Shirafuji Genta observes a group of wrestling kappa. From the series *Ghost Stories of China and Japan*. 1865. (*Wikimedia Commons*)

Tsukioka Yoshitoshi. "Takagi Umanosuke and the Ghost of a Woman." A massive ghostly head of a woman appears before the legendary swordsman Takagi Umanosuke in a print from the series *Beauty and Valor in the Novel Suikoden.* 1866. (*Los Angeles County Museum of Art*)

Tsukioka Yoshitoshi. "Takagi Toranosuke Tadakatsu Slaying a Demon." Samurai Takagi Toranosuke Tadakatsu and a demon fight in a cave as attendants light the scene with torches. 1867. (*Wikimedia Commons*)

Tsukioka Yoshitoshi. "Night Moon over Mount Manno." A winged spirit approaches Iga no Tsubone at the court at Nara in this print from the series *One Hundred Aspects of the Moon*. 1880s. (*Library of Congress*)

had happened to the other huge eel that was now nowhere to be seen?

After the man regained consciousness, he found that he could no longer even look at an eel without feeling uncomfortable. Recalling the promise he had made to the eel he had killed, he nearly ran out of the shop the next morning and fled to the home of a relative.

A year had passed when a messenger from the shop appeared at his door.

"The master of the shop is quite ill and may soon die," he reported. "Please come back soon."

Now the man had not been driven out from the shop, but had fled on his own free will. If the master died now, however, there would be no one to be his heir.

Feeling that there was nothing else he could do, the man returned to the shop and found it as prosperous as before. The people running the shop, however, were the master's wife and a young man who had worked under him when he had been employed there. The master himself had been shut up in a small dirty room in the interior of the shop. Nobody had been taking care of him and he was as frail as a withered old tree.

"What's going on here?" the man asked angrily, and calling a doctor, quickly moved the master to the sitting room.

The master, however, was hardly able to get water down his throat, much less gruel or medicine.

When the man asked the people working in the shop how the master had become so ill, they simply shook their heads. It seems that the day after they had killed the giant eel, he had taken to his bed and been unable to get up.

The master himself was unable to speak a word. He could only distend his chin like an eel and blow out his breath in puffs.

"This has got to be the giant eel's curse," the man thought, and quickly called a priest to intone a sutra for the dead eel.

Despite this, the master passed away soon after.

In the end, the man called the master's relatives together and informed them that he could not continue as heir to the shop. Formally separating himself from all connection to the place, he went off and became a wall plasterer, never wanting to see an eel again.

Living Heads and Skeletons

The Headless Ghost

A drunk was walking along the road at night, singing in a loud voice as he went, when a country samurai casually passed by from the opposite direction.

"Hey there, you!" the samurai said in a haughty tone. "I need to ask you some directions."

"Watch the way you speak, you hayseed samurai," the drunk yelled angrily. "If you want to ask somebody something, use your manners."

"You insolent cur!" the samurai shouted back and immediately unsheathed his sword and sliced neatly through the drunk's neck with a single stroke.

He did this with such speed, however, that you couldn't tell if the drunk had truly been decapitated or not. Sheathing his sword with a clink, the samurai then walked off as though on some holiday excursion.

"Hunh!" The drunk snorted. "What a coward! He only pretended to cut me down!" and muttering insults about country bumpkin samurai, he walked on.

His severed head, however, kept turning to the side.

"That's strange," the drunk mumbled. "I wonder why it's doing that," and with both hands turned his head in a forward position again.

But in a short while his head began turning to the side again.

A few more steps later, the drunk stumbled over a rock and nearly fell down. In regaining his balance, his head tumbled right down in front of him. When he put his hand to what was left of his neck, he felt blood coming out in spurts.

"Yaah!" he yelled. "I'm done for."

He realized now that his head *had* been cut off and this was terrible. If things went on this way, he was going to die! Holding his head on with both hands, he began to run.

"Fire!" someone yelled at that moment, and people came running out of their houses from every direction. Looking off in the distance, they could see that the sky was bright red.

"Where's the fire?" someone yelled.

"Over there!" shouted another

In no time at all, a mob of spectators gathered and ran in the direction of the conflagration.

If the drunk just stood there carelessly, he was going to get knocked down, and if he got knocked down, he was going to drop his head. That, for sure, would have been terrible.

The drunk now took off his head and began to run, cradling it in both hands.

"Ahem, excuse me! Excuse me!" he yelled loudly as he weaved through the crowd.

When the mob drawn by the fire saw him, they stopped dead in their tracks.

"A ... a headless ghost!" a man yelled.

A cold chill passed through them all and they completely forgot about watching the fire.

O-tsuna's Head

A long time ago, in a certain place, there was a woman named O-tsuna, who lived together with her husband.

Now, one day her husband started off on a journey connected with his work.

"I'll return as quickly as I can," he said with some concern. "Please take strict care of everything while I'm away."

After her husband left, O-tsuna began to weave straw cord for use in her household chores. As she wove, however, an old lady came into the room where she was weaving. The old lady did not say a word, but sitting down next to O-tsuna, began throwing all the straw cord O-tsuna was weaving, bit by bit, into the hearth.

"What … what are you doing?" O-tsuna asked in surprise. But no matter how she protested, the old lady did not even acknowledge her presence.

Finally, the old lady began devouring the ashes left by the burnt straw cord. O-tsuna jumped up, completely shocked, and trembling so much she could not run away.

"Well then," the old lady cackled, her mouth smeared with ashes, "I'll come again tomorrow." And out she went.

The next day, O-tsuna took three seeds from some pampas grass and hid them inside a wicker basket on the second floor. At length, the old lady returned.

"Well, now," she croaked, "She's not here, I guess."

The old lady looked around the room for a while, then began to climb to the second floor. O-tsuna thought that she would frighten the old lady and bit down on one of the pampas grass seeds with a "kachin!"

The old lady *was* surprised and stopped halfway up the stairs. The place was silent once again. As she began to climb the stairs again, once more came the sound "kachin!"

"My, my, what kind of sound is that?" the old lady muttered to herself, peering from the stairs into the second floor. After a short while, she completed her climb.

Hearing the old lady's footsteps, O-tsuna became more and more frightened and tried to stop breathing aloud. Finally making up her mind, however, she bit down hard on the third pampas grass seed, which let out a loud "kachin!"

But the old lady did not flinch.

"Woman," she half-whispered. "Are you here?" and with that started to look around the second floor.

"Ahh, I'm done for," O-tsuna sighed, and with shaking hands popped open the lid of the wicker basket.

"Today, I've come to eat *you*," the old lady chuckled, and pulling O-tsuna to her, noisily gobbled the woman up from her feet to her neck.

"My, that was delicious," she smiled. "I'll save the rest for tomorrow." With that, she put O-tsuna's head on a dish and returned the dish to the middle of the cupboard.

The next day, O-tsuna's husband, who knew nothing of these events, arrived home.

"O-tsuna! I'm back," he called out. "O-tsuna!"

But no matter how many times he called, there was no answer.

Thinking this was strange, he looked around the house, but for sure she wasn't there.

"She must have gone out somewhere," he thought, and, with nothing particular in mind, opened up the cupboard. And there on a plate was O-tsuna's head.

Waves of shock rolled over him, but just as he was about to run outside, O-tsuna's head tumbled off the shelf and bit tightly to his chest. Holding on to his wife's head, he leapt outdoors. But just then....

"Feed me some rice," the head commanded.

Hardly knowing what else to do, O-tsuna's husband cradled her head, went back inside the house and hid her head on the second floor where no one would see it. He then sent out for two portions of rice, went back upstairs and seated her head on the plate again so that she might be able to eat.

"Feed me, please," the head demanded.

No matter how much he had cared for his wife, this gave him a terrible feeling in the pit of his stomach and he was unable to put the rice in her mouth. Instead, he put the bowl over her face and wrapped it up with a sash. He then ran down the stairs and dashed outside.

O-tsuna's head, however, tumbled down the stairs and chased after him.

"Help!" he yelled. "Somebody, help!"

Finally, he fled into a thicket overgrown with mugwort and sweet flag.[1] At that moment, O-tsuna's head stopped and tumbled away in the opposite direction.

"Ahh, I'm saved!" he said aloud, and gathering up the mugwort and sweet flag he returned home, carefully placing the plants around the windows and doors.

Thanks to this, his wife's dreadful head never returned.

Ever since then, people place mugwort and sweet flag beneath the eaves of their houses on the festival held on the fifth day of the fifth month.[2] This is because flesh-eating demons and other ogres hate these plants and will never approach such protected houses to take their children away.

The Abandoned Wife

A long time ago, when Kyoto was the capital of Japan, there was a samurai who lived on the outskirts of the city. This samurai was very poor and, being unable to find employment, only secured his next meal with great difficulty. One of his acquaintances, however, had somehow become the lord of a far-off province and it was decided that the samurai would accompany him as one of his retainers.

"What do you know?" the man said happily to himself. "Even *my* luck has changed."

The samurai was overjoyed and immediately began making preparations for the journey. But the little money he had managed to save was hardly sufficient. The solution, he decided, was to abandon his long-suffering and gentle wife and to marry another woman. From this woman, he borrowed the necessary sum of money and the two of them went off to his new lord's faraway province.

---

[1] Mugwort: Japanese, *yomogi*; Latin, *Artemisia princes Pampanini*. Sweet flag: Japanese, *shobu*; Latin, *Acorus Calamus L. var. augustatus Besser*.

[2] Children's Day in Japan.

Now, poverty was never a problem and his current life, compared to that in Kyoto, was like a dream.

His new wife, however, was proud, very suspicious and incredibly willful. She spent every day enjoying herself and had nothing but complaints for the samurai. But to get to where he was, he had had to borrow money from her, so there was no way he could drive her out.

"Compared to this woman," he thought regretfully, "my first wife was gentleness itself."

Thus, he eventually began to yearn for his first wife, and after a while realized that living with her would be far preferable, even though they would be poor. At this point, even looking at his new wife's face became unbearable.

A number of years passed, and it was determined that the lord should move back to Kyoto.

"This means I'll be able to be with her again," the samurai thought happily.

When he arrived in Kyoto, the samurai returned his new wife to her former family and quickly went back to his old house.

"Can this be where I used to live?" the samurai muttered to himself as he stood before the gate.

The walls had by now lost their plaster and fallen in, the eaves slanted to one side, and the place generally had the dilapidated look of a haunted house. It had appeared nothing like this before.

"My wife must have been angry at me and moved away," he thought silently, surveying the scene.

With these sad regrets, he entered the broken-down house. To his surprise, there his wife sat where she always had.

"You ... you waited for me?" the samurai stuttered, hurrying to her side and embracing her.

"Welcome home," she said happily, and without a single complaint gazed at the samurai's face.

"Please forgive me," the samurai said, choking back his tears. "I've been horrible! But I'll never leave you again.'

The two then talked late into the night, with no thought for the time or hour. The bright light of the moon shone down into the withered garden and the crickets chirped continually.

At dawn, the two finally crawled together under the bedding. With the security of at last being in his own home, the samurai felt safe and at ease and fell into a deep sleep.

When the samurai opened his eyes, the sun was shining in from outside.

"Ahh," he yawned, "how well I slept," and with these words looked over at his wife.

With a scream, he jumped up and out from under the bedding. The woman he had been sleeping with was a withered corpse and nothing but skin and bones. Still in his nighttime clothing, he fled to the neighbor's house.

He was completely unfamiliar with the man.

"Did you know my wife, the woman who lived in this house?" he asked, still locked in dread.

"Why, yes," the man replied. "But she died last year. She was terribly sad … said something about her husband having remarried and gone off to live in a faraway province. After a while, she became sick, but there was no one to look after her and she passed away. There was no one to conduct a funeral for her either and they just left her corpse there where she died. People find the house a scary place and refuse to go near it."

This said, the man looked at the samurai's face in a strange way.

"So, did you encounter your wife's ghost last night?" he asked.

The samurai was frightened out of his wits and ran away just as he was, never to return.

At length, the people of the area heard this story and rumors spread around the capital.

"A woman's resentment is a frightening thing," it was remarked. "Even so, the samurai should have been thankful that she didn't kill him outright."

The Bleached Skull's Invitation

These events occurred over thirteen hundred years ago.

At the Gankoji, a temple in Nara, there was a very famous priest by the name of Doutou. One day, accompanied by his retainer Maro, Doutou set out for the pass at Mount Narazaka. By the side of the road there was a bleached skull that people often stepped on or kicked away.

"I don't know where this skull came from," said the priest, "but it would be a shame just to leave it here." And he had Maro pick it up and place it on top of a small tree.

Toward the end of that year, a man walked up to the temple.

"I would like to talk with Master Doutou's disciple Maro," the man declared.

Maro had no idea who this might be, but nevertheless came out to meet the man.

"Thanks to you," the man began, politely bowing his head. "I'm now quite happy. This evening, I would like to repay you for your favor, so please come with me."

Maro could not guess what this was all about, but the man was so fervent in his request that he followed along behind him. When they arrived at the man's house, the front door was tightly closed but inside the preparations for a feast had been laid out with care.

"Well now," the man said happily, "please don't be shy. Eat as much as you like."

The man asked Maro to sit down in front of the plates and ate what turned out to be quite a delicious meal along with him. Maro forgot any misgivings he might have had and ate as though in a trance.

By the time they had finished the meal and sat back to rest, it was about midnight. Suddenly, the man began to fidget.

"My older brother, who murdered me, is coming here soon," he warned. "You should leave right away."

"What are you saying?" Maro asked with surprise. "Are you telling me you're dead?"

"Yes," the man answered anxiously. "The bleached skull you kindly picked up on Mount Narazaka was mine."

"What?" Maro exclaimed in spite of himself.

"Please don't be too shocked," the man continued. "The truth is that my elder brother and I had gone out on business together and I managed to make a profit of about forty catties[3] of silver. My elder brother, however, made no profit at all. He wanted the silver for himself so he murdered me and ran away with everything. From that time, my body was left there by the roadside, kicked and stepped on by passers-by, until all that remained was my skull. Completely unexpectedly, you kindly picked up my skull and put it out of the way. Now I'm happy again."

Once again, the man bowed his head before Maro.

"Being siblings of the same family, your elder brother has done a terrible thing. Perhaps I can do something for you," Maro concluded, straightening himself as he sat.

Just at that moment, the front door opened and the man's elder brother and mother entered the house. The man himself became extremely flustered and ran out the back door. The mother and elder brother, it seems, had come to pray for the dead man's spirit and were taken aback to see Maro sitting there.

Maro made them listen to everything that had happened.

---

[3] Catty, Japanese *kin* (斤), about 1⅓ pounds.

"What is this!" the mother cried, so shocked that she nearly collapsed. "It wasn't a highway robber who killed him after all? Why, you're no kind of human being at all! To kill your own little brother…."

With that, her voice faded away and all you could hear were her sobs as she beat her older son with confused blows.

"No matter how much you cry," Maro then said tenderly, "you cannot bring your younger son back to life. Rather, you should pray for his salvation."

The mother then raised her head, nodded in agreement and turned toward the older brother.

"But you," she said flatly, "you had better pray for your murdered brother's soul for the rest of your life!"

The elder brother, as hardened as he was, suddenly was frightened of the crime he had committed, although it could never be undone. He spent the rest of his days, it seems, intoning the *nembutsu* for the repose of his younger brother's soul.

The Baby's Sneeze

There was a couple in Okinawa who had wanted a baby for a long time, and at last the wife gave birth to a baby boy.

"This is wonderful!" the boy's father declared in great joy. "We must have a celebration right away!" And off he went, inviting his neighbors and relatives to his home for the occasion. To make the day really celebratory, he went in search of a geisha who would serve sake and sing and dance.

But, unfortunately, not a single geisha was to be found.

"This is terrible," the new father muttered to himself. "Without a geisha, the celebration will be boring."

As he unhappily returned home, however, he encountered a young geisha on the road.

"I'm saved," he exclaimed. "Would you come with me to my house?"

The man explained the circumstances of his request and the geisha happily agreed to come along.

The party soon began. People were drinking sake, singing and dancing, and it was quite a raucous affair. The young geisha was very pretty and, moreover, her dancing and singing were exceptional.

"I've never seen such a wonderful geisha," someone commented.

"Please, please, dance again," another shouted ecstatically.

About this time, a man passed by the house and wondered if there was some dancing going on.

"They certainly seem to be happy," he thought.

Regretting that he was not part of the goings-on, he peeked through a chink in the wall.

There, moving gracefully among the guests, was the head of a geisha, without any body at all.

The man was so shocked that he immediately looked away. But he quickly entered the house and called over the new father.

"This is terrible," he whispered. "That geisha you have here has no body."

"What kind of foolish talk is that?" returned the father.

"Listen," the man insisted, "come outside for a moment."

The man led the new father outside to the chink in the wall, where he peeped in and gasped. Just as the man had said, the geisha's head was going here and there among the guests, moving to the sound of the singing.

The new father turned pale, but what could he do? He had expressly invited the geisha to come to his house and could not simply send her away.

After a while, however, the celebration came to an end and everyone went home in the best of spirits.

"Thanks to you, we've had a very lively bit of merrymaking," the father said gratefully to the geisha. Giving her some money, he accompanied her outside.

But, wondering where she was going, he secretly followed behind her.

The geisha had no idea that she was being followed and walked briskly along without looking back. At length, she stopped in front of the graveyard on the outskirts of the town. It would have been horrible if he had been seen, so the man hid behind a large tree off to the side. Then....

"Where have you been loitering about until this hour?" a loud voice came from the graveyard. "I can't let you come in."

"I was taken to the celebration of the birth of a baby," the geisha explained, "so I'm a little late."

"What? A baby?" the voice boomed even louder.

"As an apology for being late, I'll bring the baby here," the geisha pleaded. "So please forgive me."

"Fine. Bring the baby here and I'll let you in," the voice continued. "But how are you going to get it?"

"That will be easy," the geisha said. "I'll make the baby sneeze and take it while everyone's making a big fuss."

"All right," the voice agreed. "But be careful. Human beings are very clever, and if they hear the baby sneeze, they're liable to shout 'Eat shit!'[4] I wonder if you'll be able to grab the baby then."

"Don't worry," the geisha assured him. "I doubt if these people know that we hate these words as much as we do."

The new father heard all this and ran home as quickly as he could. He then gathered the household together and explained what he had just learned.

After that, every time the baby sneezed, everyone would shout "Eat shit!" And because of this, the ghosts in the graveyard were no longer able to take away a single child.

Thus, in Okinawa to this very day, when a baby sneezes, there are people who will shout "Eat shit!"

---

[4] Japanese, *Kuso kue* (糞くえ). The word is as vulgar, or should we say earthy, in Japanese as it is in English. *Kenkyusha's New Japanese-English Dictionary* tries to get around it with phrases like "Damn it!," "Devil take it!" and even "Heck!" but this is, as the Japanese also say, "trying to cover shit with tinsel" (糞に箔塗る).

Ghosts' Requests

The Closed Box

Many years ago, in the ancient province of Mino, there lived a man by the name of Ki no Tousuke. For a long time, his duties had been to guard his lord's mansion, but at long last he was given permission to return to his own home.

"I'll bet she's craning her neck looking out the door in expectation," he said to himself. As he thought about his wife, he could not stay still any longer. So Tousuke quickly mounted his horse, and accompanied by his retainers, made his departure.

On the way, however, he had to go over the Seta Bridge. As he began to cross this long bridge, he could see a woman in the middle of it, holding something wrapped in white.

"What can she be doing in a place like this?" he wondered, and thinking her presence rather odd, was prepared ride right past her.

"Excuse me, Sir," she suddenly called out, "but where are you going?"

"I'm just returning to my home in Mino," he replied and dismounted.

"What good luck!" the woman went on, taking out the white bundle and showing it to Tousuke. "The fact is that I'd like you to deliver this box to someone on your way. Before you get to Mino, you'll have to cross a bridge called the Kiza no hashi, and there should be a woman waiting there. Please hand this over to her, if you'll be so kind."

"That's an easy job," Tousuke replied politely as he took the box and remounted. "I'll be glad to do it. But what shall I do if the woman is not there? Just to make sure, could you tell me her name and where she lives?"

At this, the woman's face suddenly took on a frightening expression.

"She will be there for sure," she hissed. "And whatever you do, please do not open the box!"

This gave Tousuke a bad feeling in the pit of his stomach and for a moment he regretted that he had agreed to undertake this task. At this point, however, it was too late to refuse.

Tousuke's retainers had been watching their master's doings from farther up the bridge and wondered if something strange was going on.

"What happened, my Lord?" one of them asked. "We saw you

getting off your horse and talking to yourself."

"To myself?" asked Tousuke, looking dubiously at his retainer's expression. "Didn't you see the woman I was speaking to?"

"What do you mean, 'the woman'?" queried the retainer. "There was nobody there."

Hearing this, Tousuke felt a shiver go down his spine, and involuntarily looked at his horse's back. But there, for sure, was the box.

"Can you see this box?" Tousuke then asked his retainer.

"Yes, I can," came the reply. "But I have no idea when you picked it up."

Being told this by his honest and faithful retainer, Tousuke felt more and more that something strange was going on, and he quickly spurred on his horse. But by and by, he forgot all about the woman and the box and finally arrived home.

Tousuke's wife, however, soon saw the box and, thought it was a gift he had brought for her.

"What is this?" she asked, beginning to open it up.

Completely flustered, Tousuke took her hand away from the object before she could object.

"Now I've done it!" he thought in a panic. "I've forgotten to deliver this box." And he ordered his wife not to open it under any circumstances.

Tousuke explained how he had encountered a woman on the way home. His wife, however, was deeply suspicious, and thought for sure that her husband was lying, and that the box was meant for another woman.

So when Tousuke left the room for only a moment, she quickly opened the box, and with a scream fainted dead away.

The box was filled with eyeballs plucked from people's heads.

When he heard his wife's screams, Tousuke ran hurriedly back into the room. When he saw what was in the box, he, too, gasped, and without thinking, held his breath.

"What have I done bringing this thing into my home?" he wondered. "For all I know, something horrible may happen now. I've got to take it to that woman right away."

Tousuke rewrapped the box and dashed off to the bridge where the woman would be waiting. And there she was, standing in the middle of the bridge.

"I came to deliver this to you," Tousuke said nervously, holding out the box in front of the woman.

But the woman only glared at Tousuke with a horrible expression.

"Did you look inside?" she asked threateningly.

"No!" squirmed Tousuke. "Absolutely not!"

"You're lying!" she screamed, her face suddenly turning as pale as a ghost's. "You'll find out now what happens when you break a promise!"

Tousuke tried to call for help but could only throw the box at the woman. He then fled back to his home at full speed, without looking back.

Complaining that he did not feel well, he took to his bed.

"I told you emphatically not to open that box," he scolded his wife. "Now you've brought me to this…."

And barely able to finish his sentence, he breathed his last.

His wife cried and apologized, but it was too late.

So it is that you should not doubt someone without proof. Because this woman was so deeply suspicious, she wound up killing the most important person in her life.

The woman on the bridge, it is said, was the most frightening kind of "living ghost"[1] that kills people with a simple curse.

~

The Young Woman from the Oil Shop

A long time ago in a certain place, there were three samurai who loved to go fishing. One day, the three of them set out to go late-night fishing at the river. When they arrived at the river, they could see something that looked like a red fireball floating in the air on the opposite shore. Just as they wondered what this strange apparition could be, it disappeared.

The next night, however, and the next after that, the red fireball appeared and disappeared again.

---

[1] *Ikiryou* (生霊), literally, a "living spirit," but also a wraith or the apparition of a living person.

"I'm going to find out what this fireball is," declared the bravest of the three. And getting into a small boat, he crossed over to the other side of the river.

Right in the place where the fireball had been seen, the samurai found a dilapidated house and inside sat a pretty young woman.

"I've lost my way and don't know what to do," the samurai lied. "Would you please let me stay here tonight?"

"This is the house of a terrifying demon," the young woman said with a frightened expression. "You should run away as fast as you can!"

"Don't say such things," the samurai insisted. "Just let me stay one night."

"The demon really may come," the young woman declared again.

"That's all right," the samurai laughed. "What are demons to me?"

The young woman finally agreed and led him to a room in the interior of the house.

"No matter what happens, do not leave this room," she warned.

Sometime after midnight, the samurai woke to the woman's hideous screams. Leaping from his bedding, he was about to rush out to see what had happened when he remembered that he was strictly told not to leave the room. Silently opening the door, he peeked into the next room.

Nearly letting out a loud gasp, the samurai saw that a red demon was holding the young woman over a flaming fire on a large stick. Every time the flames leapt higher, she would scream and cry out.

"This is terribly cruel!" he thought, but though he was a samurai he felt weak in the knees and could not move.

After a while, the flames went out and the demon disappeared. The samurai leapt out of his room and rushed to the young woman's side. But although she was dazed and almost senseless, there was not a single burn on her entire body.

"What is this all about?" the samurai asked in shock.

"I'm from an oil shop in Osaka," the young woman began. "My father cheats customers on the amount of oil he sells them, and as a result I'm suffering like this for his crimes. This is what happens to me every night, and by now I think it would be better if the demon just went ahead and killed me. Please! Won't you go to my home in Osaka and ask them to donate their entire stock of oil to the temples on Mount Koya?"

As proof of her circumstances, the young woman ripped off a sleeve of her kimono and gave it to the samurai. The samurai took the sleeve and immediately headed to her house in Osaka.

"I've come as a messenger of the young lady of this house," he declared on arrival. "Please let me talk with the master of the shop."

"You say you're the messenger of the master's daughter?" one of the shop workers shot back. "Don't speak foolishness! His daughter is lying sick in bed and we don't know if she'll live or die. Everybody's very upset."

"Well, take a look at this, please," the samurai said and he took out the kimono sleeve that the young lady had given him.

"This belongs to the master's daughter all right," the shop worker said in amazement, and he called the master to the door.

The samurai then explained in detail why he had come all the way to Osaka to call on the oil shop.

"That's ridiculous!" the master huffed, angrily shaking his head. "My daughter is lying sick in the sitting room, the whole household is watching over her carefully, and there's no way she could have left the shop's premises."

But the sleeve that the samurai showed him was undeniably his daughter's, and just to make sure he went into sitting room and turned down the bedding. To his astonishment, one sleeve of his daughter's kimono had been ripped away.

"It's just as that samurai said," he mumbled, and he immediately asked his shop workers to take all of the shop's oil to the temples on Mount Koya.

With this, the young woman's disease disappeared as though she had never been ill. The master was overjoyed and gave his daughter to the samurai as his wife.

The Ghost that Requested a Sutra Reading

These events occurred over two hundred and seventy years ago.

In the ancient province of Etchu, there was a small temple located in the village of Ouzu. One day, one of the men living in this village was working in the rice paddies not far from the temple when he was approached by a beautiful young lady.

"Excuse me," she said, addressing him with deference. "I live in the neighboring village, and for a certain reason I cannot speak with the priest of this temple. But I would like you to give him this money and ask him to do a sutra reading."

"Of course." The man replied. "I'll go and ask him right away,"

The kind man accompanied the young lady as far as the temple and asked her to wait by the temple gate while he went inside.

"Honorable priest," he began. "Please take this and perform a sutra reading."

"There's no reason to do a sutra reading," the priest interjected. "Who would I be reciting a sutra for? What is the name of the deceased person, and when did he die?"

"Ah, yes, I didn't think of that," the man said, and went out somewhat flustered to where the woman was waiting.

"I'm so sorry. That was a lack of manners on my part," the young lady said apologetically, as she pulled a narrow piece of paper from the breast pocket of her kimono. "The name of the deceased and the day she died is written on this paper."

The man took the piece of paper and went back to the priest.

"Well, well," the priest exclaimed, looking at the skillful calligraphic handwriting. "I've never heard of this person, but fine, I'll go to her home and intone a sutra right away."

The man, however, had not asked where the woman lived.

So once again he went outside the temple but the woman was nowhere to be seen. Feeling strangely apprehensive, he went back and explained the situation to the priest.

"Well then, we'll just go off and inquire at the neighboring village," the priest declared, and with the man in tow went off to find the woman's house.

However, when they went from house to house and showed the paper to the people of that village, no one had the least idea who she was or where her house might be.

"Ahh, then the woman must have been a ghost," sighed the priest.

"What … what are you saying," the man said uneasily. "Why, she clearly had two feet!"[2]

"That doesn't mean anything," the priest went on. "She was a ghost, for sure. When she died, no one requested a sutra reading for her so she came to ask for one herself. Well, there's nothing else to be done. I'll recite a sutra for her at my temple."

So saying, the priest returned to his temple and performed a sutra reading for the woman with the correct civility and care. For, just as he had said, this had been the ghost of a woman who had passed away some years before. Coming from a poor household, no one had gone to a temple to ask the priest to read a sutra for her, so she had finally asked for one on her own.

---

[2] In Japan, as perhaps elsewhere, ghosts are not considered to have feet and are almost always depicted floating just above the ground.

Another Half

A long time ago, there was a small sake shop located near a certain bridge, and one night a shabbily dressed old man dropped in for a drink.

"Pardon me," the old man said, "just give me a half-cup of sake, please."

"Well, sure, here you are," the shopkeeper replied, thinking that this was a strange request from a customer, but nevertheless putting a half-full sake cup in front of the old man.

The old man drank it down as if it were quite delicious.

"Another half," he added, pushing the sake cup to the shopkeeper.

"Why are you ordering sake by the half-cupful?" inquired the shopkeeper, giving in to his curiosity.

"Well, you know," the old man declared, "sake is much more delicious if you drink it by the half-cup instead of pouring a full one." And as he talked, the old man downed one half-cup after another.

After a while, the old man was in a perfectly fine mood, paid the bill and left. After he had left, however, the shopkeeper noticed that a purse had been left on the bar. Examining the purse, he found it contained at least a hundred taels[3] of cash.

"Well, this is a surprise," the shopkeeper said to himself. "Was that old man carrying around this much money?"

Quite impressed, his first thought was that it would be a shame to return the purse and, fortunately, there were no other customers in the shop at the time. In the next second, he put the purse into the pocket of his kimono as though nothing had happened.

Just then, the old man came bounding back into the shop, his face as pale as a ghost's.

"Didn't I leave my purse here?" he asked nervously.

"No, there's nothing here," the shopkeeper replied with an innocent air.

"That can't be!" the old man stammered. He had completely sobered up and was ready to cry. "I'm sure I put it down right here. I beg

---

[3] A unit of weight in East Asia. In this case, probably a Japanese unit of money equal in value to a tael of silver.

of you, please give it back to me!"

But the shopkeeper insisted that he knew nothing about it, and in the end threw the old man out through the front door. Still, the old man put his palms together in supplication and implored the man.

"Listen, that's money I received for selling my only daughter," he pleaded. "Without that money, I'll die. Please, please, give it back!"

"Hunh!" the shopkeeper snorted. "I don't like being accused like that. I haven't seen your purse, I tell you!" And with that, he shut the shop door and locked it from the inside.

After banging on the door for a while, the old man seemed to have lost heart and walked away. And there in front of him, flowed the big river.

"Ahh, what a horrible man I am," he muttered. "I borrowed money just to drink sake and then had to sell my daughter just to pay my debt. And in spite of all that, the money's been taken from me. Oh, daughter, please forgive me!"

And with that, he jumped into the river and drowned.

Now, with the old man's hundred taels, the sake shopkeeper rebuilt his shop and made it into a rather splendid establishment. And thanks to that, more and more customers began to patronize the place and his business was a wonderful success.

"Well, that wasn't so good for the old man," the shopkeeper chuckled, "but it's been like a visit from the god of good fortune for me."

Feeling he was now a rich man, the shopkeeper employed a number of people and led a relaxed and easy life. And after a while, his wife became pregnant.

"My shop is a success and now I'm going to blessed with a child," the shopkeeper crowed. "What a lucky man I am!"

"It will be wonderful if this baby is a boy, won't it?" his wife suggested.

"What are you saying?" the shopkeeper replied. "It doesn't make any difference whether it's a boy or a girl. Just give me a healthy baby!"

But the baby that was born was not like others. Its hair was pure white and its face just like the old man's.

"No! Can this be *my* child?" the shopkeeper's wife wailed. As soon as she saw her child's face, she lost consciousness and died.

Even though the child's face looked like the old man's, the shopkeeper considered that it was his child after all and he hired a maid to take care of it. But almost as soon as the maid came to his house, she quit.

"If it's a matter of money," the shopkeeper implored, "I'll give you whatever you want. Just help me take care of this child."

But no matter how many maids he employed, they all quit without giving any reason.

"What can be the problem here?" the man wondered in half-panic. "No matter how strange his face is, he's still just a baby."

One night during this time, the shopkeeper went into the room where his baby was sleeping. There was nothing particularly strange there. The baby was sleeping peacefully and the shopkeeper could hear its quiet breathing.

A little after midnight, however, the baby, which had been sleeping soundly, suddenly got up and started licking the oil in the night lantern. The shopkeeper was terrified and started to run out of the room, but his legs failed him and he couldn't move an inch.

"A ... a ghost!" he gasped.

As these words escaped his mouth, the baby turned around at him and grinned. Then he lifted a wrinkled hand that looked just like the old man's, and said, "Another half...."

The Ghost That Nurtured a Child

A long time ago, in a certain village, there was a sweets shop, and one night when it was very late....

"Excuse me. I beg your pardon," a voice whispered while knocking at the front door.

"Goodness," thought the shopkeeper as he opened the door. "Who could be here at such an hour?"

There stood a woman with a pale white face.

"I'm awfully sorry, but I'd like some sweets, please," the woman said in a frail voice.

"Yes, yes, of course," the shopkeeper replied. Wrapping up some sweets, he handed them to the woman who paid him what he asked and went away.

The shopkeeper thought that this was rather strange, but the woman returned the following night and bought sweets again. And the next night, and the night after that. The woman always came to the shop just about midnight.

"Where can she be coming from this late at night?" the shopkeeper wondered, and one night followed secretly behind her when she left with her sweets. The woman never looked back but walked quickly along, almost faster than what might be considered human.

The sweets shopkeeper followed behind her pell-mell, but when the woman arrived at the temple on the outskirts of the village, she suddenly stopped. And in that instant, she disappeared.

"Now this is strange. Where could she have gone?" the shopkeeper marveled as he looked around curiously.

Suddenly, he could hear the faint sounds of a baby crying, and they seemed to be coming from a grave. Running over to the temple, he woke up the priest and the two of them returned to the grave to try and solve the matter. Indeed, the cries seemed to be coming from a freshly dug grave right before their eyes.

"This is the grave of Matsukichi's wife, who died just recently," the priest informed the shopkeeper.

"Well, let's dig it up and investigate," returned the shopkeeper, and the two of them brought hoes and got to work.

Suddenly, they both gasped at the same time. For next to the dead woman sat a fat little baby.

"This is the woman who bought the sweets," the shopkeeper said in wonder.

"So that's it," the priest replied. "This woman died when she was pregnant. She gave birth to the child in the grave and has been nurturing him with sweets ever since."

The priest picked up the child and intoned a sutra for the woman. And from that time, she never appeared at the sweets shop again.

It is said that when the child grew up, he became a well-respected priest.

People Who Were Spared

The Snow Woman

A long time ago, in the ancient province of Musashi, there were two woodcutters, Mosaku and Minokichi. Mosaku was somewhat elderly but Minokichi was still a very young man.

One cold night, the two men were returning from their work. When they arrived at the ferry crossing, a heavy snowstorm started to blow. The small ferry boat was tied up on the opposite bank but they could see neither hide nor hair of the ferryman.

"This is bad," shouted Mosaku through the swirling snow. "We'll never be able to get home like this."

"The ferryman's probably gone home because of the blizzard," Minokichi concluded.

There was nothing else they could do but to go inside the ferryman's hut. There was no place to light a fire in the small hut, nor were there any windows. Covering themselves with their straw raincoats, they lay down to sleep but the cold was almost too much to bear.

After a short while, Mosaku fell fast asleep. But young Minokichi was wide awake, listening to the sound of the wind as it swirled violently around the hut, which shook with each gust as though in an earthquake.

It was difficult to tell how much time had passed, but Minokichi suddenly felt something cold on his head and opened his eyes. The door of the hut, which they had tightly fastened, had somehow opened and was now banging in the wind. Then, something white seemed to hover over Mosaku as he lay sleeping.

Doing his best to see by the light of the snow, Minokichi could make out a woman dressed in a pure white kimono. The woman breathed what looked like white smoke over Mosaku's head.

It was all Minokichi could do to keep from shouting in terror.

The woman now approached Minokichi, squatted down next to his pillow and peered at his face for a long time. The woman was quite beautiful but there was something frightening about the way she looked at him. Then she smiled.

"I thought I would do the same thing to you as I did to your companion," she whispered, "but it seems a shame, so I'll let you go. But you must never tell anyone what you've seen tonight. If you do, I'll have to kill you."

The woman's expression suddenly became quite frightening, but then she turned and left the hut. Minokichi leapt up but the woman was nowhere to be seen.

"This must have been a dream," he thought to himself, and closing the door tightly again looked over at Mosaku.

The old man somehow looked a little strange, and when Minokichi shook him gently there was no response. He then put his hand on Mosaku's forehead, but with a gasp drew it back immediately.

Mosaku's entire body was as cold as ice.

The next morning when the snowstorm had abated, the ferryman returned to his hut and found the two men collapsed on the floor.

"Hey, pull yourself together!" he half-shouted at Minokichi, slapping him lightly on the cheeks until he opened his eyes.

"I'm alive!" the young man mumbled.

The ferryman helped Minokichi over to a hibachi, but Mosaku was dead and quite still.

When Minokichi returned to his village, he said nothing about what had occurred the night before. Even when his own mother asked questions about what had happened, he remained silent. But finally he regained his health and was ready to go out to the mountains once again.

One night the following winter, Minokichi was on his way home when he encountered a woman traveling to some destination or another. She was a young woman, tall and slender, and very pretty. As they walked along together, they talked about various things and very soon became good friends.

"If you'd like," Minokichi offered, "you could stay over at my house tonight. There's no one else there but my mother." And so saying, accompanied the young woman to his house.

The young lady's name was O-yuki,[1] and she was not only pretty but had a very gentle nature. Minokichi's mother was also completely captivated by their guest, and so asked her to stay the following night as well.

After spending a number of days together, the two young people found it hard to even think about parting. And so it was arranged that

---

[1] *Yuki* (雪) is "snow" in Japanese.

they would get married and live as husband and wife. Minokichi's mother, of course, gave her hearty approval.

"My son has found a wonderful wife," the old lady exclaimed, and from then on let O-yuki take charge of all the household affairs.

At length, one child after another was born and Minokichi found himself the father of five children. Surrounded by cute grandchildren and a gentle daughter-in-law, Minokichi's mother felt that she could now die in peace, and when her fifth grandchild was born, she passed away as though she was just going to sleep.

After that, even more children were born, until there were ten of them. Each child had beautiful pale skin and an attractive face.

The women of the village, however, looked upon O-yuki with envy.

"O-yuki never seems to get older," one of them complained. "She still looks like a young woman."

"That's true," said another. "Even though she never stops working the entire day. That's strange, isn't it?"

But when he heard these things, Minokichi was all the happier.

"Ahh," he thought, "I'm a very lucky man."

One night, however, when the children were asleep, Minokichi was drinking some sake as his wife did needlework next to a paper lantern.

"Sometimes when I look at you," he began, "I think about that night. That woman was a beautiful young lady, exactly like you.

O-yuki suddenly stopped and put down her needlework.

"Really," she said, seemingly without emotion, "where did you meet her?"

"Well, you know...," Minokichi continued, with a faraway look in his eye, and he related the entire story about what had occurred when he was a young man at the ferryman's hut that night. "But that woman was not human. She may actually have been a snow woman."

With these last words, O-yuki threw down the kimono she had been sewing and turned to Minokichi.

"How dare you break your promise!" she demanded. "That snow woman was me! Didn't I tell you that I'd kill you if you told anyone about me?" She crouched down over the reclining Minokichi.

"It ... it was you...," he stammered, turning pale. For she was undeniably the woman of that time long ago.

"If it weren't for the children, I'd kill you right now," she hissed. "But thinking of them, I just can't. You had better take good care of them though. If I ever hear that you've mistreated them, I'll finish you off on the spot!"

With that, O-yuki seemed to grow smaller and smaller, until at last she was nothing but white snow, drifting out of the window. And never once did she appear again.

⤳

The Woman-Oil Press

A long, long time ago there was a housewife living in a certain village who one day went out alone on an errand but was quite late returning home. As she approached the path over the mountain, it was already beginning to grow dark. She thought about how her children would be getting hungry and hurried up the mountain. Suddenly, a man rushed out of a thicket by the side of the road and stood in front of the woman with his hands spread out wide.

"Please!" she cried as she threw down her purse and folded her hands in supplication. "If it's money you want, I'll give you everything I have. Just please spare my life."

"I don't need money," the man replied, shaking his head. "I want you as my wife!"

"That … that's impossible," the housewife stammered. "I already have a husband and children, too."

The man grabbed the unwilling woman and dragged her deep into the mountains to a mansion that looked like a lord's. Although he indeed cast her into the house, he did not treat her in a particularly rough way.

"All you have to do is stay here," he instructed. "You don't have to *do* anything else. I'll have good meals brought to you every day, but in return you must agree never to go outside."

And with this, the man left her alone.

The housewife heaved a sigh of relief and looked around the room. As far as she could determine, it was a rather fine place, and in fact her own house could not compare to it at all. And just as the man had said, she had to do no work at all. Her only job, it seemed, was to just eat good meals every day.

After a while, the housewife forgot about her own home and simply lived a life of leisure. In the twinkling of an eye, the years passed. As time went on, the woman became quite plump and her face grew glossy and bright. Nevertheless, she grew unbearably bored just staying in the mansion all day.

One day, after the man had gone out, she secretly went outside herself. After walking a little way, she came across another fine mansion, just like the one she was living in. Wondering what kind of lord would be living in *this* place, she crept up to the mansion and peeped inside.

She was just barely able to stifle a scream.

Inside the room there were a number of women hanging upside down from the ceiling. One woman, whose long hair reached the floor, looked at the housewife in despair.

"We were all fed good meals," she said choking back her tears, "but when we became fat we were hung upside down like this and our fat is pressed from us just like oil."

Blood instantly rushed to the housewife's face.

"He'll soon do the same to you," the woman continued, "Get out of here fast before he comes back!"

And with these words, the woman began twisting her body back and forth as though in great pain. Although they were all strung together, the other women, too, wriggled about like suspended snakes.

When she witnessed this, the housewife could not just stand there any longer.

Leaping outside in confusion, she ran blindly through the mountains. But her luck ran out, and halfway home the day came to an end. She had no idea what to do, but knew that if she dallied at all, the man would surely catch her.

Suddenly, she saw a faint light in the distance and ran in its direction as if in a trance. At length, there in front of her stood a broken-down hut. Inside sat a white-haired old lady.

"Please," the housewife cried, telling the old lady everything that had befallen her. "Please help me!"

"I can't," the old lady replied, her words dropping from her wrinkled mouth like tiny drops of water.

"But, why? Why?" the housewife pleaded.

"That man and I work together," the old lady retorted. "I keep a lookout so that you women can't escape."

With a scream, the housewife ran outside to escape, but the night had already turned pitch black. To become lost on the road now would mean certain death. Coming back inside the hut, she placed her hands and head on the floor beseechingly and pleaded fervently once more.

"Well, well, if you're going that far, I guess it can't be helped," the old lady cackled, suddenly feeling sorry for her visitor. "Quick! Hide up in the rafters!"

The old lady had the housewife climb up into the ceiling rafters, and just at that moment the man burst open the door to the hut.

"Old lady!" he demanded. "Did a woman come by here trying to escape?"

"No, no one's come here," came the reply.

"That's strange," the man continued as he looked around the house in an annoying manner. "I've given her plenty of food up until now, and thought I'd put her in the press very soon. Old lady, are you telling the truth?"

"You're just one more tedious man, aren't you," the old lady angrily returned. "If you don't believe me, you'll just have to look around the house."

The man came all the way into the house and looked around carefully. Finally, he gave up in disgust.

"If a woman does come by here, inform me right away," he yelled as a parting shot.

"Thanks to you, my life has been spared," the housewife sighed after the man was gone. "I'll never forget this as long as I live."

The next morning, the housewife bowed deeply to the old lady and returned home. When she arrived, however, she found that her family thought that she had died long ago and were finally conducting a funeral for her.

"No! Can this be true?" her husband cried happily.

"We knew Mommy was still alive," the children screamed.

Not only were her husband and children overjoyed, but even the neighbors came running in an uproar.

"Hey, stop bothering me," she said irritably as she woke up to her husband and children tapping her gently.

She had overslept.

"What? Was that all a dream?" she sighed sheepishly, feeling relieved at last.

The Ghost in the Castle Keep

In Hyogo Prefecture there is a beautiful fortification called the White Heron Castle, located in the city of Himeji. Long ago, it was said there was a woman's ghost in the castle keep so that even during the day no one climbed up to the place. The keep, by the way, is the castle's highest open room, from which enemy activity and the like might be watched.

One rainy autumn night, the samurai who were making the rounds of the castle were talking about this ghost. Among them was Morita Zusho, who was really still a child.

"Tonight I'll confirm the real form of this ghost for you," the boy declared and started the climb up to the keep.

Holding a paper lantern in one hand, he climbed the first flight of stairs and then the next. Holding the lantern high above his head, he looked around the floor but found nothing particularly unusual. He then passed the fourth and fifth floors and finally reached the entrance to the room at the very top of the castle. The place was completely silent and even the plucky Zusho began to feel uneasy. He thought that perhaps he should return now, but he *had* climbed this far.

Bracing himself, he opened the door before him and a dim light leaked out from inside. Zusho gasped and stopped dead in his tracks.

In the center of the room was a single low table, and next to it a light was wavering as though in a breeze. It seemed as though someone was sitting there.

"Who is it?" a sharp voice shot out.

"My … my name is Morita Zusho," the young samurai said, sitting down at the entrance to the room, touching both hands to the floor and bowing his head.

"What are you doing here?" the voice demanded.

"Well," Zusho stammered, "I thought I would come and confirm the true form of the ghost that lives in this room."

Zusho was shaking but he told the truth.

"All right. Come in," the voice continued, as Zusho nervously entered the room. "You'd better come a little closer."

With his head still lowered, Zusho approached the low table, crawling on all fours as he came. Looking up, he found that the voice came from a woman dressed in a beautiful kimono. The woman had long hair and a nearly transparent pale complexion, and was startlingly beautiful.

"My name is Osakabe-hime," said the woman in a direct but not unkind voice. "And I am the *nushi* of this castle. You are a brave samurai to have come here, so I'm giving this to you as proof that you did so."

So saying, the woman gave him a broken-off piece of a helmet.

"Thank you very much," murmured Zusho, and putting the piece in the pocket of his robe left the room, grateful to have been spared.

Giving a sigh of relief, he started down the stairs. But he somehow sensed that someone was following him and turned around.

Zusho gulped in spite of himself. The stairs were filled with specters. And just as they fell to hideous laughter, the light in his hand blew out.

The place was pitch black and he was at a complete loss.

Thinking that there was nothing else he could do but to ask for help from Osakabe-hime, he fought his fear, once again climbed the steps and stood before the door.

"Why have you come back?" the sharp voice demanded.

"Yes, well," Zusho began hesitantly. "My light was blown out by some specters on the stairs and I came to ask you to light my lamp again."

"You are truly a brave man," the voice replied. "You did well by coming back here and not running away. All right, then, I'll relight your lamp."

The woman asked Zusho to enter the room again, took a flame from the lamp next to her low table and lit Zusho's paper lantern once more.

"Everything will be all right now," the woman said softly, but then added severely, "Do not come back here again."

Zusho took the lamp in his hand and descended the stairs. This time his return was uneventful and he finally arrived at the place where his companions were waiting.

"Hey, are you all right?" asked one of the men.

"And what about the ghost's real form?" inquired another as they all surrounded Zusho with shocked faces.

"The true form of the ghost is that of a princess," explained Zusho and showed them the piece of the helmet as he told his story.

The samurai were thoroughly impressed with what they heard and praised him for his courage and nerve. And on the following day, the story reached the ears of the castle's lord, who immediately called Zusho to his presence.

Zusho then explained to the lord all that had happened to him the night before, leaving nothing out.

"That was quite a feat climbing up alone to a place where no one else will go," the lord declared.

Praising Zusho for his courage, the lord held the broken-off piece of helmet that the young samurai had received from the princess. Suddenly, he seemed to remember something.

"I feel like I've seen this before," the lord exclaimed, and he ordered one of the samurai on duty to go to the castle warehouse and bring back a helmet. At a glance, he could see that the helmet had a piece broken off from its lower part.

"That's right! This is it!" the lord said happily, fitting the piece that Zusho had brought to the part of the helmet that was missing.

"To rip off a piece from this helmet would require great strength," he continued. "There's no mistake, the princess is certainly the *nushi* of this castle!"

Having said that, the lord climbed alone up to the keep himself. And there, just as Zusho had said, sat Osakabe-hime.

From that time on, it is said that the lord of this castle must climb to the keep once every year to formally greet the princess. Even today, the true lord of the White Heron Castle is said to be none other than Osakabe-hime herself.

⌒⊃

The Earthen Buddha Kannon

In the ancient province of Echizen, in the village of Tsuboe, is a small Buddhist temple called the Routakuji. In this temple a charming statue of Kannon, called the Earthen Buddha Kannon, is worshipped. Long ago, the priest at this temple had studied Buddhism assiduously in the capital of Kyoto.

One day, the priest was making his rounds in the village when he encountered eighteen[2] children who had gotten together to relieve their bladders in the dirt, and then to make mud pies.

"My goodness!" he scolded the children. "This is a messy business you're up to."

But then, looking carefully, he saw that they had fashioned twenty-three[3] tiny statues of Kannon. They had done quite a skillful job and the priest promptly wished he had one for himself.

"Say, now," the priest went on, "would you give one of those statues to me?" And the children gave him the best one.

The priest thanked them politely with a deep bow, but when he raised his head every one of the children and the remaining statues of Kannon disappeared like smoke.

"This statue is undoubtedly a gift from the Buddha," the priest thought to himself and carried it carefully with him wherever he went from then on.

---

[2] According to Soothill, there are eighteen different characteristics of a Buddha. There are also eighteen Japanese Buddhist sects and eighteen things a Buddhist monk should carry in the performance of his duties. Then there are the eighteen *dhatu*, or realms of sense; the eighteen layers of Hell; and the eighteen Ways a Shingon disciple meditates upon daily. The Fukukensaku Kannon particular to the Kegon and Tendai sects is sometimes depicted with eighteen arms. The reader may take his or her pick.

[3] When the priest takes his one statue, there will be twenty-two left. Does this signify the twenty-two processes in the perfect development of a Buddha?

Now a year or so later, the priest was on a journey and lost his way deep in the mountains. No matter how long he walked, he could not find his way out and eventually the sun went down.

"I'm in a fix now," he mumbled. "Surely there must be a woodcutter's hut somewhere around here."

The priest walked this way and that and finally came across a small broken-down hut.

"I've lost my way and am in difficulty," he announced at the door of the hut. "Would you please let me stay the night?"

Out from the hut came a scraggily bearded man and his wife.

"That's a shame!" the man replied. "Yes, please stay here and don't give a thought to it."

The couple welcomed the priest into their hut and even gave him a fine meal. For his part, the priest was so tired that after finishing his meal he fell asleep and soon began to snore. Seeing this, the man laughed with an evil grin.

"This is perfect," he cackled. "He's sound asleep so we can kill him right now."

"It's true," his wife smiled happily. "We haven't caught one like this for a long time."

The fact was that the two of them were a husband and wife team of frightening mountain bandits who would kill travelers lost in the mountains and take their money and clothes.

The man unsheathed his sword and neatly cut off the head of the sleeping priest, who died without making a sound. The couple looked at each other and smiled, nodding their heads in silent agreement.

"It will be all right to leave him like this," the man told his wife. "We'll take care of everything else in the morning. Let's go to bed." And he and his wife pushed the priest's body off the front step and went to sleep without further ado.

The next morning, however, the two were still sleeping when a voice intoning a sutra arose nearby.

"Hunh?" the man grunted as they suddenly woke up. For there, the priest who had supposedly been killed the night before was sitting right in front of them.

"A ... a ghost!" the wife screamed, turning pale and falling on top of her husband. The man grabbed his sword.

"Listen, ghost!" he shouted. "You may be a priest but you're a bad loser. Now go straight to Hell!"

Whereupon the priest gave a hearty laugh.

"You must be still half-asleep," he smiled. "Listen, I may be a priest but it's not polite to call me a ghost."

"But I'm sure that I cut off your head last night," the man interrupted.

"What foolishness!" the priest said flatly. "Aren't I right here in front of you and quite alive?"

The couple could still not believe what they saw and simply shook their heads, and after a while the priest began to feel a little uneasy himself.

"If the man says he cut off my head, why am I still here alive?" he wondered. "Perhaps I was saved by Kannon."

The priest took out the statue of Kannon from his robe and found that there was a mark from a sword on the nape of its neck. Indeed, the head of the statue was at the point of falling off.

"That's it!" the priest reasoned. "Kannon was merciful enough to put her own body in place of mine."

The priest placed the statue of Kannon in front of the husband and wife bandits.

"You are terrible people," he said calmly. "If I ask Kannon, she'll cut off your heads for me."

"Wait ... please wait!" the man stuttered, shaking from head to toe. "We'll never do anything evil again. Just please spare our lives!"

"All right," the priest replied sternly. "If you'll do what you've said, I'll forgive you. But from now on, you must become a monk and a nun yourselves and repeat the *nembutsu* for those you have killed."

The two of them thereupon shaved their heads, became disciples of the priest and served the Buddha from that day to the end of their lives.

The Son Who Came Back

A long time ago, a rich man's son became ill and passed away. The funeral service was over, the body had been laid to rest and everyone was about to return home. Suddenly, a groan was heard coming from the grave. Everyone was shocked to say the least, and when they removed the dirt as fast as they could, sure enough, there was the man's son, supposedly dead but quite alive.

"You've come back to life!" his parents yelled, almost out of their minds with joy. And they quickly returned home with their son.

Strangely enough, however, the son did not recognize his own house. In fact, quite to the contrary.

"This isn't my house," he complained. "Please take me home."

"You've just returned to life," his father tried to explain, "and I'm sure you're still a little confused. When you calm down, you'll see. Look, here's your old room."

His parents did their best to soothe him but he still turned a blank face to everything. Finally, they sat down and listened to what he tried to tell them, and found that he claimed to be the son of a family in the neighboring village. Just to make sure, they visited the other family and were informed that the son of that family, too, had died on the same day as their own and had been cremated.

"Well then," the father in the neighboring village said, "let me meet your son and take a look."

But when he encountered the young man, he simply shook his head.

"No, of course it's not him," he said sadly. "He doesn't look at all like our son."

Yet, when the young man saw *him*, he reacted with apparent fondness.

"Father!" he shouted happily.

"I don't know you at all," the man said.

"No, don't say that!" the young man pleaded with tears in his eyes. "You *are* my father! Please take me home right now!"

"Ahh, this is too sad," sighed the father who had just thought that his son had returned to life. "Why is he calling another man his father?" Both he and his wife could hardly bear their pain.

"All right," the man from the neighboring village finally agreed. "If you are really my son, tell me my family name and describe our house."

"Of course. That will be easy," the young man eagerly replied. And he quickly stated everything from his mother's name to details about the family business.

So now there was no doubt. He had described everything as it was, as only their real son would have been able to do. Now both families sat in a daze, thinking that the situation was completely inexplicable. Finally, the young man spoke up.

"When I died," he began, "I came back to life but my body had already been committed to the flames and I had no place to go. Circumstances were, however, that the son from this family had also passed away and had been buried without being cremated. Thus I was able to borrow his body and return to life. So while my body is that of this family's son, my soul is that of the other's."

At this point, both families got together and discussed the matter and it was agreed that the young man should go with the father he claimed as his own.

"That my son would borrow your own son's body to come back to life is unthinkable," the man from the neighboring village declared. "I hope you'll forgive him."

Still, he was overjoyed as he led the young man home.

After these events, the two families treated each other as relatives, but only two years later the young man died again, never to return.

⌒つ

The Ghost's Bowl

About three hundred years ago, there were three friends who lived in a place called Ushigome, which was within the city of Edo.

One day, the three set off to climb Mount Tateyama in the ancient province of Etchu. Within the precincts of this mountain, the Amida Buddha is worshipped as its avatar, and it is said that if you pray here to meet with a deceased loved one, that person's ghost will appear as a sort of shade.

On their way home after worshiping the avatar, the three friends sat down on a large rock at the side of the road to rest. The day was coming to an end and they were so hungry they could barely go on. Just then, they saw a man passing by with a bowl piled high with rice. Immediately, their mouths began to water.

When the man reached the place where the three men sat, he respectfully offered the bowl to them.

"You must be famished," he said reverently. "Please take this and don't give it a thought."

The three were overjoyed and with great thanks took the bowl and ate as though in a trance. Having dispatched their meal in what seemed like no time at all, they were about to return the bowl to the man when they realized he was no longer there.

"That's strange," one of them remarked.

"Do you think he might have been a ghost?" another asked.

All three of the men suddenly felt panic-stricken. Setting off quickly, they nervously walked throughout the night until arriving at a village at the foot of the mountain. Sitting down at a tea shop, they discussed the events of the night before, while the villagers gathered around them.

When the villagers heard the men's story, they turned pale.

"This is quite serious," one of them said worriedly. "Would you show me the bowl, please?"

The three men took out the bowl and placed it before the man.

"This bowl belongs to the daughter of the man who lives in the house opposite mine," he said in a low voice. "And his daughter has just passed away."

The three gasped and stood up involuntarily.

"At any rate, we should go to the girl's house and show them the bowl," the villager concluded.

The villagers accompanied the three shaken men to the girl's home and explained the story they had heard to her father. At this, both he and his wife broke down and cried.

"We were lucky enough to have both a son and a daughter," the man began, "but both of them have passed away. We put this bowl filled with rice on our daughter's grave as an offering, but it seems certain that the ghost of our son took it and gave it away to hungry travelers. He was such a good-hearted child. Now what's happened

Apparitions and Water

The Ghost Ship

Late on the last night of the year, a boat laden with goods for the New Year's celebrations was passing through the Inland Sea. It was a starless night and the wind was cold enough to cut through one like a knife.

"What's going to happen if the Ghost Ship finds us?" one of the sailors asked in a worried voice.

"Don't be nervous," his companion replied. "we're almost at port."

The sailors gathered together on the deck of the ship and talked it over. Since long ago, it was said that if a ship set sail on New Year's Eve, the Ghost Ship would be sure to appear. When it did, the ghosts of all the sailors who had died at sea would sink the ship under sail.

"Look, it's raining," someone said.

"Hunh, just when we're so close to port," complained another.

Everyone looked at the sky with anxious expressions. The sails, which had been full of wind a moment ago, now hung limply as though completely deflated. And at that moment, the ship stopped dead in the water.

"This is strange," a sailor remarked. "We've had such a strong wind."

Indeed, it felt as though they had been bewitched by foxes.

"We've no other choice," yelled the captain. "Every man to the oars!"

Everyone put their backs into it and rowed for all they were worth. The ship, however, did not move. At that moment, something like a white cloud seemed to float up ahead of them.

"It's the Ghost Ship!" several of the men yelled and let their hands drop from the oars.

The white thing gradually got bigger and bigger and quickly assumed a fearsome shape. A huge pale white face appeared, with long hair hanging down, half covering it in the still air.

"Give me a ladle!" a voice filled with malice boomed from the Ghost Ship.

Now, if a ladle was thrown to the ship in the fear of the moment, the situation would become even more perilous. The ladle itself would turn into hundreds of scoops, white arms would come out of the sea to grab hold of them and each arm would pour water into the ship without stopping. Thus, the ship would become quickly flooded and sink.

How many had been sent to the bottom of the sea in this way?

"No one is to give it a ladle!" the captain strictly ordered.

But no matter how a sailor tried to control himself at such a moment, there must have been many who gave in to the frightening voice threatening them from the Ghost Ship.

"Give me a ladle!" screamed the voice again and again, as the gunwale of the ship was breached. Everyone turned pale, feeling more dead than alive.

"Get out of here at once!" the captain yelled forcefully, striking the Ghost Ship with his oar.

But something in the Ghost Ship grabbed his oar and started to pull the captain into the sea. Even the captain, as strong as he was, was no match for this.

"Damn!" the captain grunted, and unable to hold on any longer, let go of his oar.

But at that point, however, the captain remembered an old story that the Ghost Ship cannot stand flames.

"Someone bring a fire!" he yelled.

One of the sailors immediately brought up some ignited firewood, aimed carefully at the Ghost Ship and threw it as hard as he could. The front of the ship was illuminated brightly as the sparks fell here and there. And in that instant, the Ghost Ship disappeared.

The sails of the ship then quickly filled and the ship sailed on.

"We've been saved!" the men shouted in spite of themselves, grasping each other's hands tightly.

The sailors of long ago prepared themselves for sea voyages by storing ladles with the bottoms knocked out. This, no doubt, was so that even if a ladle was thrown to the Ghost Ship, no water could be scooped up to sink their ships.

The Wet Woman and the Bull Demon

A long time ago, in the ancient province of Iwami, there lived a man by the name of Moriyama Genzo. Genzo loved to fish, and whenever he had a bit of spare time, he would pack his fishing gear and head off to the sea.

One summer evening, Genzo gathered his fishing equipment and went to do some night fishing. For some reason, it was a day when the fish were biting one after the other, and in no time at all his fish basket was full.

"If they're biting like this," Genzo chuckled to himself, "I should bring a bigger basket." And he swung his fishing pole back and forth as if in a dream.

Suddenly, he had the feeling that someone was standing behind him. He turned around with a jerk, but no one was there.

"I must be mistaken," he thought and turned back round.

With a gasp, he nearly fell back in shock. There, in the ocean right before his very eyes stood a woman in dripping wet clothes holding a small child. Genzo tried to flee but was rooted to the spot in fear.

The woman approached Genzo as though walking on top of the waves.

"This child is hungry," she said with a voice so cold it chilled Genzo to the bone. "Would you give me just one fish?"

"Of … of course," Genzo stammered, "As many as you like." And with trembling hands, he grabbed a fish and gave it to the woman.

The woman gave a thin laugh and handed the fish to the child who gobbled the still-living fish down from its head to its tail.

"I'm sorry to ask," she then said, "but one more, please."

Genzo nervously handed the woman another fish.

Smacking its lips, the child opened up its crimson mouth, and in less time than it takes to tell, gobbled the fish whole. This was so unnerving that Genzo thought he might lose his mind.

"Excuse me," the woman now asked, "would you mind holding this child for a moment?" And she thrust the child at Genzo.

Genzo began to beseech the gods in a stuttering voice, but stood there shaking, holding the child.

"Well then, please take good care of him," were the woman's parting words, and she suddenly disappeared into the waves.

Genzo shuddered and was about to toss the baby aside, but it held fast to him and was not about to let go. Unable to think, he took off running with the child in his arms, as though in a trance. Leaving the rocky jetty, he came out onto the path that ran along the shore. Behind him he heard the sound of approaching hoofs.

"Oh, no!" he thought. "It's the Bull Demon!"

Genzo was at a loss as to what to do. The Bull Demon was said to be an apparition with the head of a bull and was quick to appear after the Wet Woman.

"Som … somebody, help!" Genzo yelled, and stumbled as he ran, but the Bull Demon was coming after him with full force.

At this moment, Genzo's wife was alone at their house, and strangely enough, his sword began rattling by itself where it had been placed in the alcove.

"Something's wrong with my husband," she thought anxiously, but had no idea what to do.

Opening the front door, she was about to go outside when the sword somehow unsheathed itself and shot out like an arrow. Soaring quickly up in the sky, it just as quickly descended in a straight line down toward the seashore.

Without thinking, Genzo's wife put her hands together in supplication and prayed that her husband might be delivered from harm. At that moment, Genzo was about to be run down by the Bull Demon and gored by its horns.

"Ahh, this is the end!" he gasped and stopped running.

Suddenly, there was a horrific scream behind him. At the same time, the baby fell from his chest. Frightened out of his wits, Genzo turned around to see that his sword had pierced the Bull Demon's neck and blood was spurting everywhere.

"Now's my chance," Genzo thought, and pushed the sword down with all his might for the *coup de grace*. He then ran back to his house as quickly as he could.

The next morning, Genzo went down to the seashore with a number of men from his village, and though blood stains were everywhere, the Bull Demon was gone. And to this day, neither the Wet Woman nor the Bull Demon have returned to this shore.

The Old Man Who Stroked Faces

Long ago, there was a large, isolated mansion on the outskirts of the capital. The owner had been a man of high rank, but after he died the place took on a lonely aspect and looked like a haunted house. Now, only one man lived alone in the mansion.

One summer night, the man was sleeping out on the veranda when something cold touched his face. He opened his eyes with a start, and there before him stood a wrinkled old man only about three feet in height. The man was taken by surprise and tried to jump up, but as frightened as he was, he could not move. He pretended to be asleep but looked out through half-closed eyes to see the old man suddenly jump into the garden. Just as the old man seemed to be approaching the pond, he disappeared altogether.

"This must be some apparition that lives in the pond," the man thought to himself, and summoning up his courage went over to the water's edge. Weeds grew thick over the muddy water and the place somehow gave off an uneasy feeling. Nevertheless, the man took a piece of broken pole and poked around in the mud. But there was nothing there that was out of the ordinary.

The next night, however, and the one after that, the old man came again, and with a cold hand softly stroked the man's face. The man became increasingly frightened and fled the mansion.

Hearing this story, a robust young man declared that he would catch this loathsome fellow who liked to stroke people's faces. Taking along a straw rope, he waited impatiently for the old man to appear. His plan, of course, was to tie the old man up and take him away the second he appeared.

But the old fellow didn't show up and the young man got sleepy, and soon began to doze on the veranda.

A little after midnight, something chilly touched the young man's face.

The young man woke with a start and jumped up. The old man tried to run away, but was quickly caught and tied with the straw rope. After that, the young man tied him to a tree and called in his companions.

When they lit a lamp and looked carefully, they could see that the old man, who was wearing a light gold colored robe, seemed about to cry.

"What are you?" one of the men demanded.

"And why do you stroke people's faces?" another asked angrily.

Everyone shot questions at the old man, but he gave no answers at all, only looked around restlessly with moist eyes.

"If you don't answer, we'll take your life," the young man threatened as he unsheathed his sword.

At this the old man spoke.

"Would you please put some water in the bucket?" he squeaked, with a voice like a mosquito's.

One of the young man's companions filled a bucket with water and brought it to where the old man stood, tightly tied up with the straw rope.

"What are you going to do with that?" someone asked.

As they looked on, the old man extended his neck and gazed into the bucket, his face reflected in the water.

"I am the spirit of the water," the old man said in his tiny thin voice, and with that he leapt into the bucket. Instantly, he was nowhere to be seen, and the limp straw rope was left floating on the surface of the water. He had completely dissolved.

After this, the old man never appeared at the mansion again.

The Wrath of the Giant Abalone

A long time ago, in the ancient province of Kazusa, there lived a young *ama* in the village of Namihana. *Ama*, by the way, are women who dive down into the sea to bring up seaweed and shellfish.

Now, off the coast of this village there was a giant abalone as big as an opened umbrella, and it was said that if anyone even tossed a stone near to where it was, a huge storm would blow up immediately. The people of the village were all terribly frightened of this abalone and no one dared dive close to it.

The young *ama*, however, inadvertently angered the giant abalone somehow and the sea became rough and the rain fell in torrents. The fishermen who had gone out to work now nervously returned to shore and pulled their boats up out of the water at the port.

"And the weather was so good until now," one of the fishermen complained.

"Someone must have disturbed the giant abalone," another added.

The fishermen gathered in a small hut by the seashore and decided to wait out the storm. They were soon joined by a number of *ama*.

"There's nothing we can do," one of them concluded. "We'll just stop work for today and take it easy."

So everyone forgot about work and spent the day talking together and singing. During this time, the young *ama* and a young man became enamored with each other.

The next day, the storm abated and she went out to work, but she could not forget the young man. Although she always brought up a great number of shellfish, that day she brought up very few.

"What's the matter with her?" one of her companions asked.

"Maybe she's not feeling well," another suggested.

The women were all worried, but when they approached the young *ama* about their concerns, she had nothing to say.

The following morning, the young *ama* rowed out in a boat to the place where the giant abalone lay on the bottom of the sea. She then threw a stone into the water and hurriedly returned to shore. The sky, which had been absolutely clear, turned dark, huge waves rose up and a storm immediately blew up.

"Ahh!" one of the fishermen lamented. "A storm again?"

"We can't go on doing nothing every day," one of the *ama* said sadly.

As the fishermen and *ama* grumbled, they looked discontentedly out to sea from their houses.

"I'm sure that man is here," the young *ama* said to herself as she stood in front of the small hut.

Just as she thought, the young man, who wanted to see her as well, was standing there, too. Their eyes met and the two simultaneously ran to hold each other in a tight embrace.

"If I can't be with you, I'll go crazy," the young man declared.

"Me, too," the *ama* whispered.

From that time on, whenever the young *ama* wanted to meet her lover, she would row out to where the giant abalone lay on the bottom of the sea and throw in a stone. But in the end, she started wanting to see the young man every day, and one morning threw in a great number of stones at one time. If the storm continued for days, she thought, the men would be unable to go to work.

The young man, however, had gone out fishing the night before. Suddenly, a storm arose, the likes of which he had never seen before. The young man tried to return to shore, but the waves were too high and he was unable to get close. Desperately, he rowed his boat, but it shook like a leaf on a tree and at any moment seemed ready to capsize.

At that moment, the young *ama* realized that her lover was still out in the middle of the sea.

"I've done it now," she thought, and faced the sea with hands together in prayer. "Please, Giant Abalone, let the sea be calm again!"

But there was nothing to be done. The giant abalone had been angered beyond supplication, the sea raged horribly and the young man and his boat were swallowed up.

The young *ama* became crazy with worry and, as if in a dream, leapt into the sea. Washed by the waves and beaten by the rain, she swam farther and farther out. But no matter how good a swimmer she was, she was no match for a storm like this, and by the time she reached the young man's side, she had no strength left. The two embraced in the waves and sank to the bottom of the sea.

A few days later the storm finally subsided, but the bodies of the two young lovers had been taken away by the current and were never found. Strange to say, after this event storms never arose again when fishermen came close to where the giant abalone lay deep at the bottom of the sea.

⌒ↄ

Ghost Falls

A long time ago, in the ancient province of Houki, there was a waterfall called the Ghost Falls near the village of Kurosaka. Next to this waterfall stood a small Shinto shrine, known as the Taki Daimyojin or Bright Shining God of the Waterfall. In the village, hemp was prepared for textile materials, the work being done entirely by women. After the day's work was done, the wives and young ladies of the village would gather around the hearth and talk about this and that.

One cold winter night....

"What do you think," the eldest woman asked. "Tonight let's all tell scary stories."

"That sounds interesting," commented one of the women, " but if I get too scared, I might not be able to walk home."

"If that happens to me, my husband will have to come and get me," another added.

The women were all amused by this idea and soon agreed.

"Well then, I'll be first," the eldest woman volunteered.

After her, the women each told their favorite ghost stories, but after about ten or so, no one was laughing anymore. Several of the women, in fact, were shaking visibly.

"As a show of courage," the boldest of the young ladies then said, "Let's do something even scarier."

"Not me!" one of the women squealed.

"I'm not that manly," one of the youngest whispered.

Looking around at each other, they all shrank back from the hearth.

"If someone will walk over to Ghost Falls tonight, I'll give her all the hemp I've worked on today," the bold young lady offered.

"So will I," another woman agreed.

"I'll give her mine, too," a third said.

But no one proposed to go to the falls herself. The fact was that the people of the village felt uneasy if someone even mentioned Ghost Falls in conversation, and almost no one ever approached the place, not even during the day.

Now, however, a woman by the name of O-katsu, who was the wife of a carpenter, stood up, a two-year-old baby strapped to her back.

"Listen everyone," she began, "If I go to Ghost Falls tonight, will you really give me all your hemp?"

All the women were shocked and stared at O-katsu's face.

"I'll go," she insisted, "if you'll give me your hemp."

All the women agreed but looked at O-katsu with doubtful faces.

"Listen," one woman finally asked, "how can we know for sure that O-katsu actually goes all the way to the falls?"

"Just have her bring back the offertory box from the shrine," an old lady said.

"All right!" O-katsu declared. "I'll bring it back. You'll see!" and went off with the baby still asleep on her back.

Outside, the cold was enough to cut right through you, the doors to all the houses were tightly shut, and not even a puppy passed by. O-katsu bit her lip hard and walked towards the mountains. A pale moon had appeared in the sky. After passing through the village, she was surrounded by frozen rice paddies, and with every step the frost needles crunched under her feet. After walking on the path between the rice paddies for about half an hour, she finally entered the narrow road leading to Ghost Falls. As she continued down the slope, she realized that a careless moment would send her tumbling.

O-katsu, who was generally quite stout-hearted, began to feel increasingly nervous and wondered if she shouldn't turn back. Still, her family was poor and receiving all that hemp would be helpful indeed. Grinding her teeth, she continued down the path. Fortunately, her baby remained fast asleep.

Finally, O-katsu heard the roar of the falls. The pathway abruptly widened and the spray of the falls floated like a white curtain right before her eyes. Next to the falls, the Taki Daimyojin Shrine stood silent and deserted.

O-katsu stopped dead in her tracks, took a deep breath and ran to the front of the shrine, grabbing the offertory box.

"Hey! O-katsu!" a voice suddenly rang out from the falls.

O-katsu gasped and released the box from her hands.

"Hey! O-katsu!" the voice shouted again, more threatening than before.

O-katsu stared fearfully in the direction of the falls, but no one was there. Her body was drenched in sweat.

"But I've come this far ..." O-katsu thought to herself, and grabbing the offertory box again ran as fast as she could.

She had no idea how long she had run or even how, but when her village finally appeared, she was ready to cry. Holding tightly on to the box, she nearly flew into the women's workplace.

"O-katsu!" the eldest woman shouted. "You really brought back the offertory box!"

Everyone was shocked and crowded around the breathless woman.

"Well, what about the hemp?" O-katsu asked with a tense face.

"Of, course," one of the ladies assured her. "Just as we promised.

"But really, O-katsu, you're amazing!" a young lady interjected.

Everyone was impressed with her great courage.

"But what about your baby, O-katsu?" the eldest woman asked. "He must be awfully cold. Come over here by the fire."

Putting her arm around O-katsu, the old woman led her to the hearth and had her sit down.

"My, your back is completely drenched," she continued. "Quick, take off your nursemaid's coat!"

As the old lady began to take off O-katsu's coat, her hand was covered with blood.

"Wha ... what's this?" she stuttered.

O-katsu hurriedly pulled off her coat and screamed.

She had been carrying the blood-spattered body of her headless baby all the way back from Ghost Falls.

The Woman Who Vanished into the Water

Long ago, in the ancient province of Etchu, there was a large sake shop in the town of Isurugi called the Beniya. The master of the shop was a very mild-mannered man and many of the townspeople wanted to find work at his shop.

There was also a young woman at the shop, the daughter of the master, who was reputed to be quite beautiful.

"What kind of man would it take to be that young lady's husband?" the townspeople wondered, and often talked among themselves about her.

The young lady, however, had been born with three scaly spots under her armpit, a fact that nobody knew but her mother.

One day, this young lady, accompanied by her maid, made a pleasure trip to a place called Ryugu ga fuchi, or Pool of the Dragon Palace, and after amusing herself for a short while became thirsty.

"I'm sorry to ask you this," she said to the maid, "but would you go to one of the houses in the area and ask for a little water?"

While the maid was gone, the young lady went over to the bank of the river, and just as she seemed to be staring into its depths, suddenly jumped in.

At that point, the maid returned.

"Somebody …," she yelled in panic as she ran to the side of the river, "somebody help, please!"

But nobody came to her aid and she could not swim.

She could only kneel there and cry for her "Young Miss."

In moments, the young lady's body vanished into the water.

The maid stood there, completely cast down, but at length the sun began to go down and the surface of the water turned a bluish-black.

"I can't go back home like this," she thought. "I should apologize by dying, too."

But just as she was about to jump into the river, there was a loud noise followed by a spray of water, and the huge serpent that the girl had turned into appeared.

"I am the *nushi* of these depths," it declared. "Though I was born as a human being and raised in the Beniya, when I looked into the river I suddenly realized how much I loved the water. Please give my tender regards to my mother and father, who took good care of me for so long."

And it again sank back into the water.

The maid hurried back to the house and reported all this to the master and his wife, who immediately broke down in tears.

"Now I understand that child's scales," the mother moaned.

Even today, about six miles outside of Isurugi, you can find a scenic area called Ryugu ga fuchi, or Pool of the Dragon Palace.

Shape-shifting Cats

The Cat Monster Mansion

Many years ago, a housewife and her maid lived in a certain place along with one cat. Now, the maid treated this cat with loving care but the housewife absolutely hated it, striking and kicking it if it came near her.

"Why are you feeding that cat?" the housewife complained. "Get rid of it right away."

But no matter what the housewife said, the maid gave no indication that she was going to abandon the animal.

"If you don't get rid of that cat, you're going to have to go," the housewife finally demanded.

The maid was at a loss as to what to do, but then the cat suddenly disappeared. The housewife was happy and felt a load had been taken off her mind, but the maid was despondent. She thought about the cat every day and could do nothing but cry.

One day a traveling priest came by and said that he had seen the cat at Mount Inaba on the island of Kyushu.[1] The maid immediately asked for some time off and set out for Mount Inaba. On arriving at the mountain, however, the maid had no idea where the cat might be. Although she searched here and there, the sun finally began to set.

"Excuse me," the maid asked a man who happened to be passing by at that moment, "is there a place close by where I might stay for the night?"

"If that's what you're looking for, just go a little farther into the mountain," the man replied.

As she was instructed, the maid walked father into the mountain, when she came upon a splendid mansion. As she stood wondering why a mansion would have been built in a place like this, a beautiful young woman came out of the gate.

"I've come to find my cat," the maid explained. "but I don't know my way here and am now in a bit of a fix. May I spend the night here?"

"Have you come here to be eaten, too?" the young woman laughed with a grin.

---

[1] The third largest island of Japan, across the Kanmon Straits from Yamaguchi Prefecture, the origin of this story.

The maid felt a cold chill run down her spine and was ready to run away when an old lady came out of the house.

"If the young lady has said something strange, please forgive her," the old lady cut in. "Listen, you can stay overnight here and think nothing of it."

But the maid felt horribly uneasy about the situation and couldn't stop shaking.

"Don't worry," the old lady said kindly. "Relax and rest for a while." And she spread out some bedding for the maid.

But just about midnight, the maid suddenly opened her eyes. Somebody was talking in the next room.

Thinking that it might be flesh-eating demons, the maid got up and opened the sliding paper doors a crack. What she saw, however, were two astonishingly beautiful women sound asleep.

"That's strange," she thought. "I'm certain I heard someone talking."

Opening the paper door to the next room, she found yet two more beautiful women sleeping peacefully. Standing there for a moment, she once again heard the someone talking. Listening carefully, she felt sure it was the old woman lecturing the young lady.

"That maid is a gentle-hearted lady who wants to find the cat she was caring for," the old lady began. "Under no circumstances should you fasten your teeth on her."

With that, the maid understood that she was in the mansion of a cat monster,[2] and wondered what she had got herself into. Hardly able to keep still, she packed her bag and was about to sneak out of the room when a woman came in. Looking at the woman's face, she suddenly recognized the cat she had been so attached to.

"Goodness, it's you!" the maid said aloud, forgetting her fear.

Though the woman had a human body, her head was that of a cat.

"I'm so glad you came," the woman said softly. "But I can never go back to your place. I've become old and have decided to end my days here with my companions."

---

[2] Literally *nekomata* (猫又). In southwestern Japan, there was/is a belief that when cats get old their tails divide into two parts and they are able to bewitch people, often doing them harm. In the 89th chapter of the *Tsurezuregusa*, Yoshida Kenko (1283–1350) writes, "Deep in the mountains, there is something called a *nekomata*, which eats people.

"Please don't say that," the maid pleaded, stroking the cat's face. "Just come back with me. When you're gone, I'm so lonesome I don't know what to do. I'll find work somewhere else."

"I'll never forget what you've done for me," the cat-woman replied, handing the maid a white paper bundle. "But coming here is a cat's final success. This is the cat monster mansion that cats come to from all over Japan. All of them have been mistreated by humans, so I don't know what they will do. Please run away quickly. If you meet a cat on the way, just wave this and you'll be all right."

But when the maid hurried outside, she found an assembly of several thousand cats. Waving the white paper bundle, she walked slowly down the path. Seeing what she had in her hand, the cats all opened the way for her, and thanks to that she was able to descend the mountain without further trouble.

When the maid finally returned home, she opened the white paper bundle, only to find a picture of a dog which held a real ten-*ryo*[3] coin in its mouth.

"My! Where did you get all that money?" the housewife asked in surprise.

The maid thereupon told her the story of meeting the cat.

"Well now," the housewife said to herself. "I'd better go off to Mount Inaba myself. If a maid can get ten *ryo*, the cat's master should get at least a hundred."

So the housewife headed off to Mount Inaba, and just as the maid had said, came upon a magnificent mansion deep in the mountain.

"Excuse me," she yelled out. "I've come to see the cat I once took care of. Will you let me stay here tonight?"

At this, a beautiful woman came out of the mansion, took a sharp glance at the housewife and went back to her room. Next, the old lady appeared, led the housewife inside and spread out some bedding for her.

At midnight, though she heard no one talking, the housewife got up and slid open the paper door. There, she saw two large cats glaring steadily at her. With a gasp, the housewife shut the door and then nervously opened the sliding paper door to the next room. There, too,

---

[3] A unit of money in pre-modern Japan.

two large cats were glaring sharply at her with piercingly bright eyes. And they seemed ready to bite.

This was hardly the hundred *ryo* she had coveted. Now she held her breath in fear, and although she wanted to run away, her feet were rooted to the spot. Terrified, she was unable to move.

"Awawawawa," she cried nonsensically, and shook uncontrollably.

Just then, the cat that had lived at her house appeared.

"Ah, it's you!" the housewife gasped as she collapsed on the floor. "I've been wanting to see you. Let's go home together now."

"I'll teach you to have mistreated me!" the cat screeched as she leapt on the housewife and fastened its teeth on her throat.

And with a blood-curdling scream, the housewife gave up the ghost.

The Dancing Cat

A long time ago, a samurai, his wife and child lived together as a family of three. One day, the samurai took his child off to see a play while his wife stayed at home alone. After a while, the cat, which until then had been sleeping by the hearth, went over to the wife's side.

"Ma'am," the cat purred, "Would you like to hear the song your husband is listening to right now?" And so saying, began to sing the song being performed in the play in a high tinny tone. With the lilt of its voice and the turn of its head, it was so amusing that the wife laughed out loud in spite of herself. But when the song came to an end, the cat suddenly made a frightening face and commanded the woman never to tell anyone what she had just heard.

Not long after, the samurai returned with their child from the play. His wife kept her promise to the cat and did not mention what had happened.

One day a priest who was always coming by the samurai's house to relax, dropped in unexpectedly. He chatted for a while with the samurai and his wife, when he suddenly noticed the cat by the hearth.

"You know," he said thoughtfully, "I've seen this cat somewhere

before. Ah, I remember now. It was on a moonlit night just a while ago. A fox had put a hand towel over its head and was dancing in the garden. But it seemed as though it was a little off rhythm and this cat was mumbling to itself about helping out. In the end, the cat joined the fox and they started dancing together. Yes, this is that cat for sure."

The cat lay quietly next to the hearth and seemed not to hear what the priest was saying. After a while, the priest returned to his temple.

That night the samurai and his wife were lying down discussing what the priest had said.

"I wonder if that cat can really dance," the samurai mused. "I myself don't believe it."

"Oh, no, it can dance," his wife quickly replied. "It can even sing songs from the play." And forgetting her promise to the cat, she told her husband what had happened when he was at the play.

"Ha! Is that so?" the samurai exclaimed, very impressed. "What a rare cat."

But the next morning, the samurai opened his eyes to find his wife's throat had been ripped apart and she lay dead, spattered with blood. The cat was never seen again and nobody knew where it had gone.

The Cat's Return of a Favor

A long time ago in a certain place, there was a household that kept a cat. The cat was extraordinarily gentle and would only rarely steal food that was not its own. Once, however, it stole a fish that had been prepared for an elaborate dinner. This angered the master of the house so much that he threw one of the hearth tongs at the cat, which put out one of its eyes. The cat let out a terrifying screech and ran away.

"Now I've done it," the master thought, turning pale. Although he went around the entire neighborhood searching high and low, the cat was nowhere to be found.

A number of years passed, and one day it was necessary for the master to make a journey. His business over, he was on his way home through a broad plain when the sun went down.

"Uh, oh," he said to himself, "there must be a place to stay somewhere around here.

As he looked hard around the area, he suddenly spied a faint light off in the distance.

"Ah, I'm saved," he muttered. "Perhaps they'll let me stay there tonight."

The master trudged off in the direction of the light, and eventually, amidst thick weeds, stood a rather splendid mansion.

"Good evening! Good evening!" he shouted, and soon a one-eyed lady appeared from within.

"May I help you?" she asked politely.

"The sun is going down, and I have no place to stay," the master replied. "May I spend the night here?"

"Why, yes, please do," the one-eyed woman replied. "That would be no trouble at all."

The one-eyed woman kindly led him into the house, prepared a bath and gave him a nice meal. As it turned out, he was being very well taken care of and he relaxed now, completely at ease. At that, the one-eyed woman came into his room.

"Master, do you know who I am?" she asked with some courtesy.

"I'm not sure," he responded curiously.

"Have you forgotten already?" she continued. "I'm the cat you took good care of for so long. Look, this is the eye you put out when you threw the tong at me."

The master was in shock, and sat up straight.

"Is that so?" he said apologetically. "Ah, please forgive me. I only wanted to threaten you when I threw that tong…."

"I know that," the woman said quietly. "It was I who did wrong, stealing a fish when you had taken such good care of me."

Hearing this, the master heaved a sigh of relief. The woman, however, suddenly became quite serious.

"The fact is," she whispered, "this is the house of a ferocious cat, a monster that traps people and then eats them. You must get out of this place as quickly as possible. But there are cats on the lookout all around the house. Once you go outside, stones will rain down on you, but no matter what happens, you must run fast and be careful not to fall. If you fall, you will be killed and eaten."

The master turned pale and nervously put his pack together.

"Thank you for taking such good care of me for so long," the woman sighed. "I'm afraid that when the other cats here find out that I've told you this secret, they'll kill me in the morning. But go now, as fast as you can."

And with that, she bit off her own tongue and died.

"I'm so grateful to you. Please do forgive me," the master said under his breath, putting his hands together in a farewell prayer. Then he bounded outside.

Just as the cat had said, stones came down on him like rain. But the master just ran and ran, taking care not to stumble even once, and in the end reached home unhurt.

The Cat's Big Pumpkin

Many years ago, a cat was being kept at a certain person's home. One day, the lady of the house was sitting in front of the mirror putting on her make-up when the cat came up to her.

"Goodness," the cat said, "how pretty you are!"

This was the first time the cat had spoken words and the woman rushed to where her husband was.

"This is horrible!" she said breathlessly. "Our cat is some sort of apparition!"

"That's nonsense," the man replied, refusing to be bothered. "You're seeing things…."

"No, I'm sure it's an apparition!" she insisted. "If it isn't, how could it be speaking words? I tell you, something terrible happened just now!"

"All right then, I'll kill it," the man declared, surprised at his wife's agitation. He thereupon killed the cat and buried it in the vegetable garden at the back of the house.

The following year, a large pumpkin, bigger than anyone had ever seen, grew at the place where the cat had been buried.

"This must be the result of having killed that ghost-cat," the man thought to himself. Quite satisfied with himself, he brought the pumpkin inside and served it to his family.

The instant they ate the pumpkin, however, the entire household became sick. Everyone's stomach hurt and their groans sounded like the pitiful mewing of cats. A doctor was called in immediately, and he gave them medicine but this had no effect at all.

"This must be some sort of divine punishment," someone suggested.

At that point, one of the neighbors brought in a woman conjurer. The woman went through her trance and found that, sure enough, this was a divine punishment of some sort.

"Do you remember killing a living being sometime in the past?" she asked the husband, who was lying on his sick bed.

"The fact is, I killed the cat we were keeping and buried it in the vegetable garden," he responded in pain.

"That's it!" the conjurer said. "The cat bore you a bitter grudge and had you eat that pumpkin."

The neighbors quickly brought a hoe and went to the vegetable garden at the back of the house. Clearing away the vine of the pumpkin and digging up its roots, they found the skeleton of the cat. The pumpkin vine had been growing directly from its mouth.

"What do you know," they all agreed, "it's just like the conjurer said."

With that, the neighbors dug a grave for the cat, placed its skeleton inside and said a prayer after they had covered the grave. Strangely enough, the husband, his wife and all of their household recovered immediately.

Being Deceived by Foxes

The Fox Barber

Long ago in a place called Tachimi Pass, there lived a fox by the name of Oton. Now, Oton loved to make mischief, and his specialty was bewitching people and shaving their heads completely smooth.

As a result, the village headman gathered everyone together one day, hoping to solve this problem.

"Is there anyone here who can defeat this Oton?" he pleaded. "I'll give a good reward to anyone who can."

"We'll take care of this fox," boasted two young men who were proud of their strength. "Something like this should be as easy as eating breakfast." And they quickly agreed to do the job.

"Don't even try," one of the villagers said." This fox won't fall into your hands so easily. What are you going to do if you get your heads shaved?"

Everyone felt uneasy about this and tried to stop the two young men. But they would not give up.

"Leave it to us, Your Honor," the two said to the village headman. "We're counting on that reward." And the two quickly returned home.

That night, the two young men fixed sickles to their waists and headed out toward Tachimi Pass. Not long after, a large fox with gold-colored fur could be seen coming from the opposite direction.

"There it is! There it is!" the young men whispered, hiding nervously behind a thicket of weeds.

The fox suddenly stopped, put a large leaf on its head, and right before their eyes transformed itself into a beautiful young woman. Then it picked up a small statue of Jizo that stood by the side of the road and stroked its head. The statue quickly turned into a baby.

"You see!" said one of the young men. "It's really clever."

"It looks just like a human being," the other agreed.

As the two young men exchanged glances, the fox put the baby on its back and started to walk away. The young men stealthily followed behind.

After a while, the fox stopped in front of a house. A moment later, an old man and an old lady came out and greeted the fox with smiling faces. Then they invited the fox and the baby inside.

Peering in through a crack in the door, the two young men could see that the old man and old lady were quite overjoyed, and were treating the fox and the statue of Jizo as if they were their own daughter and grandchild.

"Those poor folks," one of the young men said sympathetically. "The old man and woman are being deceived."

"I'll take that bewitcher's hide for myself right now," the other bragged.

Standing in front of the house, the two young men were beside themselves with anger. But after a while, the old lady came outside and one of the men approached her.

"Listen, Granny," he whispered in a low voice. "It's a fox that's bewitching you in there."

But the old lady took no notice of him.

"We saw it change into a young lady right before our eyes," the other young man insisted. "And that baby is nothing more than a stone Jizo!"

At this point the old man came out of the house.

"Don't be fooled, Gramps!" the other young man demanded. "That young woman in there is a fox!"

"Such nonsense!" the old man retorted.

"No, there's no mistake about this," the young man persisted. "We saw it with our own eyes!"

"What are you saying? Are you crazy?" the old man finally spouted out in anger.

If this continued, the young men were surely going to lose that reward.

"If you think it's a lie," the other young man continued, "just throw that baby in the pot and see. It's phony skin will peel off right away."

"All right," the old man said angrily, "I'll toss it into the pot and we'll see. But if you're mistaken, you'll be dead men!"

Unmoved by the old lady's pleas, the old man leapt back into the house, grabbed the little baby and threw it into the pot of furiously boiling water. In that instant, the baby cried out as though it had been set on fire. And though moments passed, it continued to scream violently, never changing into a stone Jizo.

"It's a real baby after all," one of the young men gasped.

"How can that be?" the other whined.

The two young men became increasingly frightened. They had no idea what to do and just stood there sniveling.

When the old man saw this, he became outraged.

"I'll teach you to kill our precious grandchild," he yelled. "I'm going to turn you over to the officials and have them cut off your heads!" And grabbing the two by their arms, he pulled them outside.

"Please have mercy!" the one young man pleaded

"Just spare our lives!" the other cried.

The two young men bowed with their heads to the ground and apologized but the old man would hear none of it.

Just at that moment, however, a priest was passing by.

"What's all this commotion?" the priest asked the old man.

The old man thereupon told him the story from beginning to end.

"I see," the priest replied. "Now it's my job to help people, and no matter how angry you are, even if the heads of these young men are cut off, it won't bring the baby back to life. Listen, rather than taking these two to the officials, wouldn't it be better to have them become priests and make them pray for the baby's salvation?

"Yes," the old man consented, "if Your Holiness says so…," and he turned the two young men over to the priest.

"What do you think, you two?" the priest asked the young men. "I suppose it's better to become priests than to have your heads cut off."

"Ye … yes!" they both stammered. "We'll become priests and pray for the baby's salvation with all our hearts!"

So the priest led the two men back to his temple, quickly shaved their heads and made them priests. Having thus taken religious orders, they began by beating the temple's wooden block and intoning the *nembutsu*.

Suddenly, someone called their names.

"That's strange," one of them said. "Someone seems to have come."

The two stood up with a start, and in a moment realized that, not only had the night turned to dawn but that they had been sitting on the grass out in the middle of nowhere.

"Hey! Your head!" one of the men shouted in shock.

"What about yours?" the other yelled, equally astonished.

Each man looked at the other and involuntarily reached for his own head. Their heads had been shaved as smooth as glass, not a single hair remaining.

"We've been had!" the one said with his mouth agape. "Tricked by that fox Oton!"

"Damn him!" the other moaned.

The two stood on the grass and seethed but it was much too late.

The Old Lady's House

In a certain village lived a young man by the name of Jubei who was not very bright. One winter's day, he got up before dawn to buy some things in the town on the other side of the mountain. Climbing up the dark mountain road, he suddenly heard a rustling sound ahead. He stopped in his tracks, wondering what it might be, and looking through the thin light saw a fox digging vigorously in the dirt.

"A ha! There it is!" Jubei thought to himself. "This is the fox that always causes so much mischief in the village. I'll give it a good scare."

Jubei grasped a frozen leather horseshoe, took careful aim and threw it with all his might. His aim was good and the horseshoe fell right in front of the fox. Taken by surprise, the fox leapt into the air, slipped over a bluff and landed head first with a loud splash in the river below.

Jubei ran over to the bluff and looked down. The fox was floundering about painfully in the river, but finally swam to the other side and ran away into the mountains.

"It serves you right!" Jubei yelled after the fleeing fox, feeling quite proud of himself. And then he thought about how he would tell everyone about his exploits when he got home.

Jubei finished buying the goods he needed in the town and hurriedly started to return home. On the way, however, the sun started to go down, and by the time he reached the bluff it was completely dark.

"Well, I'm in a fix now," he said to himself. "But there must be some place around here where I could get something to light my way."

Looking around, he spied a faint light up ahead.

"Great!" he mumbled. "I'll try getting something there."

Jubei groped his way toward the light, and finally came upon a

small house in the middle of the mountain. Peeking inside, he could see an old lady sitting next to the hearth blackening her teeth.[1] The old lady's head was completely white but she was not missing even one of what looked like very strong teeth.

"Granny," he began, "I'm Jubei from the next village up the way. I was buying some things in the town but the sun's gone down and I can't see the path because it's got dark. I'm sorry to ask you, but could you lend me a torch or a paper lantern?"

The old lady paid no attention to him.

"Hey, Granny!" Jubei said again a bit louder. "Are you deaf?"

This time the old lady opened her mouth.

"I don't have a torch or a lantern," she said flatly.

"Well then, could I stay here overnight?" Jubei asked.

"I have no bedding, so you can't stay over," the old lady replied, "but why don't you come over here by the hearth?" And so saying, she added some wood to the fire.

"That would be helpful," Jubei returned thankfully. "It's so cold, my body feels like it's been frozen."

Jubei sat down at the hearth facing the old lady, but she did not say a word. She simply bared her teeth and applied more black powder

---

[1] *Haguro*, a custom for Japanese women since ancient times, it involves staining the teeth with a black powder. This was done especially at the time of marriage.

as if in a trance. This made Jubei feel uneasy and he poked at the fire to avoid looking directly at her.

After a while, the firewood was gone and the fire was about to go out.

"Don't you have any more firewood, Granny?" Jubei asked, finally looking her in the face.

Just then, the old lady bared her teeth and spoke in an astonishingly loud voice.

"What do you think?" she barked. "Glad you dropped by?"

Looking straight at Jubei, the old lady seemed to thrust out her teeth, making her face look like that of a mountain witch.

Jubei jumped up with a gasp and backed away from the hearth. Then suddenly, he fell down head over heels. When he finally came to, he was floating in the middle of the river, having swallowed an unpleasant amount of water. At length, he was able to swim to the other shore.

He glanced up at the bluff above and there was the fox staring down at him.

The Fox's Wedding

At the foot of Mount Senjo-ga-dake in Nagano Prefecture, there was once a village called Todai. In this village there was a strange phenomenon that had occurred there since times long past. This was a bright red procession that would wind its way up the mountain from a pure white plain on a snowy day.

One winter night, a long time ago, the sky was full of stars after days of heavy snow. A man who had been sent on some errand to a neighboring village, walked through the snow-covered plain late at night on his slow return.

"At last," he mumbled to himself, "it's finally stopped snowing."

Then, he became aware of something in front of him shining like a pale white light. Suddenly, it turned into a crimson-red fire and started to move around this way and that. Wondering what it might be, the man stopped dead in his tracks.

The place was a cremation ground where the dead were burned, so this was surely the fire from someone who had just died.

"What can I do now?" the man wondered, completely at a loss.

Standing there alone, he was deep in thought. He knew that he could not get back to the village without passing by the cremation ground. Nevertheless, he swallowed his fear and approached the flames, holding his nose against the possible smell of burning flesh.

Holding his sleeve over his nose and looking straight ahead, the man eventually passed by the cremation ground. For a few moments he walked as if in a trance, but then suddenly stopped. Something like the crunching sound of bones being chewed echoed through the still air. The man felt a chill go down his spine and he began to tremble uncontrollably, his feet unable to advance even a step. Filled with terror, he turned around and looked behind him.

A large fox was chewing on human bones.

The man was rooted to the spot, unable to make a sound.

The fox, having munched down the bone, just glared at the man with eyes that shone a pale blue.

The man thought his heart was going to stop. Suddenly, the fox ran off across the snowy plain in a straight line. Eyes wide open, the man gasped involuntarily for the bones that the fox had been chewing emitted a pure blue light.

After a while, the blue fire gradually turned to red and began to wind its way up the mountain, for all the world like the spirit of a dead person. Suddenly, the man came to his senses and fled back along the snowy path to his village, slipping and sliding the whole way.

When his fellow villagers heard the man's story, they agreed that this was the true form of a "fox's wedding."[2]

---

[2] A fox's wedding, or *kitsune no yomeiri* (狐の嫁入り), demonstrates at least two phenomena in Japan: one, the light/fire procession on a clear night, as in the above story, and two, a light rain falling as the sun shines.

The Crying Voice of the Ghost

A long time ago in a certain place, there lived a man by the name of Saburo. He had a younger sister who had married and gone to live with her husband in a nearby village. This younger sister, however, became ill and passed away, and Saburo rushed to where she lived to participate in her funeral.

On his way home after the burial, he thought to himself as he passed through a pine forest on the outskirts of the village, "I wonder why she died?"

The pine forest had already become quite dark and just then, behind him, he could hear the voice of a woman sobbing in grief.

Wondering who it could be crying in such a place, he turned around but could not see because of the dark. As he continued walking, the crying voice followed behind him and gradually grew louder.

"That ... that voice!" Saburo stuttered, and startled, stopped in his tracks.

The voice was that of his sister, the woman they had just buried! Saburo felt a cold chill run down his spine, and took off.

"A ... a ghost!" he screamed, running as fast as he could without looking back.

But the voice of his younger sister chased along behind him and seemed to be right at his back. Yelling for help, he finally reached his own house and leapt inside. Still, he could hear his sister's crying voice next to his ear

"What's going on?" the people of his household asked the trembling Saburo.

"Can't you hear it?" Saburo sobbed. "Listen! It's my little sister's voice!"

"We can't hear anything," came the response. "I suppose you've gotten drunk on sake."

Nobody, it seemed, believed a word Saburo was saying.

"Well now, take a bath and calm down," someone added.

Saburo gave up and tried to take a bath. But everywhere he went in the house, he could still hear his sister's crying voice. Even as he sat in the bathtub, he could hear her voice nearby.

"Older brother … older brother," it cried.

Saburo nearly went crazy. Putting his hands over his ears, he glanced at the bathroom wall. Through a chink in the wall, a long narrow pale hand slithered its way inside.

"Older brother … older brother," came the cry, as the hand twisted itself around Saburo's neck.

Saburo shrieked, flew out of the bathroom still naked and hid underneath his bedding. Unable to shake off his fear, he refused to come out from under his mattress until a conjurer was called in to dispel the ghost, which some believed was nothing more than a fox.

Friendly Ghosts

The Land of the One-eyes

There was once a monk traveling around the country, who stopped one night to visit a foreman who set up show tents[1] at religious festivals. The priest thanked the foreman for all his past favors and entertained him with some curious stories.

"I've been to a number of different places," the priest began, "but the most surprising was the land of the one-eyes. Everyone there has only one eye. If you brought back one of them, I imagine your tent shows would be a big success."

So saying, he drew a detailed map of the land of the one-eyes.

"This is a real boon," the foreman declared. "I'll bring one of them back right away."

The next day, after the monk had gone home, the foreman quickly set out for the land of the one-eyes. His journey took him a number of days, but he finally arrived.

Inspecting the place, he found that the people walking along the road, the people going in and out of their houses, in fact, everyone had only one eye.

"A hah!" he said to himself, "It's just like the priest said." And as he ambled along, he couldn't help staring at everyone he saw.

The one-eyes were looking curiously at the foreman, too.

"Another two-eyed human being has come," they whispered to each other.

The foreman, all the while, was wondering which of the one-eyes he might take back with him when he saw a little girl playing by the side of the road. As luck would have it, no one else was around.

"All right!" he thought. "I'll take this kid."

The foreman grabbed the little girl and tried to put her in his basket, but she screamed in surprise. Kicking and struggling inside the basket, she raised quite a racket.

People nearby heard her screams and came running.

[1] *Yashi* (香具師) are men who set up little booths much like the sideshows at American county fairs, only on a smaller scale. The word is defined as "showman," "racketeer," and "charlatan," so we can imagine that the *yashi* are held in fascination but not in great repute.

"What's going on here?" one demanded in a loud voice.

"He's kidnapping her!" another yelled.

"Grab him!" shouted yet another.

Very quickly a large crowd of people gathered, and in the end the foreman himself was taken captive and tied up with a straw rope.

"Hey! This man has two eyes!" someone yelled.

"Take him to the official!" someone else suggested.

The foreman turned pale as he was marched off to the official, wondering if he was going to be killed.

"Say, this man has two eyes!" the official said incredulously. "It would be a shame to kill him. Let's display him in a show tent instead."

And so the unfortunate foreman was taken to a festival show tent and exhibited as a rare item for all to see.

The Man Who Changed into a Corpse

Many years ago, there were three men who lived in the ancient province of Ise. The three, who were brave young men, were good friends.

One day, the three of them decided to take a trip to the province of Omi. To do so, however, they would have to climb over Mount Suzuka, a frightening mountain that lay between the two provinces. To make matters worse, there was said to be a flesh-eating demon living in an old deserted temple that stood on the mountain.

Now, the fastest path that led over this mountain passed right in front of the temple, but out of fear everyone took the long way around.

As the three young men were passing by the temple, it suddenly started to rain. They hastily took shelter under a large tree, but the rain was not about to stop and after a while the sun also started to go down.

"There's nothing else we can do," one of the men said. "We'll have to spend the night in that temple."

"But what about the flesh-eating demon that lives there?" queried the second.

"I didn't come here to be eaten," added the third.

"But we've come this far," the first man replied. "Let's see if there's really a demon here or not. A human being is eventually going to die. What difference does it make if you die being eaten by a demon or by getting sick?"

With this indisputable logic, the other two men agreed.

The three then entered the pitch-black temple, which was filled with spider webs and smelled horribly of mildew.

"Somehow, I don't think I can sleep in here," one of the men complained.

"You're right!" another added. "I'm wide awake."

"I wonder if a demon really lives here," the other thought out loud.

The three men talked together for a while, but then one of them came up with an idea.

"It's boring just sitting here doing nothing," he suggested. "Why don't we have a test of courage?"

"A test of courage?" came the response.

"Sure," the man continued. "Look, as we were coming over the mountain today, we saw a corpse lying by the side of the road. Who's brave enough to go out there and carry it back?"

"What? That's stupid!" interjected one of the others.

But then, the man who had initially suggested staying overnight at the temple spoke up.

"That sounds interesting," he agreed as he stood up. "Let's start."

"Wa ... wait a minute!" protested the other man. "Should we really go out in the middle of the night when it's raining this hard?"

"If it's that unpleasant for you, stay here," the first man said. "We'll go without you." And without further ado, he stripped down to his loincloth and ran out of the temple.

The man who had proposed this test of courage was not about to let himself be outdone, so he stripped down as well and chased after his friend.

The third man, now left alone in the temple, felt a breeze come up that smelled something like blood.

"That's strange," he thought, and quickly grasped his sword.

Suddenly, he heard weird laughter coming from nowhere in particular, and at the same time a pale light shone from the rafters. In an instant the light transformed itself into the head of a ghost, with a mouth that stretched from ear to ear and sharp glinting eyes.

"You wretch! Come and get me!" the man yelled as he stood up and unsheathed his sword.

But the ghost's head disappeared, and in its place a little one-eyed temple boy[2] showed his face, laughing in a high-pitched voice and extending a long red tongue. The man, however, did not flinch, but stood glaring at the rafters as motionless as the statue of the Nio[3] temple guardians, with his sword raised. The face of the one-eyed temple boy then evaporated and nothing else appeared.

In the meantime, the man who had chased after his friend, secretly took a short cut and thus arrived first at the place where the corpse lay. Putting his arms around the corpse, he dragged it over to a river, tossed it into the water and then lay down where the corpse had been. At this point, the man who had run out of the temple first, arrived.

---

[2] *Hitotsu-me kozo*, a traditional Japanese apparition.

[3] Nio (仁王), the pair of Kongo gods whose statues are often found at the entrance to Buddhist temples in Japan.

"Hunh!" he grunted. "Why should I be afraid of a corpse?" And so saying, he shouldered the man who was lying there in place of the corpse.

As they went along, the man who was being carried bit down on his friend's shoulder. His friend, however, was not in the least bit frightened.

"No, no," he said calmly. "Don't bite me. There's no reason to take out your anger on me."

The man, together with what he thought was a corpse on his back, finally arrived at the front of the temple and put the body down.

"Hey, you two!" he shouted proudly, "I've brought you the dead man!" And he went inside the temple to get his friends.

But the man who had been carried on the other's back, sprang up and ran away to hide.

So when the man who had carried the "corpse" back brought out the man who had stayed at the temple to see the dead body, there was nothing there.

"Hey! What happened to the corpse?" the man shouted in dismay.

"Did you really bring it back?" the other asked skeptically.

"Of course I did," the first man retorted. "Do you think I'd lie about that?"

But search as he might, there was neither substance nor shadow of a corpse to be found. Assuring each other that this was strange indeed, the two men cocked their heads and wondered what to do.

Just then, the man who had been hiding walked up. With a grin, he told them the truth of the matter.

"What? Is that right?" the first man laughed. "You really put one over me!"

The three men laughed until their sides hurt, proof of how brave they really were. Then, when day broke, they continued on over the mountain and walked down to the province of Omi.

People who heard this story decided that there was no demon living in the temple after all, and if there was, it was really only a fox. And from that time on, they walked by the temple with total indifference.

The Ghost's Drinking Bout

There was once an antique dealer who one day discovered in town a rare painting of a ghost.

"Hmm. This is something I should take and put up for sale," he thought to himself.

The dealer then bought the painting, went back to his shop and priced it at ten times the cost he had paid for it. Not long after, a customer entered the shop and asked to purchase the item, saying he would come back with the money the next day. The painting was the work of a famous artist by the name of Oukyo,[4] and the female ghost he had depicted looked absolutely alive.

"I've made a ten-fold profit thanks to this ghost," the dealer chuckled happily, and hung the painting temporarily in the alcove of his house.[5]

That night he placed some sake in front of the painting as an offering and then began to sip a little himself. After a while, the paper lanterns began to gutter and grow dark, and suddenly someone appeared to sitting in front of the tray from which he was drinking.

"Goodness, who are you?" he asked.

"I'm the ghost in the painting," came the reply.

"A gh ... ghost!" the dealer stuttered, spilling his sake in surprise.

"Please don't be afraid," the ghost said calmly. "I didn't appear because I have any anger toward you. Everyone else seemed afraid of my painting and put it out of sight, but you've put it in your alcove and have even offered it sake. So as a gesture of thanks, I thought I'd fill your cup this evening."

When the dealer looked carefully, he could see that the ghost had already drunk a bit of sake and that her face was turning as red as his.

"That's very kind of you," he replied, no longer feeling frightened. "This is the first time I've ever been served sake by a ghost."

---

[4] Maruyama Oukyo (1733–95).

[5] The *tokonoma*, or alcove in a Japanese house where scrolls and other art objects are displayed.

The dealer now felt completely relaxed, and he and the ghost began drinking a good deal of sake. After a while, they were both quite drunk. Bringing out a shamisen, they started playing and singing and having a good, but noisy, time.

"What's going on in there?" the dealer's wife yelled all of a sudden, hearing the racket and coming into the sitting room.

"This is terrible! Somebody's coming," the ghost whispered and hastily returned to the painting.

"Was somebody in here with you?" the dealer's wife asked suspiciously as she held the paper lamp high and looked around the room.

"No, it's just me," the dealer replied sheepishly.

After his wife left the room, the dealer looked up at the painting and gasped. The drunken ghost was now lying down with her head propped on her arm and was sleeping soundly. There was nothing ghostly about the painting now and it could probably not be sold.

"This is terrible," the dealer muttered, "Maybe she'll sleep it off before tomorrow morning."

Sick with worry, the antique dealer was now, himself, as sober as a judge.

The Clog Ghost

A long time ago there was a family that treated their footwear very roughly. At that time, of course, "footwear" meant clogs and straw sandals, for there were as yet no shoes in Japan.

Now this particular family, from the wife right on down to the maid, would simply throw away their footwear if a clog was missing a tooth[6] or the cords were a little tight.

One night, after everyone in the family had gone to sleep, the maid was still up alone. Suddenly, from just outside the front of the house, she heard someone singing:

> *Gararin, gororon, gararin, gororon,*
> *With three holes, I have two teeth.*

Thinking this to be a rather strange song for someone to be singing at such an hour, she stealthily opened the door a crack and peeped outside. No one was there. A little while later, however, she heard the sound of clogs going by and once again the song:

> *Gararin, gororon, gararin, gororon,*
> *With three holes, I have two teeth.*

The maid became frightened and could not sleep. In the end, she stayed awake the whole night.

The next morning, the maid went straight to the woman of the house and told her what had happened.

"Don't be silly!" the housewife scolded her. "You just had a dream, don't you think?" and did not believe her story.

---

[6] *Geta* (下駄). These are basically made of a flat, rectangular foot-sized horizontal piece of wood supported underneath by two vertical pieces called "teeth" about half an inch thick and anywhere from one and a half and two inches tall, spaced at about the ball of the foot in front and the mid-heel behind. Three holes are drilled through the horizontal wood through which the cords are strung to hold down the foot; the front hole at the juncture of the big and second toes, the two rear holes at the sides of the foot about two inches to the rear.

"But it's true!" the maid insisted, still trembling as she spoke. "If you think I'm lying, just come to my room tonight."

"All right," retorted the housewife. "If you're that upset, I'll sleep in your room tonight."

That night, the housewife duly went to the maid's room and went to sleep. But at about midnight, she could hear the sound of someone walking by in clogs, singing a song:

> *Gararin, gororon, gararin, gororon,*
> *With three holes, I have two teeth.*

"Goodness, it's just as you said," the housewife admitted, getting up with a start.

However, this housewife was a woman of great courage.

"I'm going to see the true form of this ghost with my own eyes," she said flatly, and with the trembling maid in tow quietly went and stood just inside the front door. Sliding the door open a crack, she looked outside. There she saw it, a huge clog ghost singing away as it walked around in front of the house:

> *Gararin, gororon, gararin, gororon,*
> *With three holes, I have two teeth.*

After walking around in the front of the house for a while, it moved around to the back. The housewife followed stealthily and at length saw the clog ghost disappear into the shed where the household had always thrown their worn-out footwear, earning the rancor of the clogs and sandals that could have been repaired.

The Doll that Chased off the Bandits

Many years ago in a town in the prefecture of Tottori, there was a very wealthy man by the name of Sakunoya. One night, five bandits broke into his mansion, tying up the entire household except for the master himself.

"All right," demanded the bandits' leader, "take us to where you keep your money."

The bandits poked the master's sides with their swords as he led them to a large storehouse. When the master opened the storehouse with the key, the bandits went inside, leaving him with a warning.

"Wait here," they threatened. "If you try to run away, we'll kill all of you."

Inside the storehouse, there were boxes of gold piled one on top of the other.

"This is just what you'd think of Sakunoya," admitted one of the bandits, with wide-open eyes.

"He sure saved up a lot of gold," said another in admiration.

The bandits were quite impressed. At length each shouldered one of the boxes and they started to go outside.

"Wait! Or I'll crush you like fleas!" boomed a voice. And a huge sumo wrestler, standing there like one of the Nio, appeared before their eyes. His face crimson red and his eyes glittering with light, he waved his arms which were as thick as logs.

"Wa … wait a moment!" squealed one of the bandits.

"Just spare our lives!" pleaded another.

The bandits threw down the boxes of gold and ran away without looking back, while the master, quite beside himself with joy, flew back to the house and untied the people who had been bound with straw rope.

"Everybody rejoice!" he beamed. "The bandits ran away empty-handed!" And with that, he told them everything he had seen.

"That must have been the spirit[7] of the sumo wrestler doll that's been in our possession for generations," the master's grandmother suggested.

The master, accompanied by his entire household, then went into the spacious storehouse and looked into every corner. Finally, on the second floor they found the doll of a sumo wrestler carved from wood. Strangely enough, the doll was wet with sweat and there was fresh dirt on both of its firmly planted feet.

"That's it!" the master exclaimed. "It was this doll that saved me!"

The master was truly overjoyed and had a shrine built for the doll. Placing the doll inside the shrine, he performed services for it and, it is said, prayed to it every day.

---

[7] *Seikon* (精魂), the pure spirit or vital energy of a thing. The first character can mean anything from spirit, ghost, energy and vitality to semen, while the second character can mean the soul or spirit, or the yang soul distinguished from the yin soul. This *seikon* is believed to be able to leave the body and manifest itself as a ghost in the form of its prior being.

Snakes, Wild Boars and Crabs

The Younger Sister Who Turned into a Snake

A long time ago there was a couple who had two children, an older boy and a younger girl, who was a very beautiful. The children got along very well and even slept together at night. Strangely enough, just about midnight the younger sister's feet invariably got cold.

"Strange things happen, you know," the elder brother said anxiously. "Do you think there's something wrong with you?"

The elder brother was quite worried about his sister. One night, around midnight, she slipped quietly out of the house. Wondering where she might be going at such an hour, her brother followed secretly behind her. At length she stood on the bank of a river, loosened her long hair, and after moistening it with water began beating it against the trunk of a willow tree.

"Please make me into a snake," she murmured.

Her brother was shocked and immediately ran home to tell his parents what he had seen.

"This is terrible," he sputtered. "If we don't kill my younger sister soon, something horrible is bound to happen. Please! Let me kill my younger sister!"

"You're talking nonsense!" his parents scolded him. "How can an elder brother kill his little sister? Have you gone insane?"

"She's going to bite us all to death," the elder brother pleaded. "Please, let me take care of this!"

"You're saying unspeakable things," his father replied, becoming quite angry. "We can't live together with a dreadful person like you. Get out at once!"

"If you won't listen to me, there's nothing more I can do," the elder brother said sadly. "I'll leave at once." And packing his few belongings, he fled the house.

The elder brother spent several years traveling constantly, but when passing through a certain village he fell in love and got married. Now with a wife, he could no longer continue traveling, so he rented a house in the village and settled down. He had loved animals since he was a child and began keeping a white-tailed eagle and a hawk. Both these birds are rough-spirited but when they become accustomed to their trainers, no other bird can match them for usefulness. As was his habit, the elder brother went out hunting with them every day.

As the days went by, however, the elder brother could not help thinking about his mother and father. Wondering what had become of them, he could finally sit still no longer. So one year he made up his mind and returned to his home village. But before he left, he gave his wife a small mirror.

"I have always carried this mirror with me," he instructed her. "If it becomes cloudy, you will know that something bad is happening to me and you should release the white-tailed eagle and the hawk."

Thinking that he would soon be able to see his beloved parents whom he had not met for years, the elder brother quickened his pace and after a number of days of continuous travel arrived at the house where he was born.

Everything was just as it had been long ago and he was overjoyed. But no one appeared to be there.

"Perhaps they're all out somewhere," he thought to himself, and stepped inside.

The place was completely quiet, but he went back to look in the sitting room. There, coiled up in sleep, was a huge snake.

The elder brother let out a gasp and the snake instantly transformed itself into his younger sister.

"My goodness, Elder Brother," she said happily. "Welcome home!" And without thinking, she rushed forward and grasped her brother's hand.

"Yah!" the elder brother yelled, turning pale, "He ... help!"

"Why are you so afraid?" his sister asked soothingly. "We haven't seen each other for so long!"

"But you ... you're a snake, aren't you?" he stuttered.

"Don't be silly," she went on. "And it's the middle of the day. How could you be dreaming?"

The elder brother stared hard at his little sister's face. Without a doubt, this was the same pretty young lady. At last he regained control of himself.

"Well, what about Mother and Father?" he asked.

"Three years ago they became ill and passed away," she replied, looking down sadly.

Suddenly, however, she brightened up with a smile.

"But you must be hungry," she started, "so I'm going to fix you a nice meal. In the meantime, why don't you play this drum?" And she left the room.

Left to his own devices, the elder brother began vacantly to play the drum, when two mice, one white, one black, slid down from the rafters along a pillar.

"We are your parents!" one of them squeaked. "We were bitten to death by our own daughter and turned into mice. If you linger here, you'll be killed, too. We'll continue playing the drum for you, so run away now!"

The elder brother now knew that he had been right all along. Looking at the two mice, tears flowed down his cheeks. He should not hesitate. Rushing out into the back garden, he found a horse tied up to the shed, and leaping onto it, struck it with a whip.

Hearing the sound of the hoofbeats, the younger sister climbed quickly up to the roof and saw her elder brother riding away.

"Now you've done it!" she screamed. "I'll show you!"

In an instant, the beautiful young woman transformed herself back into a huge snake and set off after the horse. In no time at all, the distance between them shortened, and after a short while the horse was so tired it could no longer go on.

"This … this is it!" the elder brother stammered. But as he was about to be swallowed by the snake, he was able to climb to the top of a tree.

A crimson red tongue slithered from the snake's mouth and it glared at the top of the tree. Soon, the snake began to chew at the roots of the tree, and the tree seemed about to topple over at any moment.

The elder brother was shaken but managed to jump to the next tree. After doing this twice, two trees had fallen over and only one remained. Just at that moment, his wife noticed that the mirror had completely clouded over.

"Oh, no!" she cried, and hurriedly released the white-tailed eagle and the hawk from their tethers.

The two birds flew in a straight line up into the sky and disappeared.

"Ahh," his wife sighed. "It's too late."

The snake had now chewed into the last tree and it had fallen over with a crash. But at that instant, the two birds descended from the sky, aiming right at the snake.

Even this huge snake was no match for the sharp beaks and claws of the two birds, and in no time at all was bitten to death.

"I've been saved," the elder brother sighed, still holding tightly to the tree, his eyes closed tight.

Kuro-hime and the Nushi of the Lake

A long time ago in the ancient province of Shinshu, there was a famous lord by the name of Takanashi Masamori. He was an extraordinarily strong ruler and could easily defeat any of his enemies. He also had a very beautiful daughter called Kuro-hime.

One spring this lord, accompanied by his retainers, took Kuro-hime to a place called Mount Higashi to view the cherry blossoms. For a while they drank sake and sang, then suddenly a white snake slithered down a nearby cherry tree and stopped next to Kuro-hime.

Since ancient times, a white snake has been said to be a messenger of the gods, and seeing this snake the lord was overjoyed.

"A white snake coming to your side is a blessing," the lord declared. "Give it some sake, Princess."

Kuro-hime presented the snake with a full cup of sake and the snake, in turn, flicked out its tongue and lapped up the sake as though it was quite delicious. It then stared at Kuro-hime for some time, but at length climbed back up the tree and disappeared.

Two or three days later, the lord suddenly woke up in the middle of the night, aware that someone was sitting next to his pillow. Leaping up with a shout, he grabbed his sword from its stand. When he looked carefully, however, he saw that it was a young high-class man, who bowed reverentially with the palms of his hands on the floor.

"I am the *nushi* of the great marsh at Mount Yu," he said politely. "The other day I took on the form of a white snake and went flow-er-viewing. Quite by chance I met the princess, who was kind enough to offer me sake. Since that time, I have been unable to forget her and have come to ask for her hand in marriage."

The lord was shocked, and looked carefully at the young man's face. He seemed to be a fine youth whom you would never suspect to be the *nushi* of a swamp. Yet, he was not about to hand over his beloved Kuro-hime to something that was not a human being.

"Your offer is a kind one," the lord replied decisively, "but I must refuse."

The next night, however, and the one after, the young man came again about midnight and each time he asked for Kuro-hime to become his bride.

This went on for ninety-nine nights. On the hundredth night the young man came back for a final time.

"I have beseeched you with all my heart," he said plaintively. "Now, if you will give me the princess of your own free will, I will strictly command the *nushi* of the forty-eight lakes around Mount Yu to protect your castle from destruction. But if that's not good enough, I will bring your castle to ruin right away."

Hearing those words, the lord – as strong as he was – was in a quandary. He was, indeed, quite famous and it would be unthinkable if his castle were destroyed. Yet, he could not give up his darling Kuro-hime to the *nushi* of a swamp.

Thinking about it for a moment or two, he hit upon a plan.

"All right," he began, "I understand. Tomorrow morning I'm going to mount my horse and ride around the castle twenty-one times. If you can keep up with me until the very end, the princess is yours. But if you should fall behind at some point, you must give up on having her."

"Thank you so much," the young man replied happily. "I will be here in the morning for sure." He then returned home.

Very early the next morning, however, the lord ordered his retainers to plant thousands of swords, blades up, in the grasses around the castle.

"That should do it," he thought to himself, and when he finally mounted his horse and went outside the castle, the young man was waiting for him.

After a quick greeting, the lord struck his horse with his whip and the horse galloped off with remarkable energy. But the young man was not about to lose this contest, and set off after him as though in flight.

After running a number of times around the castle, however, the young man was breathing hard, his feet were beginning to lag, and the gap between him and the horse was widening.

"That will teach him!" the lord gloated as he glanced over his shoulder. "He'll have to give up on the princess now." And he applied the whip to his horse all the more.

The horse flew like the wind.

At that moment, the figure of the young man disappeared and was replaced by a huge snake. Having transformed itself into a human being had proved too painful, so now it appeared in its true form. And soon it was on the heels of the horse.

But the thousands of swords that had been planted, blades up, in the grass now tore the snake's body into shreds every time it advanced, and its blood covered the ground. The faster it slithered along, the more the swords cut away at it.

Nevertheless, the giant snake would not give up. Having dyed the grass a crimson red, it finally completed the twenty-first round of the castle, and blood-stained, it undulated painfully towards the lord.

"According to our agreement," it barely pronounced, "I'll take the princess now."

"Don't talk foolishness!" the lord spit out. "Do you think I would let the princess be taken by a big snake like you?"

"What!" the snake cried. "Are you breaking your promise? All right, see what happens now."

As it spoke, a red fire flared from its mouth, black clouds instantly gathered in what had been a clear blue sky, and a violent storm blew up. In moments, lightning flashed and rain fell in torrents. Suddenly, as a sound echoed from deep in the earth, the forty-eight lakes around Mount Yu crumbled and the floodwaters pushed their way towards the castle.

Bells in the villages surrounding the castle rang out in warning, and the villagers all fled to the mountain opposite Mount Yu. The lord, meanwhile ensconced inside the castle, was forced to climb from one floor to the next as the water rose higher and higher.

Shouting to the gods, this once strong lord raised his prayerful hands to the heavens.

But with a great "crack!" the mountain collapsed and the fleeing villagers and samurai were swallowed up.

"It's all over!" the lord called out. "I'm completely ruined!"

Just then, Kuro-hime leapt from the castle into the rising waters.
"Great *nushi* of the swamp!" she shouted above the din. "Please
forgive him! I'm coming to you!"

In that moment the storm subsided as though it had been just a
dream, and the sky became clear again. But the houses, people and rice
paddies of the village had been swept away. And Kuro-hime was never
seen again.

The beautiful Mount Yu still soars above the horizon in the north
of Nagano Prefecture. Since that time, however, it has gone by the name
of Mount Kuro-hime.

The Brave Brothers

Long ago in a certain province there were two brothers who were quite
brave young men. When their mother became ill and died, they put
her body in a round wooden coffin and placed it in the sitting room
of the cottage detached from the main house. Then they waited for the
day of the funeral.

However, one day a man came by.

"Last night there was a suspicious light coming from your detached
cottage," he reported.

"That might be Mother's spirit," the eldest brother said. "Or it
could be a ghost."

The two brothers talked it over and decided to find out what the
true form of this suspicious light might be.

"Tonight I'll sleep next to our mother's body," the younger brother
said. "If you hear me call out, bring a lamp right away."

"Will you be all right by yourself?" the older brother asked anxiously.

"I'll be fine," the younger brother replied, striking his chest with a
thud. "Leave it to me."

That night the younger brother went over to the detached cottage
where they had placed the dead body of their mother, and turned the
lid of the coffin upside down. There he lay down, face up, holding
tightly onto his sword.

Everything was completely still, and not a sound could be heard. When he thought about the fact that his dead mother's corpse was just beneath his back, even this brave young man felt a bit uneasy. Nevertheless, he was stubbornly patient and waited for whatever strange thing might appear.

A little after midnight, he saw something like a light moving in the rafters.

"It's come!" he said to himself and adjusted his grip on the sword.

At length, a plank opened up in the ceiling and the light began to descend. Then, with a sort of thud, the light flamed up in a bluish white and approached the coffin lid upon which the younger brother was lying.

"Now!" the younger brother yelled as he grabbed the light and pierced it with his sword.

In an instant, the light disappeared, and something black fell on the floor.

"Elder Brother!" he shouted, "Come quickly!"

The elder brother ran into the sitting room, holding his lamp high, and the two gasped at what they saw. There lay a dead large wild boar, its stomach pierced by a sword.

"This is it!" the elder brother said, looking at his younger brother. "The true form of that suspicious light."

The story soon spread to the people in the neighborhood.

"Sleeping next to a dead person was a bold feat!" one of them said admiringly.

"You're right," said another. "That light might have been a flesh-eating demon."

And everyone praised the brothers' courage.

The Crab's Return of a Favor

A long time ago in the ancient province of Yamashiro, a young unmarried lady lived in a place called Kii. It was her nature to be kind-hearted and she never killed a living thing.

One day some cowherds had caught a crab in the river and were about to roast and eat it. Just then the young lady was passing by and saw what was happening.

"Listen," she pleaded, "would you give this crab to me?"

"Absolutely not!" one of the cowherds replied, shaking his head. "We're going to cook it and eat it."

"Well then, take this in exchange," she said, taking off the kimono she was wearing and handing it over.

The kimono was of excellent quality and would fetch a high price if sold.

"Sure!" the boys said, and handed her the crab. "We'll never do this again."

The young lady let the crab escape back into the river as she recited a sutra.

Sometime later, the young lady was in the mountain and saw a large snake about to swallow a frog. Forgetting her fear, she ran up to the snake.

"Please give this frog to me," she cried. "In return, I'll treat you as a god and present you with many offerings."

The snake, regardless, starting swallowing the frog bit by bit.

"If that's not good enough, I'll become your wife," the young lady finally begged. "So please release the frog."

Immediately, the snake raised its head, looked at the young lady and vomited out the frog whole. The young lady picked up the frog, let it come back to its senses and then released it into the woods. Then she turned to the snake.

"In seven days I'll become your bride," she declared.

The snake, apparently quite pleased, wiggled its red tongue and disappeared into the interior of the mountain.

When the young lady returned home, she told her parents what had happened.

"What?" her father exclaimed. "How could you make a ridiculous promise like that?"

Her shocked mother and father went off to discuss the matter with a very respected priest. But....

"There's nothing you can do," he said plainly. "Just believe in the Buddha."

The young lady's parents then prayed to the Buddha for help every day, their hands together in supplication.

The night of the seventh day finally arrived. The young lady's parents shut the door to their house tightly, put her between them and sat in front of the Buddhist altar. At length, the roar of a sudden wind announced that the huge snake had arrived. A heavy knock was heard on the closed rain shutters.

The three people began to intone the *nembutsu* with all their hearts. The snake, however, climbed up on the roof, broke through the ceiling and fell down in front of the young lady.

"Ahh, it's all over!" her parents cried, closing their eyes tightly.

But the huge snake suddenly began writhing and convulsing as if in great pain. It seemed to be intertwined with something and struggling with all its might. After a moment or two, its head fell to the floor.

The young lady looked down with a start. There at her feet lay the dead body of the snake, cut to ribbons, and beneath it a great number of dead crabs, their pincers raised in the air.

"Ahh," she sobbed, "the crab I helped the other day came to my rescue." And without thinking, she turned to the crabs with her palms together in gratitude.

The next day, the young lady made a grave for the crabs and intoned a sutra for them. After that, when people found crabs in this province they took good care of them and returned them to their rivers.

Afterword

Mount Kurama rises 1,870 feet above sea level just to the northeast of Kyoto. In that position it is believed to protect the old capital from the evil spirits said to come from that direction. The mountain is covered with tall ancient Japanese cypresses and other conifers, the roots of which spread over the ground in eerie patterns. It was traditionally thought to be a daunting climb, not so much because of its steep incline or height but because of the strange and dark nature of its ambiance.

In 770 A.D., a priest by the name of Gantei was led up the mountain by a vision of a white horse. After a terrifying encounter with a huge snake, which he defeated by chanting an esoteric incantation, he founded a small temple there. This he dedicated to the god Bishamonten, a deity with his own past in demonic forces, who eventually became a guardian of Buddhism and of the imperial city. Bishamonten is worshipped there to this day, along with the Thousand Arm Kannon and the god Maoson, who is believed to have descended to Mount Kurama from the Planet Venus some 6,500,000 years ago.

Mount Kurama is also well known as the abode of *tengu*, beings sometimes in the form of half kites, half humans, although their more advanced forms are fully like human beings with the exception of their long noses. In ancient times, these beings were considered forces of evil, causing disasters and illnesses or kidnapping people. Later, some became protectors of Buddhism, although they still enjoyed confounding arrogant priests with difficult questions and repartee concerning their religion. *Tengu* can fly swiftly either by wings or the aid of fans, and are extraordinarily adept at swordsmanship and the martial arts. The most famous *tengu* at Mount Kurama is Sojobo, who, with the aid of *tengu* from various other mountains, taught martial arts to the Young Minamoto Yoshitsune, who would go on to defeat the rival Heike clan in the 12th century. Other martial artists, the most prominent of whom is the founder of *aikido*, Uyeshiba Morihei, have and still do train at the mountain, hoping for assistance from these liminal beings.

In 2005, a friend of mine and I decided to walk over the mountain, stop to pray at the temple near the peak, and then continue on over to the village of Kibune, home of a Shinto shrine, traditional restaurants situated over a mountain stream, and a number of inns. It was mid-November, but there had been an early heavy snow and the scant footprints on ancient stone steps indicated how few visitors had preceded us. Drifts on the branches above us periodically gave way, dumping their burden on our heads. The climb is a steep one, and we eventually became separated, with my friend, a martial arts master himself, taking the lead. At one point, in a quiet place not far beyond the temple, I heard a hoarse, high-pitched voice chanting a sutra, mantra or dharani—I couldn't tell which—as I approached a sort of trellis over the path. Seated on the ground in front of this empty gate was a woman of maybe fifty or sixty with a hawk-like nose and almost burning blue eyes. She ignored me as I got closer, continued her chanting, and the hair stood up on the back of my neck. Not knowing what else to do, I made the common Japanese hand signal of "Excuse me, I'm coming through," and walked quickly by, her chanting becoming dimmer as I carried on. I was not sure what I had seen or heard, but was shaken enough by the experience that I stepped up my pace for the rest of the walk. In thirty minutes or so, I arrived at Kibune and found my friend waiting for me. Questioning him about what I had seen, he claimed to have no idea of what I was talking about, but was concerned about my agitated state. A few minutes later, we sat down in a restaurant next to a small river, ate bowls of noodles coming down a wooden chute, and watched the snow drifts and leaves float by. I recalled that at the temple, when I bought a set of prayer beads, I had flippantly asked the woman behind the counter if she had ever seen a *tengu*. Her response was a polite, but faintly nervous "No, not yet."

Published by Tuttle Publishing, an imprint of Periplus Editions (HK) Ltd.

www.tuttlepublishing.com

Copyright © 2021 Periplus Editions (HK) Ltd.

First Tuttle edition, 2021
ISBN 978-4-8053-1660-3

LCCN 2021934624

27 26 25 24 23
13 12 11 10 9 8 7   2309TP

Printed in Singapore

TUTTLE PUBLISHING® is a registered trademark of Tuttle Publishing, a division of Periplus Editions (HK) Ltd.

Distributed by:

North America, Latin American & Europe
Tuttle Publishing
364 Innovation Drive
North Clarendon
VT 05759-9436 U.S.A.
Tel: 1 (802) 773-8930
Fax: 1 (802) 773-6993
info@tuttlepublishing.com
www.tuttlepublishing.com

Asia Pacific
Berkeley Books Pte. Ltd.
3 Kallang Sector #04-01
Singapore 349278
Tel: (65) 6741 2178
Fax: (65) 6741 2179
inquiries@periplus.com.sg
www.tuttlepublishing.com

Japan
Tuttle Publishing
Yaekari Building, 3rd Floor
5-4-12 Osaki Shinagawa-ku
Tokyo 141 0032
Tel: (81) 3 5437-0171
Fax: (81) 3 5437-0755
sales@tuttle.co.jp
www.tuttle.co.jp